D1334842

ABOUT THE AUTHOR

John Hardy was born in 1934 in Marske-by-the-Sea, then a small village in North Yorkshire. He has worked in various parts of the UK as a quantity surveyor, lecturer, homoeopath, acupuncturist, and guest house proprietor/chef.

In 1994 he moved with his wife Wendy to Sedella, a small village in the Axarquía in Málaga province. Since then, in his retirement, he has from time to time continued practising natural medicine, done sundry building work around the finca and taken up writing.

He has published articles on natural medicine, a book on civil engineering measurement, and various short stories. For information on John and his other books, please visit www.johnhardybooks.com

MURDER, EXTORTION, OBSESSION...

MALAGA MYSTERIES

A COLLECTION OF SHORT STORIES

JOHN HARDY

Matador
9 Priory Business Park,
Wistow Road, Kibworth Beauchamp,
Leicestershire. LE8 0RX
Tel: (+44) 116 279 2299
Fax: (+44) 116 279 2277
Email: books@troubador.co.uk
Web: www.troubador.co.uk/matador

ISBN 978 1784622 756

British Library Cataloguing in Publication Data.
A catalogue record for this book is available from the British Library.

Printed and bound by CPI Group (UK) Ltd, Croydon, CR0 4YY
Typeset in 11pt Minion Pro by Troubador Publishing Ltd, Leicester, UK

Matador is an imprint of Troubador Publishing Ltd

MIX
Paper from
responsible sources
FSC® C013604

ACKNOWLEDGEMENTS

I would like to dedicate this book to Wendy, without whose help and encouragement it would not have been produced. Not to mention her typing of the work and her mastering of Word to get it into the right format. In her conquest of computer skills, we would both wish to credit the help given by Don and Jane.

I would also like to thank Paco, painter and decorator, saxophone player but above all photographer and friend, and Adele his partner, for the photos of Sedella on the front and back covers.

Lastly I must thank *"la gente de mi pueblo"*, the people of my village, who have made Wendy and me welcome.

John Hardy Sedella 2014
www.johnhardybooks.com

CONTENTS

PREFACE

MALAGA MYSTERIES IS A collection of short stories set in southern Spain, mainly in the Axarquía, a region in Málaga province in Andalucía. Most of the stories first appeared in 'Andalucían Mysteries' and 'More Andalucían Mysteries', published in 2013 and 2014 respectively.

The stories contain murder, extortion, robbery, obsession, child abuse, identity fraud, people trafficking and other dark subjects, but usually with a light touch and in many cases humour. In some there is a sense of uncertainty and ambiguity as to the actual events. All have a twist in the tail.

The stories themselves are all fictional but many of the events used in the stories are based on actual incidents, some of which happened to, or were witnessed by myself, but once again the stories bear no relation to the factual occasion. An example of this is the bar in 'The Vine', where a local English resident was always given, as a wind-up by the barman, hot milk with her tea, not cold as she wanted. Another example of this is the interplay in the bar between the young barman and the English diner in 'Happy Families'.

With the exception of such places as Málaga, Torre del Mar, Nerja and Vélez-Málaga, all the village names are fictitious, though some are based on an actual location or even a combination of more than one. As an example of this, the bank and village described in 'Bank Robbery' actually exists as portrayed in the story, however the name and location of the village are fictional.

There is one exception to this. In 'Only a Painting', Finca El Cerillo near Canillas de Albaida is a real location, and Sue, Gordon, David and Christine are real people. When I outlined the story to them they wanted their actual names to be used. The hotel is as described in the story a first class place in a lovely setting, well worth a visit. To my knowledge however there has never been a body in their pool, or a murder committed on the premises.

All the stories together try to give a picture of the area, from the beaches of the Costa del Sol into the mountainous hinterland. The day to day life, the fiestas and the interplay between the local populace, the expat community and the hordes of holidaymakers who together inhabit the region. The dark background is of course entirely of my making, as are any factual errors in the plots. For both of these I apologise.

THE VINE

IT WAS MID AFTERNOON and the man was sitting outside a bar in the hot September sun, somewhere in what he had discovered on his map to be the Axarquía in southern Spain. From where he sat, just to the side of the door, he could see over his right shoulder the barman, alone now in the empty bar, busily catching up washing glasses after what must have been a busy lunchtime trade. As he looked inside the barman caught sight of his glance and smiled, raising his shoulders. "Mucho trabajo, poco dinero," he called out. Not understanding a word, but unwilling to show his ignorance, the man grinned back. "Er, yes," he replied and then quickly corrected himself, "Sí, sí, OK, yes." It was no good, he thought, he must concentrate on the phrase book he had bought only two days ago at Gatwick airport. He turned his glance away from the bar and looked down at the novel he was trying to read. That was no good either, he thought, why hadn't he bought some books to read as well as the Spanish/English phrase book at the airport? He had picked this one at random from his bookcase just before leaving home. It was one left over from his childhood, Dickens' 'Tale of Two Cities'. Listlessly he tried to concentrate once more on its contents but his mind would not focus on it at all.

"It was the best of times, it was the worst of times," he thought morosely. No, it was only the worst of times. What was he doing here anyway? He never went on holidays, never, and if he took time off at all, he spent it watching cricket or football or decorating, either that or watching the telly, he added honestly. It was all Jennifer's fault, she, his sister, had insisted. "Get away, get some sun, relax," she had gone on and on until he had agreed, just for a bit of peace. She had done all the arranging, booked his flight, and his hire car, bought him some pesetas and waved him off. "See you in two weeks, enjoy yourself," she had called out as he went through the barrier at the airport. Enjoy yourself, he thought, gazing unseeing at the page in front of him, as if. But he was tired, he needed rest he mentally agreed, he was drained after a damaging six months.

He took stock, he was 34 and a successful Detective Inspector with the Eastshire force. A rising talent! That was part of the trouble, he was totally immersed in his work, one reason why he did not, and had not for years, taken a holiday. He had not even taken his full quota of leave, he admitted to himself. It was time to be honest, to face up to things, that was what this holiday was supposed to be about, that and having a break. Just a few months ago Jill, his wife, had walked out demanding a divorce. "You're never here," she had complained. "Always working, we never go anywhere, do anything together. Thank God we've no kids. So that's it, Andrew, I'm off. It's not too late for me, I'm only 30 and young enough to make a fresh start."

He had been stunned and unable to reply, or even, he admitted now from the safety of both time and place, to take it all in. He had just started a new case, a devastating dreadful and time consuming case, of child abuse and murder. He was fully consumed and psychologically numbed by it, and focussed on solving it to the exclusion of everything else, his own situation included. So Jill had disappeared from his life almost without his awareness, on the surface at least. And then, just two weeks ago, the case was solved, but the suspect, knowing he had been discovered, had killed himself rather messily, and he blamed himself for that too, because he had not, by his own reasoning, moved fast enough.

"Look Andrew, you can't take everything on to yourself," his Superintendent had said. "You're drained, the case, a nasty one, your divorce, Elliot's suicide. Go on leave, that's an order, you're due God knows how much time off, and you're no good to us in this state. Go away! Come back when you've sorted things out a bit. Got them in balance."

And so here he was, in the sun, sipping an ice-cold beer, outside a bar in God knows where, trying to read a book he had once found enjoyable but could not now be bothered with…

His deepening gloom and self pity were interrupted by voices, English ones. Two women were coming down the steps leading from the road on to the terrace. Middle-aged, engrossed in a conversation.

"I thought we'd stop here for a drink before we go on, it's not far now, and then you can have a lay down after your journey. I don't know about you, but I'm parched." The speaker was dressed casually in a cotton dress and sunhat, black hair showing under it. Her companion was more formally attired, and sweating in a two piece suit. They entered the bar, and the one who obviously lived locally said, "Tea alright, Dot? Dos té, Paco, con leche," this last to the barman. "We'll have leche, sorry milk, Dot, is that alright? He does a good tea here, in a pot, not in the cups."

The barman turned to his gleaming coffee machine behind him, put two teabags into a stainless steel pot and filled it with hot water, that came hissing and steaming out of the pipe. Then he took a small metal jug and filled it with milk, and putting it under the same spout, proceeded to steam-heat it.

"Cold milk, Paco, cold, oh! bother the man. Frío, frío, leche FRÍO," she was almost shouting. She turned to her companion, "He always does this to me, he should know by now I always have cold milk."

The barman paused and turned to face her. "Fría, leche fría?" he asked with raised eyebrows and exaggerated surprise. "Fría, no caliente?" "No, not hot, no caliente," replied the woman crossly. The barman caught sight of Andrew looking at him from over his shoulder, and his eyes sparkled briefly, a half smile forming about his lips. He's sending her up, Andrew thought, he obviously always does it, he smiled back as the barman poured out a second jug of, this time, cold milk.

Andrew went back to his book, but something was buzzing in the back of his mind, he knew the woman. Don't be silly, he told himself, but the thought persisted. Something about her, the way she had reacted, her anger, her voice. His mind, used to worrying at problems, would not let it go. The women were leaving, he looked at his watch amazed, fifteen minutes had passed, then as they passed him and she looked sideways at him, he had it. Jane Hobson, wife of Alfie, who he had met after Alfie had escaped from prison, about ten years ago. Alf Hobson was in prison for a bank robbery, but had been found not guilty of the murder of a bank clerk during the robbery. Then he had escaped, never to be found, and no money had been recovered. Andrew had been only 24 and a new Detective Constable when he had gone to check out Alfie's wife, Jane, to see if there was any sign of the wanted man. He remembered her defiance at the time, her anger. "He won't come anywhere near me," she'd shouted at him. "Go away and leave me alone, I've done nothing wrong."

Even as he was thinking, Andrew had risen, paid for the beer and started up the steps after the two women. What should he do? Jane Hobson had vanished about a year later when the surveillance on her had had to be reduced. What should he do? he asked himself again. He was on holiday, in a strange land, he had no authority here, did not even know the law. But two million pounds was still missing, as well as Alfie. He saw the two women reach a car parked down the road and get in. He got into his own car, fortunately facing the same way, and pulled out after them. He must at least find out where they were going, where Jane lived, and Alfie too? He wondered.

The car in front led him through the small village of Tejedos, near the bar, and out the other side. About two kilometres or so after that it turned into an entrance to a villa. The villa was enclosed inside a high hedge. He drove past the entrance and pulled off the road some way past. Locking the car, he walked back to the gateway and looked cautiously in at the house. Jane's car was parked on some gravel in front of the house, but there was no sign of life at all. He walked back to the corner of the garden, and made his way along the edge of a vineyard until he found a small gap in the hedge and looked through. He was looking at a terrace with a swimming pool at the back of the villa. In the water was a girl with long black hair. Jane Hobson came out of the back door, calling out over her shoulder, "Just put your things in the room, Dot, and then have a lie down, a siesta. Hi Molly," she called to the girl in the water, "Aunt Dot's here, go in and say hello before she dozes off."

Molly Hobson, Andrew thought, watching as the girl came out of the pool, water cascading off her attractive body. She was only a frightened ten year old the last time he had seen her, large dark eyes fearfully peering at him from a thin face, with an awkward skinny body. A bit different now, he mused, looking at her shapely form in a miniscule bikini. She disappeared into the house, returning a few minutes later in a pair of shorts and a brightly coloured top. "I'm just going into Tejedos to see María, mum, Aunt Dot's fine, nearly asleep. See you in a bit," and she was gone. The harsh rattle of a moped started at the front of the house, and then went off down the road and quiet descended on the scene. What now, he thought.

He made his way back to the corner of the field, along the road to the gate and walked up the drive. He went down the side of the villa and cautiously looked across the terrace to where the woman sat, a jug of orange juice beside her on the table.

"Come in," she called quietly, startling him, "Constable Farthing, isn't it? Or is it Sergeant now?" "Inspector, actually," he managed as he advanced. Trust Jane, he thought, everyone always said she was a quick thinker, and intelligent. How she had got mixed up with the likes of Alfie Hobson was always a mystery to the whole team who had been on the case. He had been violent to her as well, he recalled, a vicious thug, suspected of at least two murders and numerous assaults.

"Congratulations, Inspector hey? You were a bit wet behind the ears when we met," she said. "Are you here officially?"

"No, I'm just on holiday, but I recognised you at the bar. How did you know I was here?"

"I recognised you too, as we were leaving," she answered. "Though you've filled out a bit. And you shouldn't wear a white shirt if you want to hide, I could see it through the hedge. I saw you get into your car and follow me too. Now not too much noise, as my sister's asleep. If you're looking for Alf, he's not here, I haven't seen him for years. Sit down and have a glass of orange."

He saw that a second glass had been placed ready for him on the table, she was obviously a clever lady.

"Thanks," he sat down. "You must realise I've no standing here, but I have a duty to find your husband." There was ice in the orange, which was freshly squeezed, and it was pleasant on the terrace, and cool in the shade of a large vine that grew in the corner and spread out over the whole area.

"I'll be honest with you," she began, "I did follow Alfie out here, he sent for me when things cooled off. I was never married to him, ah I see you didn't know that, someone slipped up there." Superintendent Dodds, Andrew thought, just about to retire and one of the old school, bang a confession out of somebody, and don't bother with too much clever stuff. But someone should have looked into her background. She was going on, "Well, I had a passport in my own name. That's Johnson, so I'm Jane Johnson, or Juana as they call me here now. Alf bought himself a new passport in the same name after he escaped, he had enough money to buy himself what he wanted," she added bitterly. "He'd also bought this place and was well settled by the time I arrived. But the locals didn't like him, well it was hard to like Alf. So Molly and me, we settled down too, but things were never good. He'd always hit me of course." She paused. Looking at her Andrew thought, she's tough, no sign now of a battered wife, as there had been at their first meeting. "He'd always hit me," she took up the story again, "but I could cope, then one day he hit Molly. She was only thirteen, going on fourteen, we'd been here about a year then and she was well in with the local kids. She went to school here, well one night they all went to some disco or other, and she got back late. He couldn't abide being defied, and he'd told her to be back by midnight, well it was two in the morning when she got back, things tend to go on late here you know. There was no harm in it, she was with a group, and you don't get problems here like in England." She paused again, gazing into the distance, then continued again. "That was it as far as I was concerned, I told him, me yes, her no. I made him go away for good."

Andrew sat there thinking, was it true? Should he just leave it? But how had she 'made him go away for good?' Had she threatened to split on him, contact the police, tell them who he was? And what about the money? That was still missing. Even if she really didn't know where Alf was, she might know about that.

"You really have no idea where he is, he really went away and you've not heard from him since?" he asked, playing for time. She was silent for a long time, dreamily looking up into the leaves of the vine over their heads. At last she broke the silence, cutting into his thoughts. "Antonio, an old man in the village, just after I arrived here when I was planning this terrace, told me that if I wanted to grow a big healthy vine, I should do what the locals used to do at one time. He said they would bury a donkey beneath the plant, and that it would feed on it for years."

The sound of the moped entering the gate came to them, followed by rapid steps down the side of the house, and Molly appeared at the corner. "Hi mum, oh hello, who are you?"

"This is an old friend," replied Jane. "He just turned up unexpectedly, he's on holiday and… well, looked me up. Andrew, meet Molly, my daughter, Molly meet Andrew. Now, Molly, Aunt Dot and I are going into the village to eat tonight, will you come with us as well, or have you other plans?" Molly was eyeing Andrew with a certain look in her eyes. He's not bad, she thought, and presumably on his own. He sensed her interest and was smitten in return. He felt fresh and alive for the first time in months. If Alf really had gone, he decided he would do nothing to disturb the life of either Molly or her mother. To hell with the money, but he must make sure Alf was not still here.

Molly kept her eyes on him as she answered her mother with a look of what? promise? challenge? "Sure, I'll come with you, and you'll join us Andrew, won't you? Then I'll have someone to talk to when Mum and Aunt Dot talk family together."

"Well, er, I'm not sure…" he trailed off, wanting to say yes, but knowing he couldn't intrude in this family, him of all people. Yet he had not felt so carefree, so refreshed, for years. This was the cure he needed, but… "Yes, do, Andrew," said Jane, smiling at him. "Great, that's settled," said Molly. "I'm going for a shower, see you in a while."

Jane reached above her head and picked a bunch of grapes. "What was I saying, yes, well, I was finished with Alfie when he hit Molly, you can imagine, she's everything to me. He was a violent man you know, always beating up someone, and he had killed three people to my knowledge. Violent and vicious he was, I don't know how I ever got involved with him. Well I do, but I was younger then, and wild myself. Oh well, as I said, that was the end, hitting Molly like that." She broke a grape off, and put it into her mouth, handing another to Andrew. "Have a grape, they're so juicy, Antonio says he's never seen such a strong healthy plant as this vine. I said to him, Antonio, when I planted it, that I didn't have a donkey to bury under it." She paused again and ate another grape. Andrew felt a chill settle over him, despite the heat of the early evening, cold shivers running up his spine.

"You asked about Alf, yes, he's gone for good. What did everyone call him? An ox of a man, that's right, and he was stubborn, oh he was stubborn. Stubborn as a… as a mule, isn't it?" Andrew felt himself relax, with a light heart he followed Jane across the terrace and into the house. "I'll just get my car," he said, "then if I could, I'll have a shower and change before we go to eat."

Outside, on the empty terrace, the vine cast its cooling shade.

CAVEAT EMPTOR

"DID YOU HAVE A good holiday?"

"What?" I looked up from my paper in annoyance and turned to the man in the next seat.

"Sorry, didn't you hear me? Noise of the engines I expect. I only asked if you had had a good holiday."

The plane from Málaga to Gatwick had just taken off and was banking steeply over the sea, turning to head back over the city and on to its destination. In the departure lounge, on the short bus ride from the departure gate to the plane, and after sitting in my seat, I had avoided contact with the other passengers. Since then I had been quietly reading my newspaper, not wanting to join in a conversation with strangers.

"Actually I'm going on holiday, not coming back, I live in Spain," I said, turning back to my paper and hoping he would take the hint and stop disturbing me.

"Do you?" he persisted. "That's interesting, I'm in the process of trying to buy out here too. No luck this time though."

"Right," I responded, without looking up. A discreet noise sounded over the loudspeakers and the seat belt sign went off. We were informed about the height at which we would be flying, the speed of the plane, its arrival time in London and advised to keep our seat belts fastened for our own safety, first in Spanish and then in English. Taking advantage of the hiatus in my reading as I waited for the announcement to finish, my neighbour went on to tell me that he had spent the previous week touring the area "from Mojácar to La Linea", looking for property. He had visited several estate agents, "on the spur of the moment, you know, no appointments, just turned up at their offices." This was, he assured me, the best way, they had no time to "dream up scams". He hadn't however had any luck.

I kept my eyes on the page, hoping in vain he'd get the message, hearing his voice drone on next to me, some bits piercing my thoughts, other bits just a background noise. "I'd had no trouble with any of them, except one. A real cowboy he was, tried all sorts of fast ones on me. Tall man, black spade-like beard and long black hair. Well spoken type, now what was his name?"

"Jack Pendlebury," I thought, my attention caught at last.

"Jack something or other, Penter... Peddler... Pen... "

"Pendlebury," I said, lowering my paper.

"That's right, Jack Pendlebury. Do you know him? Not a friend or anything, I hope."

"No. Not a friend. Met him once," I answered.

All around us, suddenly, there was a surge of movement. Tables being lowered, meal trays handed out. During this break in our conversation, I looked out of the window and gazed down through the thin white streaks of cloud at the brown barren land of central Iberia. Here and there darker patches of land patterned the landscape, whilst in the distance a line of sierras was visible. Yes, I had met Jack Pendlebury once, and it had stuck in my memory ever since. It must have been over twelve years ago, when I too was house hunting, but the event was as clear as if it were yesterday.

I had sent the outline of what I was looking for to his agency the week before my visit, so that he could sort out suitable sites to look at. That way we would not waste each other's time. "Somewhere in the campo, not in a town or village. Some way inland, say six or so miles minimum, with plenty of land. I don't care if there's a building or not, or what state it's in. I can build or refurbish as necessary. The site is what's important." That or something like it is what I'd told him in the letter. I'd turned up at his office at 10 am as arranged and, fortunately as it turned out, decided to follow him in my hire car, rather than go in his, so that I could move on from wherever we ended up. He'd taken me out of the town, Mojácar, and driven off inland. We'd passed under the N340 motorway and then gone on into the dry, brown, dusty hinterland before turning off the small country road on to a dirt track. About 500 metres down the track he'd pulled up next to an electricity pylon, and we'd both got out. He was standing at the edge of a small 'valley', looking down into it. The 'valley' was about 400 metres across and about 15 metres deep, with a flat wide base.

"That's where you'll be able to get your power," he'd said, pointing at the pylon. "And there's a water main under the track. The site stretches from this side of the valley to the other and about a kilometre of its length." He paused and pointed down into the 'valley'. "That's where you'll build your house, on the level bit at the bottom."

I'd looked at him. I didn't know much about Spain then, but I did know there had been a drought for a few years, and

I could tell a dry river bed from a 'valley'. When the rains came, and come they would, any house built down there wouldn't last five minutes.

"Thanks a lot," I'd said. "Goodbye," and without any more ado I'd got back into my car and driven off.

"Wait," his voice had followed me. "If you don't like it, I've more…"

"This looks good, doesn't it," my fellow passenger's voice brought me back to the present. I looked down at my tray. On it was a small salad, a bread bun, some meat and veg, and what looked like a peach sponge or some suchlike.

"Uh. Well, so-so," I managed. "Vino tinto," I added to the stewardess who had just put the tray in front of me. All around people were taking off plastic wrapping and starting to eat. I broke the seal on my wine and poured some into my plastic glass before tackling the salad.

"He was a right cowboy, that Pendlebury, don't know how well you know him, but he really tried to do me. But nobody does that to me and gets away with it."

"Right," I said, at a loss for words. "I don't really know him, just met him the once, house hunting you know."

I looked more directly at my fellow passenger. He was a big raw-looking man with strong heavy arms, on one of which I could see a tattoo of a snake. He looked strong and tough and there was an angry glint in his eyes.

"Told him I wanted a place just outside the town, enough land for a pool. That sort of thing. First he took me to a place in the town, no room to swing a cat. Then out into the country to an old villa, nearly falling down, and right next to a pig farm. Then another with no track to it, and then one with no room for a fish pond never mind a swimming pool. A whole day he wasted, my first one it was, just over a week ago, and I had to get to Marbella the next day to look round there. Nothing he showed me was anything like what I wanted. And some of the problems weren't obvious, I had to work them out for myself."

"Caveat emptor," I murmured.

"What?"

"Buyer beware."

"Oh. Right. Yeah. He tried all sorts of things, good job I'd my wits about me. But the last one really got my goat. Sent me over the top I can tell you."

Again there was a welcome break as the trays were gathered up. Once more I looked out of the window, but all I could see was cloud, rolling away in all directions.

"Do you know what he tried next?" His voice once more cut into my thoughts that had gone, reluctantly, back to the purpose of my visit to England. My sister had left her husband, or rather he had left her, and she had begged me to come back and help her sort things out.

"You'll have to go," my wife had insisted. "Just for a week. Help her with finances, the house, the children, all that sort of thing." So with a heavy heart, I'd taken the first available flight.

I shook my head. "No, what did he try?"

"We were looking round this finca place. Just right in many ways. Fair size, quite good nick, a fair bit of land, and only about a mile or so out of Mojácar. He says to me that it would take a bit of renovating but that there was power and water. He pointed to a pipe that came through the wall with a tap on. "It'll need plumbing of course," he said. I tried the tap but nothing came out. "Oh, it's turned off," he said to me, "but the town hall will soon turn it on again when you pay the water rates."

He paused, looking at me in a grim way.

"What then?" I asked. "What was the problem?"

He nodded at me with a small smile on his lips, that didn't reach his eyes. "Later on, I walked round the house, looking at the land, and do you know what I noticed?"

"No." I couldn't imagine, but I didn't like the look on his face.

"I saw the end of a pipe. There was no water, that pipe was just poked through the wall. Not connected to anything. I lost my temper with him then."

During the silence that followed, the pilot's voice came over the speakers to tell us that we would be landing in a short time at Gatwick, to fasten our seat belts, that the temperature in London was twelve degrees, that it was raining, and that he hoped that we would fly with them again. I looked out of the window and saw green fields with a road winding through them, over in the distance was a lake and nearer a village. Soon we would be landing where I would be met by my sister and be plunged into her chaos and misery. I glanced again at my paper and folded it away. My neighbour had now finally stopped talking and lapsed into a moody silence.

The last I saw of him he was striding away from baggage reclaim with his luggage which had been one of the first off the belt, whilst mine as usual was obviously going to be the last. As I stood waiting I opened my paper again, it was that day's copy of 'Sur in English' and, because of the interruptions of my fellow passenger, I'd not got past the first page. Now I looked inside and read the main headline on the second page.

"Mysterious death of English Estate Agent". Pushing my trolley of cases, I read on. Apparently an English estate agent, Jack Pendlebury, had been found battered to death at a remote deserted finca near Mojácar the previous week. No one knew what he was doing there, or who if anyone he'd been showing around. "It's been on our books for ages," his assistant was quoted as saying, "but it's in a poor state, and has no water, we just couldn't sell it."

I went through the barrier in a turmoil of thought. What should I do? Who was the man who had sat next to me and was he anything to do with it? Or had the agent taken someone else to view the house? Or was his death connected to something else altogether?

Suddenly my thoughts were interrupted by my sister, shaking me by the arm. "Where are you going, didn't you see me? Oh, I don't know what I'm going to do… "

Later in the car, still being deluged by her woes, I realised I'd dropped or mislaid the paper. At least it was no longer in my possession.

What should I do, what would you do?

"And then there's the bank account to sort out, it's a joint one, and the insurance policies, and where am I going to live? He wants to sell the house. Are you listening to me at all?"

What can I do?

FLOWERS FOR MANOLITO

JOSEFINA HAD WALKED THE three kilometres from the *aldea,* hamlet, of Tierra Verdes down the *carril,* lane, between the tall bamboos to the crossroads every Friday since the fatal accident. She came down on Fridays because that was the day, over three months ago now, when Manolito her eldest grandson had been knocked down by the Englishman. And also because Manolo her eldest son and father of Manolito went to the market in Vélez-Málaga every Thursday and brought home flowers for her to take with her the following day.

The six kilometre trip, down the hill to the crossroads and then back up again, together with a half hour or so rest at the bottom to fix the flowers to the concrete post and say a prayer to the Virgin, took up all morning. But it was the least she could do in memory of her beloved *nieto,* grandson.

This Friday was no exception, so after Manolo and his wife, María, had left to go to the court where a verdict on the trial of the Englishman was expected that morning, she set out down the carril as normal. She had rejected as she always did Manolo's offer of a lift down to the spot, just as she had rejected similar offers every week from all her sons. She saw it as part of her duty to walk there and back and leave the flowers at the spot where the boy had died.

As she walked between the tall rustling *cañas,* canes, she could catch glimpses through them of the land to either side.

Groves of olive and almond trees, orchards of oranges and lemons, vineyards and the occasional view of the newly popular avocado interspersed with a fig tree or *algarrobo,* carob. At one point she stopped for some time and gazed through an opening between the caña to what had once been Miguel's vineyard. Miguel, at 82, was a contemporary and friend of hers and she knew he had been proud of his vines. He had made wine from some of the crop and then sold the rest to Larios in Málaga, who made Málaga wine from it. But two years ago Miguel had become too old to work the large vineyard anymore, and had given it to his sons to avoid paying death duties on the gift. Both his sons lived in Málaga and had well paid jobs with little time left to cultivate a vineyard, which required a lot of attention all year long. They had grubbed up all the vines, terraced the land and planted avocados, the new and increasingly popular crop of the area. She knew Miguel was saddened by this and despite him explaining to her the logic of his sons' actions, she too was also upset both on his behalf and her own. She had known the vineyard since childhood when Miguel's father worked it. She had played there as a child and drunk many a glass of the *terreno,* wine, made from the grapes. Sighing and shaking her head, she moved on down the lane.

At the end of the carril, it joined the road from Casavieja to the coast. It joined it at a slight curve. Here partly obscuring the view round the bend was an old carob tree with a girth of over a metre, and a tall concrete post signing the way to Tierra Verdes. She took last week's withered flowers from the post and tied on the fresh ones she had brought with her in their place.

It was at this spot that the Englishman's car had collided with Manolito's moped at just after 3.30pm on that fatal day many weeks before.

Everyone knew that the car driver had had too much to drink. They also knew that that was the main cause of the accident and not simply, as he claimed, because his vision was obscured by the tree, post and bend.

Josefina sat down on the bank at the roadside and went over in her mind all the facts that had become known over the weeks since the event.

Manolito had left home just before 3.30 that afternoon to go to the *gasolinera,* petrol station, to work his afternoon shift. When he reached the junction, his moped had been hit by the car which was travelling rapidly down the hill, far too fast for the conditions. Manolito together with his moped and the car, had ended up in the ditch at the side of the road. He had died on impact and the car driver, who had hit his head on the windscreen as he was not wearing a seatbelt, had suffered mild concussion.

Earlier that morning a group of *extranjeros,* foreigners, the Englishman amongst them, had met up in Bar Jeromo in Casavieja, as they did every Friday for a few tapas and drinks.

The Englishman had drunk several litres of draught lager and finished with a couple of whiskies and cokes. As a Spanish whisky is about four English measures, he was well over the limit when he came to leave. He was well-known in the area for drinking to excess and no one was surprised or worried by this. When questioned later by the Guardia only old Pedro was prepared to speak out. The barman, who did not want to lose his foreign trade, would not be precise. He would only say he thought that the man had probably had, perhaps, a bit too much but could not say for certain. Other locals, who didn't want to appear in court, simply shrugged and claimed not to have noticed. Pedro was the only one to speak out and agree to be a witness in court. His evidence was destroyed by a clever lawyer from Málaga, who derided it and made much of Pedro's age and eyesight problems, together with the fact that he too was befuddled with drink.

The Englishman had been the first of the group to leave the bar and drive off down the hill. His route home took him down the road to the bottom of the hill past the junction to the aldea. Here it took him along the main road at the bottom before reaching a turn off which went back up the hill again to Las Pasas where he lived. If there had been a road directly from the bar to his home it would have saved many kilometres and gone past Tierra Verdes. His route was roughly along three sides of a square. However on that fateful day when he reached the junction to the hamlet he collided with Manolito and his moped, and knew little more until he woke up in hospital.

Close on his heels two more cars driven by the extranjeros came upon the scene. They quickly called the ambulance on their mobiles and gave what help they could. When the *Guardia Tráfico,* traffic police, came on the scene they did a less than perfect job. Concentrating on directing traffic around the incident and taking statements, they failed to take a blood test from the driver. Then later at the hospital they were not allowed near him by the doctor, until he was satisfied about his concussed state. By then it was too late and so it could not be proved in court that he was over the limit.

Josefina finished mulling over the events in her mind, said a prayer, crossed herself and rising from the ground, began to walk back up the hill to Tierra Verdes. Slower now than on the way down, it was gone one o'clock when she reached home.

It was later that afternoon when Manolo and María returned from the court and told the assembled family of the verdict. Josefina's three sons and two daughters were there, together with their respective partners and children. Seven grandchildren in total, the eldest being Pepe, Manolito's younger brother.

The verdict had been accidental death. A lack of evidence and witnesses and the clever lawyer making sure that the Englishman received no more than a stern warning, together with a fine he could well afford to pay. The family were dismayed but felt powerless to do anything about the situation.

The next morning Pepe, who at eighteen was two years younger than Manolito, was working on the family land when his mobile rang. It was his friend Antonio who lived in Casavieja and was in Bar Jeromo. Antonio told him that the extranjeros were in the bar celebrating the result, and that the Englishman was once more the worse for drink, apparently taking no notice of the warning given him by the judge to be careful in the future.

Pepe was incensed and returned home, and without saying anything to anyone else, took his father's hunting rifle and set out across country to the *pueblo,* village, of Las Pasas

23

which, whilst it was over ten kilometres by road away from the aldea, was barely four by footpath over the sierra. The first part of the route took him over the old Roman humpback packhorse bridge and up a steep hillside, where the stone paved footpath had deep pockets worn in it by the passage of countless mules over the centuries. Then where the ancient track turned sharp left he went off on a faint footpath across the hillside, through a small pinewood and came out just outside Las Pasas. Keeping out of sight he made his way to the home of the Englishman and found a spot hidden from the windows of the house. From here he had a clear sight of the area in front of the house where one car was parked and where he knew, in time, the man would park his own car on his return. Here he sat down to wait, the rifle across his knees.

From the house he could hear music of a radio and also occasionally the clatter of crockery as the man's wife prepared a meal.

In the bar the group of extranjeros became louder as they celebrated the result of the case, whilst the locals left and the bar owner became more worried about the situation. At last the party broke up and all the men went on their way, most of them much the worse for wear.

Pepe, sitting in the hot afternoon sun with the sound of the cicadas becoming louder and louder, fell into a doze and then dropped into an even deeper sleep as he waited for his prey to come home.

It was here, just off the road outside the gate of the house that the Guardia officers found him when they came to speak to the Englishman's wife. He was still asleep with the gun on the ground beside him where it had slipped off his lap.

The Guardia had grave news for the Englishman's wife. On his way home, as he came round the bend at the junction to Tierra Verdes, her husband's car had left the road and driven straight into the tree and concrete post, killing him outright.

His last vision, just before the impact, would have been of the bunch of flowers on the post.

SPRINGBOARD

THEY SAY THAT IN times of greatest danger, during life threatening events, your past life runs through your mind in a very few seconds. Certainly the circumstances leading up to Neil's ungainly plunge into the pool flashed in front of Petra's eyes as she ran to the side and dived in after him. Or at least that's what she claimed later. Not that she was in any danger, but by the way he had dropped into the water, she knew that he certainly was.

She had been enjoying a late afternoon's sunbathing, after a morning shopping with Neil in Málaga, which had become a habit during their stay in the villa. He, also as usual, had decided to have a dip in the pool. Through half closed eyes she'd watched him come out of their patio doors and saunter to the side, dip a toe in the water, and then go back a few steps and ready himself to dive in. Before he could run to the edge she had sat up and called out, "Do you think you should swim today, Neil? I don't think you're quite sober." When they had finished their shopping, they had met up with a few of their friends and spent a couple of hours in a bar, drinking and eating tapas. To her knowledge, and she hadn't been closely watching him or counting, he had sunk two gin and tonics and several glasses of wine. And a gin and tonic here was about a triple in English measures. As she had known he would, he'd turned to her and almost sneered, "Don't fuss, Petra," before facing the pool once more and diving in.

That first dive off the side had been almost perfect, as if to refute her claim of his being not fully in charge of his faculties. She followed him with her eyes as he swam up and down the pool. He certainly was in good shape for someone well over forty five, she thought, watching his lean brown body cleave through the water. Standing up, she'd glanced casually around the small garden, which was nearly all taken up with the terrace and pool, enclosed by a wall which made it almost fully secluded. The area was only overlooked by the villas on either side, and only by them if their occupants sat at the very edge of their terraces and looked through the patterned concrete blocks set on top of the metre high dividing walls. She and Neil could only look into their neighbours' gardens by similarly going to the extreme sides of their patio.

Looking to her left she had seen that the two young Spanish women staying next door, as usual when Neil was giving his regular late afternoon performance, were watching him. She could never decide if they were attracted or amused by his antics, but whatever it was, they almost always managed to be on the corner of their terrace at this time of day, when he was in the water. Today they were there as normal, she noted with satisfaction.

Half turning to her right she'd noted, again with pleasure, that Mr Turner, who owned the villa on that side had also, as he usually did, found a reason to be on the edge of his property peering through. She had no doubt why he habitually came to stare into their garden at this time of day, as when Neil was swimming she always sunbathed topless, wearing only the skimpiest briefs.

Neil did not seem to mind that their neighbours on both sides regularly spied on their afternoon ritual, in fact he positively appeared to welcome their attention. No doubt he enjoyed showing off to the women and got vicarious pleasure from old Turner drooling over her. It was probably a case of "You can look all you like, but don't touch", she decided. She'd turned to one side and the other, moving her breasts up and down, just to keep his attention, before once more lying on the sun lounger.

She'd watched as Neil had come out of the water and gone to the deep end where the springboard was. As usual he'd gone back to the edge of the tiled area to get a run then sprinted forward on to the board. His trick was to run up the plank, give a skip, bounce on the end and flip high into the air, jack knife and cleave cleanly into the water.

Today, halfway along the board he'd slipped, fallen awkwardly and struck his head on the corner of the plank before dropping into the pool with a loud cry and splash.

The shouts of her three neighbours had mingled with her own as she'd jumped up and ran to the pool, diving in after him. It was during this brief period that all the events leading up to the incident had flashed through her mind. Or so she'd said afterwards. But perhaps it was just that she'd been going over and over their life together of late and it only seemed that way. Whatever the truth, she was convinced they had.

She had first met Neil when she was twenty-one and working for a firm of architects in Darlington. He owned a building firm and had come into the office to discuss a tender his firm had submitted. He was nearly forty and divorced, and had been smitten by her as soon as he saw her. She had left school at eighteen with few qualifications, with only GCE's in Maths and English. She was good at shorthand and typing, which the school taught, and could work a computer. She got a job in the typing pool of the architects and soon became their senior clerical assistant. "Well, the other two are useless," she told her parents, when she was promoted. One day when she had been with the firm for about a year, the senior partner called her into his office. His PA, a women of about fifty, had had an accident on her way to work in her car and was in hospital. He asked Petra to fill in for her until he knew what would happen. In the event, his PA did not come back to work, but decided to retire to take things easier. Petra had done so well in the job that she was offered it permanently. So there she was with a top job and no qualifications.

It was about two years later that she met Neil and, despite their age difference, they struck up a relationship and eventually married. He owned two houses, one in Darlington and one in Hawes, in the Pennines, 'for the weekends' as he put it, as well as the villa in Spain. He was, in Petra's words, 'stinking rich' and for about six months she was happy and thought herself very lucky. She had her job, which she loved, had left her grotty flat in Stockton, and was living in the lap of luxury with a partner she loved and whom she thought loved her. Neil was in very good shape and she told her parents that everything was 'tickety boo', as her grandma used to say.

Then one day Neil came home, just after she had arrived back from work herself, and told her that she had to give up her job and stay at home full time, to "make the place a decent home" as he put it. She had laughed and told him that she was happy as things were, and that she didn't want to give up work yet and that she thought they had a good home already. She told him she'd think about it in a year or so, if they wanted to start a family.

"It all came back to me as I ran to the pool, dived in and swam up to him. He was floating, face down in the water, with a crimson stain of blood from the cut on his head spreading on the surface beside it," she said to Madge much later, when they were discussing the affair. Madge was her only confidant in those days as Neil had made her give up her friends one by one over the years. Neil of course did not even know she knew Madge, never mind had made a friend of her.

"Well, when I laughed and told him I didn't want to give up my job," she continued to Madge. "He hit me, hard, in the solar plexus. Drove all the air from my body and made me retch. Then he just walked out of the house. He came back after about an hour and calmly told me that there was more of that if I didn't do as he said. I was terrified. I handed in my notice the next day.

"Over the next three years I led a dog's life. He was a wife beater, but subtle with it. He never hit me where it would show, so I had no black eyes or bruises to explain away, and he used psychological pressure as well. He broke my spirit and I lost all confidence. I'd no one to turn to as I'd no friends left and my parents both thought the world of him, and that I was more than lucky. They wouldn't hear a word against him, and in any case had retired to Wales, and I seldom saw them and never without him. I thought of going to a shelter for battered wives, but felt a fraud, being so well off, for he never stinted with money, and I had no bruises to show. In the end I steeled myself and told him I wanted a divorce. I expected him to flare up and braced myself for an onslaught.

"He just laughed and told me about you."

He had told Petra that his previous wife, Madge, had divorced him, and boasted that she hadn't got a penny out of him. He said that he had had a good lawyer and that he'd paid someone to say that Madge had been having an affair for years, and had then run out on him. He told her that he'd do the same with her and she would be penniless. That was when she'd hunted out Madge and gone to see her. Madge had confirmed the story, adding that the judge had ruled that he had been the innocent party, and told her that she had acted disgracefully. Then she had described how one of Neil's foremen had stood up for her and helped her out, and eventually married her. Neil had sacked the man and had tried to ensure that he never got a job again. However, she had continued, one of Neil's rivals, who didn't like him, had taken her husband on as a Contracts Manager, so in the end he had got a better job.

Madge's story had made her think and she'd realised that she'd have to find somewhere to go if she left Neil. She'd need a flat, money to live on and a job. With no qualifications she'd known that wouldn't be easy. But she'd made up her mind and began to salt away some cash from the money Neil gave her. This was how things had stood when they had come away to Spain for their latest holiday. And all this, she claimed, had flashed before her as she dived in and went to his aid.

She surfaced beside his body floating in the pool and slowly pulled it to the side. The two Spanish women were meanwhile climbing over the screen and lowering themselves on to the patio. It was a good four minutes before they managed this and ran across the paving and leaned down to help pull him from the water. Mr Turner was calling over from his garden. "I've rung O61 emergencies and they're sending an ambulance. If you'll unbolt your back gate I'll come round and help. I can't climb this fence, I'm too old." Both the Spaniards spoke English and understood him, so one of them went across to let him in. When he arrived, he turned Neil over on to his stomach and lifted him from the middle to drain water from his lungs. Then he put him on his back and pulled his tongue from his mouth. Kneeling beside him, he started to give mouth to mouth resuscitation. It was now nearly ten minutes since Neil had first gone into the water.

Suddenly the garden filled with people. Two paramedics took over from Mr Turner and two Policía Local started asking questions of her neighbours. Petra turned from the scene and went and sat on a patio chair, and poured herself a whisky from the bottle on the table.

A short time later an officer from the Policía Nacional arrived and took over from the local policemen. He had a woman officer with him, and she crossed over to where Petra was sitting, still only wearing bikini bottoms. She took her by the arm and led her indoors away from the busy scene by the pool.

"Come inside. Now go and put some clothes on, then I'll sit with you till the Captain comes in."

She spoke English with an easy manner and a pleasant accent. Despite the fact that the sun was now dropping in the sky, the evening was still hot and so Petra just pulled on a tee shirt. She then made a couple of telephone calls to tell her parents and Madge what had happened. After about half an hour, the police officer entered and had a muttered conversation with his assistant. He then came over to Petra and, with the female officer translating, questioned her.

"We have already spoken to your neighbours," he began. "They have told me what happened, as they saw it clearly. It was obviously an unfortunate accident, however if you are able I would just like to clarify a few points."

"Of course. Can you tell me how Neil is?"

"The doctor is with him now and we will know better in a short time. Now, your husband slipped off the springboard. You can confirm this?"

"Yes, whilst he was running up to dive."

"Your neighbours say you had called out to him not to swim, as you had been drinking at lunchtime."

She nodded a reply.

"How much had he had? Was he drunk?"

"Not drunk, I don't think so. How much? I'm not sure, two gins and a few wines, I believe."

"But you didn't think him sober enough to swim?"

"Water can be dangerous, if you've been drinking."

He considered this and then gave a nod of agreement. He went on. "Your neighbours say you were not swimming, just sunbathing. Then you went to his rescue and pulled him out?"

"Yes. I seldom swim in the afternoon. I pulled him to the side, but couldn't get him from the pool until the others came."

"Hm. But you didn't do anything to start his breathing? Mr Turner did that later when he arrived."

"I don't know how. All I did was try to stop the bleeding from his cut."

"Was it bleeding much?" he asked quite sharply.

"No. No, I think it had stopped, or at least nearly."

He nodded and relaxed, concern showing on his face. Before he could speak, the doctor came into the room and spoke rapidly in Spanish to the two officers. The two men went out into the garden and the woman police officer came over to Petra.

"I'm sorry, the doctor has just informed us that your husband is dead. In his opinion, he was already dead when you pulled him out of the pool. They're taking him to the hospital to carry out a post mortem now, but it will only be a formality. Can I get you anything?"

Petra shook her head and poured herself another drink, then phoned her mother and Madge again to give them the latest news. She was quite calm, but could hear the satisfaction in Madge's voice when she said, "At least he won't be able to harm you, or any other woman, again. Look, I'll fly out tomorrow and be with you at the funeral."

The daylight was almost gone when the police captain came back into the room.

"I'm sorry, Mrs Slingsby, Petra, but don't blame yourself, you did all you could. Is there anyone who can come and spend the night with you? Would you like my officer here to stay?"

"No, thank you," she replied. "The doctor has given me some sleeping pills, so I'll be alright. I just want to be alone. A friend and my mother are flying out tomorrow, so I won't be alone for the funeral."

"I'll come back in the morning with a colleague, when it's light, he'll take a few samples for forensics. You know, the blood on the diving board where your husband hit his head, and so on. Don't worry, it's only routine, all three witnesses gave very clear statements as to what happened, it was clearly an accident. We won't come too early, to give you time to sleep in and recover from the shock."

He smiled at her in sympathy and went back outside. Then at last everyone had gone, and she was left alone.

She sat sipping her drink, recalling the look in Neil's eyes, half dazed from the blow to his head, when she had first reached him in the pool and turned him over. It had been fierce as he tried, even then, to dominate her and force her to keep him afloat. It had turned to first pleading and then terror, as he realised what she was doing. She had calmly pushed his head back under the water and held it there, he was too stunned and weakened from the blow to resist. She had towed him face down, slowly, to the edge, but had still had to wait for the two women to arrive and help her haul him out. She had already known he was dead before Mr Turner began his ministrations.

As the evening turned to night she took several decisions. She would sell this villa, but buy somewhere else nearby, as she had come to love Málaga and the surrounding area. Madge's husband could be given the job of running the business for her, that would really rub salt into Neil's wounds, wherever he was, and she herself could take over the office administration. To be going back to work once more was a pleasant thought. She had all night to sit and plan, for she didn't intend to take any pills to make her sleep, and a tired, pale face would help when she met her mother at the airport, and faced the police captain again. Besides, she had to wait until she was sure her neighbours were all asleep, and that nobody was on the edge of their terraces, looking into her garden.

Then she would crawl out on to the springboard and carefully wash off the grease she had spread there early that morning, before the police came back to examine the blood at its end.

EASY MONEY

IN THE MIRROR BEHIND the counter George could see the entrance to the bar. He could also see his own reflection and he quickly checked his appearance. Distinguished, clean-shaven, expensive business suit, conservative tie, everything as it should be. On the bar beside him a copy of 'Sur in English' as arranged, this week's copy, not the one in which his advert had appeared. Inserted under Meeting Point, it had read: "Mature, successful business man, too busy to socialise, seeks attractive English speaking lady aged 30 – 50 years for lasting and meaningful relationship. Box No… "

Tonight he was meeting the one he had selected from the six replies he had received. Sonia Willmot was 35 years old, a widow, very attractive and very well off. His research consisted of an unobserved scrutiny of her at the hotel where she was staying in Marbella, and a phone call to a private detective in England.

He had given the agent, one he used often, her name and the address in Newcastle she had given him in her letter replying to the advert. His instructions had been a rapid reply, and at low cost. The agent had therefore simply carried out an enquiry by phone. The results were encouraging, her husband had left her very well off on his demise some six months earlier. She was by far the best choice, George had decided, and as his finances were low, he had to move fast.

Sonia came into the bar with her copy of Sur under her

arm, but he pretended not to see her, looking down into his drink. She paused and glanced round the room. He was, she decided, the only possible person she was seeking amongst the small crowd of local Spaniards and casually dressed holiday makers, and he had his copy of Sur beside him.

They got on well together and decided to allow the relationship to evolve by having lunch together the next day. He was never in any doubt, having already picked her out, but she had to be carefully fostered and encouraged. On the other hand speed was also essential, his rent had only a few weeks to go before he would be homeless and his cash was running out. His last two unsuccessful sorties had left him almost penniless. This time he must succeed.

Over the next few days they met for lunch and dinner, and went on outings to Selwo Safari Park and Ronda. He described to her how he made his living. He told her that he bought and sold shares and currency, and made prudent investments with the profits. She in turn told him of the death of her husband, and of being in receipt of a large sum of money from the sale of his assets. He carefully made no early moves.

It was Sonia who, hesitantly, made the approach however. "George, don't think me presumptuous, but could you help me, if you would, to invest some of it? If it's not improper to ask?"

Elated, he pretended to think for a few moments. "Well," he paused. "I'm putting a twenty thousand pound package together, that's about thirty thousand euros, with my agent on Friday. I could get about 10% interest, all being well. Is that the sort of thing you want?"

"Oh yes, that sounds fine, but how would I go about it?"

He arranged a meeting for her with his agent, Bruno, the next day. Bruno came down from Madrid the following morning on the train. George used him for this sort of deal, for a fee of 10%. This time it would be more as Bruno would also have to loan him the twenty thousand for a day or two. When Sonia told Bruno that she wanted to invest one hundred thousand pounds, he agreed to only charge George 1% on the loan.

There would be no problem with the money. She had an account with Barclays, whose branch in Marbella was only too pleased to transfer the money from her Newcastle branch and make it available in euros.

Bruno explained he would need it in cash, in two days time. She arranged to have it delivered to her hotel. George was with her as a messenger arrived with a small parcel and watched her deposit it in the hotel safe.

She was no fool, however, and was obviously worried about handing out such a large sum to anyone, despite Bruno's solid appearance and impressive paperwork. This was what George paid him for, to give confidence to the deal. George now played his master card, it never failed.

"Look Sonia, I can't be here to meet Bruno, I have to go off on business for a few days. Could I leave my money with you, and you see to it for me?"

So George put his twenty thousand pounds in her hotel safe, beside her own package. On the morning of the meeting Bruno arrived at the hotel at half past ten as they had agreed, to take charge of the money and give Sonia the worthless documents in return. He phoned George shortly after to report.

"What do you mean, she's checked out earlier this morning?" George shouted into the phone, breaking out into a sweat. "Where's the money? You can't be serious."

He rang off in a panic. He had no money, no flat after next Tuesday and he owed Bruno twenty thousand pounds, plus interest, plus his expenses for his trip from Madrid. He had to run and run quickly, before Bruno brought in his heavies. What had gone wrong, he thought despairingly, as he packed in a hurry.

Sitting on the plane to Gatwick Polly King, alias Sonia Willmot, thought, "How gullible can some people be?" For the cost of a four week holiday on the Costa del Sol, a bit of research in England to find a suitable person to imitate, and the cost of having a parcel full of newspaper (the same 'Sur in English' that had carried the advert, a nice touch that, she thought) delivered to her hotel by a courier, she had made twenty thousand pounds. She hoped George and Bruno could afford it.

HAPPY FAMILIES

THAT FRIDAY EVENING I was the only customer in Bar Cádiz, although there were several groups in the restaurant. I could hear the subdued murmur of voices and the occasional clatter of crockery through the half-open door. Paco the owner was constantly in and out with various plates of food, and I could hear Francesca his wife in the kitchen. Their son *Paquito*, little Paco, was behind the bar, even though at 15 he probably shouldn't have been. I was drinking *vino tinto*, red wine, whilst waiting for Esperanza, "Esi", my novia. An interesting word novia, or novio, the masculine equivalent. It could mean anything from boyfriend or girlfriend (its literal translation), fiancée or even a cohabiting partner. I wasn't exactly sure just what it meant for Esi and me. We certainly weren't cohabiting, but although not officially engaged I hoped that we were more than just boy and girlfriend.

I'd better explain. I'd been coming to stay with my Aunt Lizzie, my mother's sister, who lived in Las Parras de la Sierra, a small village in the Axarquía, ever since I could travel unattended in aeroplanes. As I'm now 26 and a qualified architect, that's for a lot of years. I've always come over several times a year and so by now I know the village and its inhabitants very well. Esi, who is 23, and I have been friends for years and something more for the last two. That Friday evening she had been at choir practice. The village

41

boasts a town band, a choir and a dance group, Esi being in the last two.

Just then one of the groups dining in the restaurant came out into the bar, their meal finished, to pay the bill. It was the Ramshaws, an English family who stayed in the village at least once a year. They were a family of four, Martin, Doris and their two children Toby, the eldest, and Ruth who was about five or six. I knew them by sight as Aunt Lizzie did the cleaning and turn rounds at the villa they usually stayed in, and Doris often borrowed Aunt Lizzie's scooter. Martin was a tall, heavy built man who usually, in my opinion, wore an expression of dissatisfaction, a bit of a brute of a man I thought, perhaps uncharitably. He certainly refused to let Doris go off on her own in the hire car, which is why she used Lizzie's bike. Doris looked to me to be always pale and drawn, unhappy and even fearful.

Martin asked loudly in English for the bill, to which Paquito answered in slow clear Spanish. Mutual incomprehension. Martin grew louder and redder and Paquito more animated with much arm movement. I kept my head down and sipped my wine whilst pretending to watch the telly in the corner, which was showing some unfathomable game show. The object of which seemed to be that the contestants, all carrying various small animals, appeared to have to dismantle a tower of plastic cubes on which they were standing.

At last the bill was settled and the Ramshaws left the bar, Martin now quite angry muttering about 'bloody Spanish' and loudly chastising his wife and children. I turned to Paquito, who I knew spoke reasonable English, and said in my less reasonable Spanish that he had known all the time what Martin had been saying and could have dealt with him quite well in that language.

To which Paquito replied with irrefutable logic, "Si, Carlos, pero estamos en España."

I am always Carlos to the villagers, Charles being my christened name, and yes, as he said, this was indeed Spain. Presumably he thought that Martin, who had been coming for years to Las Parras, could by now have made some effort to learn at least the rudiments of the language. Or maybe he just didn't like Martin.

Just then Esi and a couple of her friends arrived and I lost interest in the whole incident. As I said, Esi and I had been novios for a few years now and I was hoping to take the relationship to a new and more formal level very soon. Esi, who spoke both English and German to a reasonable level, worked in Vélez-Málaga down the hill, in a mobile phone shop. It has always amazed me how Spaniards who speak one or two foreign languages reasonably well often work in quite modest jobs. In England two or three languages are seldom spoken and if they were, qualified the speaker for a good position. I knew however that Esi did not want to leave the village, let alone Spain. Now however I was almost in a position to move into the area myself. On Monday I had an interview for a job in Málaga with the building firm Hermanos Costillos. Miguel Costillos, the senior partner and elder brother, was a cousin of a neighbour of Esi's parents, and had agreed to talk to me about the possibility of my joining the firm. Here, in southern Spain, everybody seemed to have a *primo*, cousin, somewhere and everywhere. A vast family network which was now working to my advantage. If I got the job, I intended to formally propose to Esi.

Going home that evening I walked past the villa rented by the Ramshaws, which was not far from my aunt's, and heard a fearful row going on. At least I heard Martin shouting, the children crying and Doris trying to calm him down and comfort them. The man's a brute, I remember thinking. In fact during that weekend, I seemed to come across them everywhere. He always appeared to be angry, she even paler and haunted in her looks, and the children unhappy. But I was too occupied with thoughts of my coming interview on Monday to take in anything more than a surface impression. And why should I have done anyway, they were nothing to do with me and I hardly knew them.

Monday morning dawned and I walked down the narrow *calle*, street, to where my hire car was parked in one of the wider roads at the edge of the pueblo. As I went past the Ramshaws' rental I noticed the lights on and the usual rumpus coming from within. Soon however I was driving down the mountain road to the motorway at the bottom, and on to Málaga, and the dysfunctional family that had recently seemed to intrude on my life was forgotten.

The interview with Miguel lasted nearly all morning. Hermanos Costillos was a fairly large building contractors who constructed flats, houses and factories in the Málaga area. They wanted a designer and someone who could oversee the construction of the projects and deal with their English clients. As a fairly newly qualified architect with site experience, I was ideal for the job. Miguel obviously thought the same and offered me the position. We agreed terms and elated I drove back to Vélez to meet up with Esi. Her shop was in a large shopping complex that was open all day, and that week she was on the morning shift. When she came out at about 2.30 I was waiting and we went for a bite to eat. I told her the news, proposed, was accepted, explained that I would return to England the next day to hand in my notice, work it, and then return to live permanently in Las Parras de la Sierra. All that and it was still not 3 pm.

Driving back up the hill to the pueblo I followed Esi in her car, lost in plans for the next few weeks which were going to be hectic. Halfway to the village there is a large lay-by with picnic tables where two or three walks into the hills start. As we approached it I noticed Martin Ramshaw walking up one of the paths away from his hire car parked at the spot. By his clothes and the pack he was carrying it was obvious he was going for an afternoon hike in the sierras. A scooter with a woman driving it was just pulling into the lay-by. As I passed she got off the bike, took off her helmet and started walking up the same path as Martin who was by now some way ahead. Then I was past and once more involved in my many thoughts and plans.

As I walked back to my aunt's with Esi to tell her the news, I noticed the two children playing outside the Ramshaws' house and observed how quiet and peaceful it was. Although I am recalling these facts now, months later, at the time they made little impression on me. But I am fairly sure of them as I think back.

The next morning I left my aunt's house at 5.30 am to catch an early flight. The village was still and silent with no one awake and the street lights still shining. As I passed the Ramshaws I saw Doris through the lighted kitchen window moving about. Driving down the hill I only passed two vans, nobody else was about that early. I was surprised to see a car parked at the picnic area, putting it down to a teenage couple who had spent the night there. I dismissed from my mind the thought that came to me that it was the Ramshaws' car. It was the same make and colour and, I thought, in about the same position but that must be just coincidence. He wouldn't have spent the night there, of that I was sure.

The next few weeks were indeed hectic as I finished all my outstanding tasks at work, sorted and packed my things for the move and spent time with my friends and family who I would now only see spasmodically in the future. I spoke to both Esi and my aunt on the phone several times and though they told me about village happenings and gossip, it went clean over my head. All I wanted to talk and think about was the future. At last the time came to move, at the end of what one minute appeared an eternity and then shortly after seemed not long enough to get everything done on time. Then of course it was the new job, buying a car, finding a place to live, the wedding, one thing after the other with no time to stop or draw breath.

All in all, nearly a year must have passed when once again on a Friday evening I was sitting in Bar Cádiz, drinking red wine. Again I was the only customer in the bar that early in the evening. Once more hearing the sounds of people eating in the restaurant and watching Paco go back and forth to his wife in the kitchen. But this time I was waiting not for my novia, but for my wife. Paquito behind the bar was chatting to me about football. He was a Betis supporter whilst I went regularly, now that I was resident in the pueblo, to watch Málaga at the Rosaleda stadium. Why he travelled all the way to Sevilla was a mystery to me, then I remembered Paco, his father, came from there and was an avid fan.

A woman and two children came out of the restaurant and up to the bar to pay. The woman was good looking, well groomed and the family were obviously happy to be on holiday together. The boy and girl were well looked after, I thought, and obviously knew Paquito who, as was his way with children, made much of them. When they left he said to me, "That tragedy last year was a blessing in disguise for them, wasn't it."

The remark startled me in several ways. In the first instance he was speaking in English. I knew he could speak English but not with that fluidity. When I mentioned this he grinned and told me he learnt it from the many English girls who came out on holiday. The second reason was that I didn't know the family or what tragedy he was talking about.

"You do," he said. "It's Doris, Toby and Ruth Ramshaw, and Esi must have told you what happened to Martin."

She probably had, as had my aunt, but at the time I'd been in England too busy to listen to or take in village news. What had happened apparently was that Martin Ramshaw had gone walking one day in the hills, parking his car at the start of a footpath and had somehow fallen off the path into a deep *arroyo,* stream, hitting his head on a rock and, unconscious, had bled to death. He had not been missed until the next day as Doris had put the children to bed, taken painkillers for a migraine and gone to bed herself, not waking until late the next morning. On finding Martin had not returned, she had raised the alarm and first the car and then the body had been found.

"She's been a changed woman since then," said my aunt, "no longer browbeaten and downtrodden. The children too have both blossomed. Good can come out of ill, you know. Everyone but him benefitted. And he was a bully you know, I never liked him."

As I came to see more of them during that holiday, I realised that they were indeed the same family I'd known before, just made initially unrecognisable by the change in their lives.

It was over a week later when I asked Aunt Lizzie just when Martin Ramshaw had had his accident.

"Why, the day before you left to go back to England to work your notice," she replied. "I did tell you on the phone. You must have passed his car on the way to the airport. Of course you wouldn't have known it was his or even seen it in the half light at that time of the morning."

But I had seen it of course and Doris didn't sleep in that morning, I thought. And, if she was the woman I saw go up the path after him, then she was either with or following him on that walk. I never said anything to anyone of course, as preoccupied as I had been at the time, I could have had it all wrong. And Doris wouldn't have left the children alone and gone off to walk with Martin, would she?

Then again she did have access to my aunt's scooter.

MISSING

THE BODY OF A young woman was found, stumbled over would be more correct, by a fisherman returning home at first light after a night spent angling off the beach between Torrox Costa and Nerja. Because the body was naked and the head had been shaved clean of hair he had literally not noticed her against the sand on which she lay, her lightly tanned skin almost the same colour as its surroundings.

The two uniformed Guardia and their Sergeant, called from Nerja by the almost incoherent angler on his mobile, parked their land rover on the edge of the road and made their way to the lone figure standing awaiting their arrival at the water's edge. They soon established that she had been killed by a gunshot wound to the head. A wound that obliterated much of her features. Leaving one of his men to guard the body and take a statement from the fisherman, the Sergeant and the other Guardia began questioning the inhabitants of the line of houses that faced the beach.

Mario was awakened by their pounding on his door. He was a barman at the luxury Hotel Dila in Nerja, had been on duty until the early hours and was not pleased to be woken so early. He knew both the Guardia officers and soon assured them that neither he nor Inma, who was a maid at the same hotel and still in bed, had heard or seen anything.

With no clues, no identification and no missing person report that could in any way fit the corpse, their first assessment was that the death was probably drug related. The phrase 'a settling of scores between dealers' used in such cases was given to the media. The woman was clearly North European with blue eyes, probably fair-haired and about twenty-five years old. Her fingerprints were not on record and although local dentists were contacted, none of them could match her teeth to their records. No further action could be or was taken and her file was left on the Sergeant's desk pending any more information that became available.

The previous Wednesday evening, five days before the body was found on the beach, Sally was sitting in the bar of the Hotel Dila, studying a couple sitting nearby. The woman was certainly striking, she thought. Striking rather than beautiful. Dramatic. That was the word, she decided, dramatic. The woman's hair was ash blonde, almost bleached white by the sun, and worn in a style that looked windblown, finger-raked, but was in fact perfectly styled to look just that way. Running through this white tangle of hair were several seemingly random strands dyed bright green. She wore a low-cut flimsy blouse of the same green, that clung to her half-exposed breasts, and a long purple skirt slashed to the hip showing smooth shapely legs. White gold earrings, bracelets on wrists and one ankle set with small diamonds, and a ruby pendant nestling between her breasts, glinted in the subdued lights of the bar. Her voice was sharp and clear, cutting through the soft background music.

"Mark, be a dear, get me another of these. I seem to have finished this." She held out a glass to her companion. Very definitely dramatic, Sally thought.

Mario served the drinks to Mark, who he knew was the

blonde's husband, with a smile. They had been here for several days now, Mark and Lavinia, and he was fascinated by her.

"Obsessed, more like," snapped Inma, who noticed his eyes following the blonde whenever she was near. But it wasn't sexual attraction, Mario insisted.

"You are more beautiful, my Inma," he protested. "It is just that she is so…so…"

He couldn't find a word for it. Odd certainly wasn't right, pretty and beautiful were no good either. She was certainly not beautiful and pretty was too pale a word. In the end he hit on the same word as Sally.

"*Dramática, eso es, es dramática.*" Dramatic, that's it, she's dramatic. Bringing a snort from Inma.

Mario looked round the bar and caught Sally's eye. He smiled at her. Now there was a beauty, he thought. About the same age as Lavinia, with the same sharpish chin and nose, just as good a body, but more discreetly clothed and with short black hair that framed her face to perfection, and dark clear eyes. He glanced quickly away so that Inma wouldn't see him looking at her. But the blonde was a magnet to him and he once again turned to look at her. He was, he decided, bewitched.

The day before the body was found Sally checked out of the hotel. On the forecourt, waiting for her taxi, she bumped into Mark. It looked like an accidental meeting. But Mark was tense, strain showing in his eyes.

"All set, Sal?" he queried. "Everything ready for tonight?"

"Don't worry, nothing can go wrong. Relax, we'll soon be together." Sally smiled casually and moved away. Just a chance encounter.

On the evening after the body's discovery Mario was once again on duty in the bar. He was telling two locals of the morning's events and the discovery of the dead woman. Mark and Lavinia were sitting at their usual table with pre-dinner drinks. Lavinia tonight was wearing a white off-the-shoulder full-length silk sheath, once again slashed to the hip. Her voice, clear and shrill as usual, cut through the air.

"I'll just go and phone daddy and tell him I'm coming back for a couple of days. He can meet me at Heathrow."

She came up to the bar to use the phone at the end, smiling at Mario.

"Daddy? Lavinia. Listen, I'm coming back for two days, no, Mark's staying here. Meet me at the airport, will you? No, nothing's wrong, why should there be? I just have to come back, I want to talk to you, and have my hair done, and you know only André will do. Here's Mark, bye, see you tomorrow."

Mario listened with half an ear to Mark giving details of the flight to his father-in-law. There was a slight frown on his face. Something was worrying him, but what, he couldn't quite place it. He glanced across at Lavinia, once more seated at the table, sipping her martini. Then he was called to the other end of the bar to serve a German guest. Mario spoke English as well as Spanish, but no German. The guest only spoke German and no other language, so by the time they'd finished Mario had quite forgotten his earlier thoughts. Mark and Lavinia had left the bar to go into dinner as had the couple of Spaniards he'd been telling about the body on the beach. Inma came in with an order for wine from the restaurant.

"Lost your lady love," she said sarcastically, bringing the usual response from him.

Sir William Brownleigh, Lavinia's father, waited in the bar at arrivals. It was too much, he thought, Lavinia had just expected him to drop everything and come and meet her. He'd had to cancel two appointments and trust them to his PA. The trouble with his daughter, he thought, staring moodily into his whisky, was that she was spoilt, and had too much money. That was the fault of his first wife, she'd spoilt her as a child and then died, leaving her a fortune. She had grown up wild and wilful. He'd thought she'd settled down since she'd married Mark, of who he thoroughly approved. To show this approval he'd given them a handsome wedding gift of cash, equal to Lavinia's inheritance from her mother, on the condition that they held the two sums in a joint account. Not being a fool, he'd also insisted on a pre-nuptial agreement whereby it all reverted to his daughter if Mark left or divorced her.

Everything had been fine for the last two years, since the marriage. Lavinia had controlled her excesses, he'd taken Mark into the business and the perpetual crises in his life initiated by her behaviour had become a thing of the past. Till now. This was more like the Lavinia he knew of old, to call and expect him to drop everything to meet her. And to come all the way back from Spain to London to 'speak to him', about what he pondered, and to go to her hairdressers. Didn't they have hairdressers in Spain? Not as good as André, according to his daughter.

Several hours after her flight had landed, she still had not shown up. Sir William rang Mark. Yes, she had caught the flight Mark told him, or at least gone through to departures in good time. Sir William then checked with the airline office. Yes, certainly a Lavinia Perry had boarded the plane at Málaga. A stewardess was found who remembered her leaving the plane at Heathrow. She was in no doubt about it. There never was any doubt, Sir William thought, given Lavinia's appearance and manner. But she certainly hadn't come out of the arrivals gate. That Sir William could swear to.

Sir William Brownleigh was a prominent figure in the city and had several high level contacts in the police and the foreign office. Within hours Scotland Yard had initiated an investigation and search at Heathrow, and the British Consulate in Málaga had stirred the Guardia into action there. No trace of Lavinia could be found at either airport. Several indisputable facts were established. She had checked in at Málaga; she had boarded and left the plane; she had not checked in or boarded any other flight; she was nowhere to be found. When all possible explanations had failed, the police began to explore the improbable and impossible ones. The search was widened at both ends.

Mark told his father-in-law that he would stay in Nerja for a few days.

"If she's been off on one of her escapades she'll just as likely come back here as turn up in England. And if she does, she'll expect me to be waiting. Anyway I can try to help the police search at this end."

Sir William had agreed, adding, "If she turns up here, I'll let you know at once, Mark. Where can she have got to? What is she playing at?"

Three days after the body was discovered on the beach

outside Mario's house, and two days after Lavinia's disappearance, Sally returned to the Hotel Dila in Nerja. That evening she sat in the bar chatting to Mark. Mario was behind the bar and Inma, who had just come off duty, was sitting there chatting to him and the Guardia Sergeant.

"Still no news on who the woman was who was found on the beach?" Mario enquired.

"Who? Oh her, no," the Sergeant replied. He had almost forgotten her as he had been leading the search locally for Lavinia. That was his excuse for sitting at the bar chatting. He had been talking to the staff trying to see if any of them could throw any light on where she had gone, or why.

Mario glanced across at the English couple. He frowned.

"They seem too close and cosy, seeing that his wife has gone missing," he said.

"You're just annoyed because your beautiful blonde's not here," Inma snapped at him.

The Guardia smiled at them as they started to bicker about Mario's attraction to Lavinia. He tended to agree with the barman. Mark seemed too relaxed, too absorbed with the brunette for a husband whose wife had run off. He'd just interviewed Mark again about his wife's disappearance, but had learned nothing new.

"The last I saw of her was when she went through to the departure lounge. Then her father, Sir William, rang to say she hadn't turned up. She does these things from time to time," Mark had told him, and then frowning, "or at least she used to, she hasn't for the last year or two. Since we were married."

Sally came over to the bar and asked Mario for two more

drinks. How different from Lavinia, Mario thought, she never came to the bar, she always sent her husband. He served the two brandies and looked into her eyes smiling. Sally returned to Mark with the drinks and Mario stood transfixed, staring after her.

"Don't start getting ideas about her as well," Inma started, but Mario ignored her and spoke to the Sergeant.

"Paco, listen. She had brown eyes. That was the thing."

"Who had?" The Sergeant said, following Mario's gaze. "So what? She's a brunette, what else do you expect?"

"No, listen, not her…"

Two hours later the Sergeant and his men entered Sally's and Mark's rooms. In hers they found an ash-blonde wig with green strands running through it. In his they found a gun and Mark and Sally in bed.

"I still don't understand, Mario," Inma complained when they finally got home late that night.

"It was the night they found the body on the beach," he explained. "Lavinia came up to the bar to make a phone call. She had brown eyes, not blue ones. It was Sally in the wig. They'd shot Lavinia and shaved off her distinctive hair. It was her body over there."

Inma looked across the sand to the sea lapping the shore and shivered. Moonlight reflected off the small waves, reminding Mario of the jewellery Lavinia used to wear. He tore his gaze away and followed Inma into the house.

BEST LAID PLANS

HEATHER DECIDED TO KILL Amanda Carter between the pre-dinner olives and dry sherry, and the brandy and coffee after the meal. It was a decision she reached slowly and hesitantly as she watched Amanda, at a nearby table, ruin the evening of an elderly couple, the Hendersons, who Amanda was dining with.

The restaurant, *El Castaño*, the chestnut tree, in the Alpujarran village of Cabra, was quite full that evening but Heather was close enough to see and hear most of what was happening at their table. She knew it was the Hendersons' wedding anniversary and that they had been looking forward to it for quite a while. Amanda had, in her usual overriding way, hijacked the event.

"They couldn't be left alone on their special day," she had told everyone who would listen to her. "In any case, they wouldn't be able to arrange it properly, with the language and all that, poor dears," she had added, despite the couple's adequate Spanish and obvious wish to be alone.

So she'd taken it over, overruled their protests, joined them at their expense and, as Heather could see and hear, spoiled their evening. The Hendersons, too polite and unassertive to object with sufficient insistence, had given in to her pressure and allowed her to take over and intrude on their evening.

Heather, Amanda, the Hendersons and a few other

English families, all lived on a small *urbanización,* estate, just outside the Spanish town of Cabra in the hills to the south east of Granada. The expatriate community had all got on reasonably well together until the arrival of the Carters two years before. Amanda Carter was a leech. Under the guise of 'good works' and 'neighbourliness' she intruded into the lives of the others. Her special targets were those who could be classified as inadequate or needy in any way. Such people she took under her wing, brooking no refusal, and feeding on their impotence to stand up to her. This was normally all done at the expense of her victims as she was an expert at never using her own money.

Bill Carter, her husband, was always away on business and Heather suspected that he had arranged their move to Spain whilst maintaining his commercial commitments in the rest of Europe, as a means of getting away from his dominant wife. He also had a good eye for making a profit and she knew that he had made a substantial sum from selling his UK residence and buying in Cabra. As the majority of the other residents of the urbanisation were either single, as Heather was, or retired and elderly, like the Hendersons, Amanda had a good supply of victims for her ministrations. She fed, Heather had come to realise, on the weaknesses and cash balances of those less adequate than herself.

It was time to do something about it, Heather had decided by the time her prawns were put in front of her at the start of her meal, but what? Over the goat stew with accompanying salad, the idea of somehow removing Amanda from the village was reached. Whilst chewing the garlic-flavoured meat, several ideas of how to do this were, one by one, dismissed by her as being too fanciful and impractical. Whilst eating her flan, notions of kidnapping and terrorising her neighbour were finally discounted as being both impossible to arrange and unlikely to succeed. The notion of murder came, as all such thoughts should, with the first sip of brandy. Now the only question left was, how?

When she awoke the next morning Heather would have probably dismissed the previous evening's decision as merely foolish nonsense, brought on by the alcohol, if it hadn't been for the arrival of Amanda on her doorstep.

"Good morning, dear," she began, sweeping past Heather into the house.

How I hate being called dear, Heather thought, trailing behind her.

"Sorry I couldn't join you last night, I hate to see you eating all alone, so miserable," Amanda continued. "But as you know I was pledged to seeing that our anniversary couple next door enjoyed their evening. However, I'm here now to make up, join you for a coffee. Have a good chat."

Heather, who had been more than happy to be alone the previous evening, and this morning was looking forward to a quiet read with her coffee, experienced a sinking feeling.

"Really, Amanda," she objected. "I'm rather busy this morning. I haven't time to stop for a break."

"Nonsense, dear," Amanda overrode her. "Of course you must stop for a bit. All work you know. What you need is some company to bring you out of yourself. Now you sit still and I'll make the coffee. You have some biscuits, haven't you?"

The idea of murder resurfaced as a now vital, not just a possible, option.

Later in the day Heather went into the walk-in storeroom of her villa and searched amongst the boxes of the possessions she had hoarded there. Her father had been a soldier during the second world war and among his souvenirs had been a service revolver. Heather had inherited this together with some ammunition on his death. She had brought them with her when she moved out to Spain some years before. He had also taught her how to clean, load and fire it, although she had never been very proficient in the art. After a short search she found the weapon, took it out of its holster and as she held it considered her next moves.

First she went up into the high sierras above the village and found an isolated spot where she could practise. She chose a Thursday, which was a day allowed for hunting at that time of the year, so her few shots wouldn't raise any suspicions. She had never been a good shot, despite her father's instruction, in fact she had always been a bit afraid of the gun. But now needs must, she decided, and she would have to reacquaint herself with the wretched thing. Before leaving home she took it to pieces, oiled and cleaned it and then reassembled it, finding to her pleasure that she still remembered how it was done. Then she went up to her chosen spot and fired it several times. She was, she now decided, ready for action. The time for that action would be during the fiesta of San José, the village patron saint, in mid March, she resolved. That gave her just a few more weeks to make her final plans.

She chose the Saturday night of the fiesta, when there

would be a fireworks display, to carry out the actual deed. First she checked that Amanda intended to go to the fiesta that night. This was not too difficult as several of the other residents of the estate told her that Amanda had arranged to take them in her car. She then made sure that Amanda couldn't include her in this group by explaining that she would be away from home that day, shopping in Granada.

In the week before the fiesta ETA made an abortive attempt to assassinate a prominent politician who was visiting Granada. The police failed to catch them and they vanished into the countryside. During that time the radio and television carried warnings about their danger to the local populace. People were advised not to approach suspicious characters but to warn the authorities of any strangers in the area.

At about half past ten on Saturday evening the float carrying the statue of San José left the village church in procession to go to the small *ermita,* chapel, at the other end of the village. At the head of the procession were two of the *mayordomos,* stewards, letting off rockets every few yards. Behind them came the statue followed by the village band and then the villagers. Explosions, music and raised voices filled the air. As they passed several of the houses on the route, displays of sparklers and coloured fireworks were set off on their balconies. When the procession reached the square in front of the ermita, the statue was rested on metal stands and the band formed up to one side of it. Once the crowd had all assembled in the square the firework display started. Rockets, roman candles and set displays filled the night air with light, colour and loud explosions.

Heather had planned to shoot Amanda under cover of the noise of the fireworks. She pushed through the crowd and positioned herself a few feet away from her target. During a particularly noisy period when everyone was shouting out and looking up into the sky with the band playing close by, under cover of a barrage of rapid explosions, she fired four shots in quick succession.

Her aim let her down. It was as usual inaccurate, and she had had to go further away from Amanda than she had wanted, into a recess in a wall on the edge of the crowd, to avoid being seen. She had also had to fire from a crouching position and aim upwards to ensure that once past Amanda, the bullets would go over the heads of those beyond her. Two of the bullets nicked Amanda's arm whilst the others missed her completely. Seeing Amanda shaken but still alive, she was overcome by a feeling of both relief and exasperation.

"All for nothing," she muttered, hiding her gun in a large pocket of her warm winter coat.

The police, when they were called over to Amanda after the shooting, could not understand or explain the event. Who would shoot at an English resident of the village? That the minor wounds had been caused by bullets was not in doubt. Both the local doctor and the Guardia Sergeant who examined them were quite sure of that. She was just unfortunate, they concluded. Perhaps she had got in the way of an argument between drug dealers, or even been the victim of the ETA terrorists known to be in the area. In any case she was not badly hurt, nobody had noticed anything and their interest soon waned.

Heather awoke the next morning in a depressed state. She was not normally a violent person and had been keyed up for days preparing herself for the task. Now she felt a great sense of anticlimax and despair. She thought she had probably just made matters worse. When there was a knock on her door and she opened it to Amanda, her spirits could not have been lower.

Over coffee her visitor described the events of the previous night and showed her the dressings on the wounds.

"It's a dangerous place this, dear," she said. "You must be careful in future not to go out at night alone. What with drug runners and terrorists on the loose, anything can happen."

Heather looked back at her glumly. I'm right, she thought, she'll be even more domineering in the future, she'll take over completely, oh what have I done? Her mind had blanked out what Amanda was saying as her thoughts became more and more despondent. She pulled herself together to hear the end of Amanda's news.

"… fortunately, for me at least, it won't be a problem. Bill's had a really good offer for the house, he's been trying to get me to agree to move for weeks now without success… but after last night… well! And it's much too good to turn down and he's found a really marvellous place, fantastically cheap, in Portugal. So we'll be moving soon, but I'm ever so worried about you, and the others who'll still be left here. Do you think you ought to consider moving as well? I'm sure Bill could find you a buyer, at a good price. You could buy near us in Portugal, there's more for sale nearby."

Relief and surprise flooded over Heather. In the event it

had been enough. All's well that ends well. Move to Portugal with Amanda? Not on your nellie, she thought.

"Oh no, I'm quite happy here. I'm sure there's no real danger to anyone really," she said smiling.

"Especially after I throw father's gun away," she added silently to herself.

BLACK DIAMONDS

"I FIRST MET PETER Firth when he came to lecture at the same college as me, and bought the Old Forge just down the road. The Old Forge is a large rambling listed building, and Peter lived there with his wife Glenda and her cousin Alan. Peter had worked in West Africa somewhere as a mining engineer, then for the National Coal Board in South Yorkshire before becoming a lecturer. He moved to Bradbury College of Higher Education, where I teach, from a technical college somewhere in the north. Because of his background, his main subjects as a lecturer were Geology, Soil Mechanics and Land Surveying. Together with his wife and cousin, who was something of a DIY expert, he set about renovating and modernising the Old Forge, so that when he moved on and sold it some nine years later it brought a very good price.

"Peter was at the college for nearly ten years and because we were neighbours and taught in the same department, we got to know each other quite well. But there was always a point beyond which he would not go in our friendship. I put it down, at the time, to him being reserved by nature.

"An example of this reserve was in the way he would never talk about their holiday home in southern Spain. This despite the fact that he knew that I took Naomi and the children away to the Costa del Sol every year for two weeks. He never explained where the villa was except that it was 'somewhere near Málaga'. Despite this, I knew that he spent every holiday there. At Christmas he, Glenda and Alan would all go off together, but at Easter and for the whole of the long summer break, he would go alone, explaining that 'Glenda and Alan couldn't stand the heat'.

"One year, shortly before they sold the Old Forge and Peter left the college, a strange incident occurred. I had taken the family, as usual, for our annual fortnight's holiday to Spain, where we were renting a holiday flat in a town called Torre del Mar. We hadn't been there before, having usually rented either on the other side of Málaga from Torre, or beyond Nerja in the other direction. It had become our custom over the years for me to go off once or twice for the day, leaving Naomi and the children on the beach. The children were growing up by then of course, in fact it was the last time all five of us went off together on holiday. But I still took two days off by myself, driving into the hills above the town and exploring the countryside.

"On one of these trips that year I went into the Montes de Málaga, and then turned east towards the Axarquía. I stopped at a small village en route to have a morning coffee. Whilst I was sitting outside the bar I saw, to my surprise, Peter walking towards me, holding hands with a handsome black woman. They were obviously very much together as a couple and to stop him from noticing me I hid behind an English newspaper I had bought that morning in Torre.

"It wasn't the fact that she was black that caused me any embarrassment. I'm not at all prejudiced, well I can't be, can I, as Naomi is a second generation immigrant from Tobago, as black as you can get, and our three children range from light brown to almost Naomi's colour. No, what made me hide behind the newspaper was the fact that Peter's wife was back in England, and also that he obviously didn't want anyone at college to know where his holiday home was. Anyway, they went past and walked off down the road without noticing me.

"I didn't tell Naomi anything about the incident.

"Then, three years ago, some six years after they had moved, we got three visitors. Rachel, our eldest girl, the one who is almost as black as Naomi, answered the door and then came into the kitchen where Naomi and I were and said, 'There's three… black people at the door asking for you, Dad.' It was the way she said black that startled us, with a sort of a distasteful tone, one of disapproval.

"This from a black girl who knows from experience all about racial prejudice and is normally very PC. She explained in a sarcastic voice in response to our surprised expressions, 'West African gentlemen, except one's a woman, and the other two ain't gentlemen. They're not very nice at all, if you ask me.'

"We went to the door and found three people, all clearly African as Rachel had said, standing there. There was a tall thin man with hostile eyes and an angry expression; a shorter fatter man who wore a false smile; and a woman who had the coldest eyes and look I have ever seen.

"'We are trying to trace a Peter Firth who used to live just down the road,' the fat man began. 'Mrs West next door to where he used to live said if anyone would know where he'd gone, you would.'

"I remember thinking at first, Peter Firth, who's that? He

had been gone for six years, and then I remembered. I explained, quite politely, that no, I had not kept in touch with him, and that I had no idea where he had gone to.

"'We must find him – if you deliberately try to stop…,' the tall angry man began, until the woman cut in icily, 'Morgan,' and he lapsed into hostile silence. The fat man, who was beginning to sweat, smiled ingratiatingly and continued, 'We understand he had a house abroad, in Spain, Mrs West thought, or perhaps Malta, according to their neighbour on the other side.'

"I felt Naomi's fingers digging into my arm, a signal she uses to caution and warn me. 'Don't tell them anything, I don't trust them,' was her message. 'I believe it was in Italy,' she said. I said it may have been Spain, feeling her fingers once more dig in hard, relaxing when I added, 'Somewhere in the north, near Barcelona perhaps.' 'If you are trying to fool us…,' began the tall man, to be stopped once again by a look from the woman.

"I tried to appear helpful and suggested that the confusion between northern Spain, Italy and Malta might be because the villa was in fact on an island, somewhere in the Mediterranean, perhaps the Balearics or even off the coast of Greece. I finished by saying it could even be in 'one of those two bits of Spain on the African mainland.' 'Ceuta and Melilla,' the black woman said thoughtfully. At last they went away.

"'They gave me the shivers,' said Naomi. 'They were up to no good at all.'

"I agreed with her, but thought that we had managed to raise quite a smokescreen around the location of Peter's villa.

"Last year Naomi and I went to Spain as usual for our holiday, on our own of course, as the children no longer come with us. For a treat we stayed at the Parador in Málaga. I still kept to my practice of going off by myself for the odd day, and so one day whilst Naomi was shopping in Málaga, I drove back to the village where I had seen Peter years before. I had some trouble finding it as I had forgotten its name and it was quite a small place. I had no trouble however tracking down 'the Englishman with the black wife' once I had got there.

"When Peter came to the door he was not at all pleased to see me, but I asked him to hear me out. I told him how I knew he lived there, and that I had told no one else of this, not even Naomi. I then described to him, and to the black woman who had joined him, the visit of the three Africans. 'Tell him everything, Peter,' she said.

"He then explained that the black woman, Sara, was his real wife, who he had met whilst working in West Africa. She had been promised to the son of a neighbour. 'That would be the tall man who visited you. The short fatter one and the woman would be my brother and sister,' Sara explained. 'We were a rich family, owners of the mine where Peter worked. We had to run off together to get married, and I took some of the diamonds from the mine with us. The family honour was disgraced by my actions. In our customs, that is punishable by death, and we have moved around ever since. They have been looking for us all this time and will not give up easily. Once they nearly caught up with us, and that's when I came to live here, and Peter's sister Glenda and her husband Alan went with him to the Old Forge in the guise of his wife and her cousin. Well, we'll have to move on again now. They have a large area to cover, thanks to you and your wife, but they'll track us down eventually.' 'And you, you must be careful,' Peter continued. 'If they think you've helped us and deliberately misled them, then you'll be in danger too.'

"I didn't tell Naomi of the meeting, not wanting to worry her, but towards the end of our holiday I heard on a local English radio station of a house that burned down in their village, and the lucky escape of the two British occupants. I also caught a glimpse of someone in the street who may have been the shorter of the two black men, but as it is several years since I saw him last, I cannot be sure.

"I have written this account of the affair however, and intend to leave it with my Will in case anything happens to me."

The solicitor stopped reading and looked across at the grieving widow.

"I was not sure what to do with this," he said. "But thought I ought to read it out to you."

"If only he'd told me," she replied, tears glistening in her eyes. "If I'd known, I wouldn't have told anyone where he'd gone last weekend, especially not her of all people."

"Who?"

"The 'tall cold featured woman' he writes about. She came here again, said she had a message for him from his old friend Peter. I said he wasn't here, that he had gone to a conference in Cambridge and wouldn't be back until Tuesday. For her to come back then. If only I'd known… "

"But it was a car accident he died in," the solicitor replied unsteadily. "It was an accident… wasn't it?"

THE PENANCE OF THE
MAIDEN AUNT

MISS SHILITOE WAS A formidable old lady, there was no doubt about that. At almost eighty she was still a fine looking woman, her face unlined, her figure firm and well proportioned, and it was obvious that in her youth she had been quite a beauty. When she was, as today, in her English mode, dressed in a severe black suit and jacket, a white lace blouse and wide brimmed hat to keep off the sun, she looked the picture of an English spinster. Almost a caricature.

Her nephew Charles, anxious and sweating in the hot Andalucían sun, knew that whilst that was so, there was also another side to her character. She had lived for nearly sixty years, since 1922, in Churriana, a suburb to the north of Málaga, one of her claims to fame being that she had been an acquaintance of Gerald Brennan. This other side of her character took her from being, on the surface, a respectable English maiden lady, to that of a more flamboyant Spanish señorita of advanced years. Her time in Churriana had given her almost fluent Spanish and a seemingly endless number of friends and acquaintances amongst the locals. When mixing with them she joined in their lives to the full and became vibrant and animated.

Charles, who was very fond of her and visited her regularly, had witnessed this change of character many times. Today, just when he needed her to be relaxed and approachable, she appeared to be in her least amenable mood. When she was like this, he knew she could wither even the strongest with her straight-laced impregnable respectability.

She was a Quaker, or so she claimed, but he knew that if she was, she was surely an unorthodox one. On the other hand, he admitted, he knew little or nothing about the Society of Friends, and they may all have been like her, but he doubted it. When in her Spanish persona she worshipped in the local Catholic church and was on friendly terms with the priest, as she was with others in the area including the Bishop. One day, Charles had witnessed her turn on and verbally demolish an official of one of the English Free Churches in the vicinity, by her scorn and a few withering words. The man was some sort of sidesman, or churchwarden or lay pastor, he was not sure exactly what as his knowledge of Free Church terms was even less than that of the Quakers. Charles himself was a staunch Anglican. He knew his aunt didn't like the man, who was a short, tubby, red-faced, fussy individual. She considered him to be insincere, condescending and a bore. "Besides which, he dresses in a black cassock, as if he were the Minister," she always said by way of a final assassination of his character. That day, the man had overheard her telling some of the congregation how she often went to the local Catholic church in her village to celebrate Mass. "Miss Shilitoe," he had butted in stentoriously. "Don't tell me you go to Popish services, you a Quaker, or so you claim." All round them a silence had fallen over the worshippers who were leaving the church. The Minister had stood appalled but unsure of how to intervene and Charles had felt discomforted. His aunt had not been at all put out, she had turned to the man and said icily, "I don't recall telling YOU anything. I WAS having a private conversation. If you make a habit of eavesdropping then you must expect to hear much you do not like. I should say that most people here would share few, if any, of your views. As to Popery, I prefer their open fellowship to your bigotry any day. Come, Charles."

And with that she had left, followed by her nephew, to whom the Minister had winked and raised a thumb. Her adversary had stood red-faced, to the amusement of those around him.

This morning also, as she and Charles sat sipping pre-lunch sherries in the bar in Churriana, she was very much in her English maiden aunt role, he thought glumly. And he had an urgent and delicate, almost desperate, matter to raise with her. How exactly could he go about it without raising her ire, he pondered miserably.

"Let me bring you up to speed on our plans for tomorrow…"

The voice of a young Englishman at the next table brought a frown to his aunt's face.

"What is that young man talking about? Why do the young not use language correctly?" she said acidly, in a voice that carried to the man, who stopped talking and glared at her.

Charles coloured and stuttered out a reply, sotto voce. "It's a sort of, er, Americanism, I suppose. It means, er, to, er, bring you up to date…"

"I know what it means, I object to debasement of the English tongue." Again she spoke icily and clearly.

"What's with you, you old biddy." The man, long-haired and tattooed, had risen and stood over her. She looked back at him calmly. Behind the man a huge Spaniard, of about fifty, had also got up from his seat and sauntered nearer.

"I believe you heard, young man. You have a perfectly good language to use, why do you have to debase it so?" She was polite but adamant.

"I'll give you debase…" he began, to be interrupted by a stream of Spanish from the large man at his shoulder. Miss Shilitoe answered, just as rapidly, in the same tongue, then smiling slightly said to the young man, "Manolito here asks if I need his assistance, but I have assured him that we are simply chatting. That is so, is it not?"

As she spoke the Englishman turned and saw the large burly figure standing behind him. She went on, "Manolito means little Manolo, you can observe that the title little is given in jest."

"Yeah, well, I suppose we are. Just chatting, that is. Come on, let's get out of here." And with that he and his companion left the bar. Manolito, the fifth of her lovers who she had given up, reluctantly, several years ago because of their age disparity, sat down again with a grin.

Miss Shilitoe turned back to her nephew with a sigh. She was extremely fond of Charles, her youngest sister's son, and he visited her more than any of the others of her family. None of them, she knew, could understand why she lived here, in Andalucía, far from them. He was the only one of them, she believed, who knew of her second Spanish persona. But even he did not know it all, of the lovers she had had over the years. Manolito, who she had broken with almost ten years ago, had probably been the most indulgent on her part. Charles obviously had something on his mind, some worry that he wished to share with her, but couldn't bring himself to speak about it. Perhaps she looked too forbidding. She softened her expression and spoke gently.

"What is it, Charles? Why are you looking so pensive?" When he didn't answer, she finished her sherry, rose and led the way into the restaurant. "Come, you can tell me over lunch."

Everyone in the place seemed to know her and it was ages before the waiters had finished fussing around them, and they were left alone with their soup.

"Now, out with it, what's the problem?" she commanded. At last he managed to speak, the sherry and wine they were now drinking and his aunt's subtly changed manner, loosening his tongue. "I've met this girl. Well, I met her several months ago during a previous visit to you. She lives in Cártama. Her name's Elena. We're in love with each other."

The sentences came out in short bursts with long gaps in between, but she didn't interrupt. Over the second course he went on more easily.

"This visit, sometime after I returned, just a few days ago, I sensed something was wrong. At first it was fine, as it always had been, and then one day she seemed worried and more reserved. I can't get her to say what it is and my Spanish isn't good enough to prize out the reason. I'm not fluent enough. Could you help me, Aunt? Try to find out what the problem is?"

She concentrated on eating, considering, and then said, "I would like to meet your Elena. Could you possibly arrange it for tomorrow?"

The following morning when they set out in Charles' car to drive the short distance to Cártama, she had changed from an English spinster to a Spanish señorita by subtly altering her appearance. Wearing a simple black dress, with her grey hair pulled back and held by a red comb, it was perhaps more her bearing that made the real difference.

She took to Elena at once. The Spanish woman was about two years younger than Charles, had black hair and bright flashing eyes. Soon the two of them were chatting animatedly as she drew out the younger woman's background. Second youngest of a large family, a pharmaceutical chemist with good prospects, she thought her an ideal match for her nephew. She both sang and danced the flamenco, and obviously loved her region and home. There was however, as Charles had said, a certain reserve and worry which clouded her eyes from time to time and raised a barrier between them, when she appeared to withdraw into herself and fall silent.

After a while she sent Charles away, telling him that she wanted to talk to Elena alone. When he had gone, albeit reluctantly, she came straight to the point. She may have been in her Spanish persona, but she was still a formidable commanding old lady. Perhaps even more so than in her English mode to Elena, who was reminded of her late autocratic grandmother.

"Now, tell me, what troubles you, child?" Miss Shilitoe demanded rather than asked. "You can trust me utterly, nothing you tell me will go any further, or shock me, no matter what it is. My nephew tells me that he loves you deeply and I will do anything, and I mean anything, to aid his happiness. He has always shown me love and devotion, far more than any other of my relatives, who I see little of. And I feel drawn to you too, so out with it."

The tale took some extracting but at last, bit by bit, Elena told the old lady everything. It was quite simple, but devastating in its potential. Elena's younger brother had fallen in with a crowd of his contemporaries who experimented with soft drugs. Then, one day, a pusher had sold them some heroin and crack cocaine. One of the group had become seriously ill, and ended up in hospital. She, Elena, had heard stories of others who had been addicted to such drugs and ruined their lives, some of them even dying. She had become sick with worry for her younger brother and had approached the man and tried to warn him off. He had turned violent and in defending herself she had killed him and, in panic, hidden the body. She had stabbed him with a sharp knife she had taken along to the meeting for protection. She told Miss Shilitoe that the idea of killing him, if he didn't agree to stop dealing with the locals her brother mixed with, had been in the back of her mind all the time. She had felt strongly and now wasn't in the least sorry for what she had done. The trouble was that the Guardia had found the body and worked out the time of his death. One of the Sergeants suspected her and if he could find enough evidence, which he might at any time, she would be arrested and imprisoned. She would not involve Charles in any of the mess.

Miss Shilitoe thought for a few minutes after she had heard Elena's story and then said, "What a strange coincidence," a remark that mystified the other woman. Then she went on.

"What I am about to tell you now must go no further, not even to my nephew. As I honour your confidence, so you too must honour mine. During my life in Spain I have had several lovers. The first three I gave up for certain reasons, not important here, and the fifth was sheer indulgence on my part. In the end I had to let him go, against his wishes, as I considered it not fair for a forty year old man to be saddled with a seventy year old woman as I was then. I did so reluctantly for he was, and remains for that matter, a fine man and we are still very good friends."

Elena looked at the somewhat prim figure in amazement.

"Incredible, you are truly formidable," she gasped.

"Yes, well, be that as it may, but now to the fourth man, who concerns us here," the old lady continued. "He above all the others was my true love. Or so I thought. Then one day I discovered he was a dealer in hard drugs. I won't bore you with all the details, but I've always detested such people, I've seen too many of their victims. So despite my strong Quaker views on violence, I killed him. I have done my penance in many ways since then to atone, but unlike you faced no human judgement, for no one ever discovered his body, or knew what had happened to him. He simply mysteriously disappeared."

"Thank you for your confidence in me," Elena replied. "It is, as you said, an amazing coincidence. I am sure we both did the correct thing. May I call you tía? For you are like an aunt to me as well as to Charles."

"Of course, and I will call you sobrina in turn, for if I am to be your aunt then you must become my niece. But I had a reason for telling you my story, not just to show that we both have faced the same issue, and resolved it in the same way. Tell me when the man died, and I will say that you were visiting Charles and me at the time, and couldn't possibly have done the deed, I know he will agree to collaborate with us in this. If the Sergeant should come to you, refer him to me. Now, you must come to Churriana with us and confess to our priest. He is a good man and will give you a suitable penance and will hold to his vows of secrecy. He is a close friend of mine and will see you at once if I ask it. Then you can set Charles' mind at rest, and in due course you can marry."

When Charles returned they told him a little of their conversation and he agreed at once to say that Elena had been with him and his aunt on the night in question. They didn't tell him of his aunt's crime, but only of Elena's.

Two days later the Guardia Sergeant visited them and they gave him Elena's alibi. He wasn't fully convinced but when he approached the local *alcalde,* mayor, who had been one of Miss Shilitoe's lovers, he assured him of her probity. The mayor also sent him to the Bishop who affirmed that she was a reliable witness, and a personal friend. With that the sergeant had to be satisfied, and accept that Elena could not have carried out the crime.

Miss Shilitoe then spoke with her friend the priest and confessed her knowledge of the affair. He looked at her with a wan smile. "I doubt you seek absolution from me. But rest assured, Elena has her penance. Part of it, which affects you, is that she is to keep away from that nephew of yours for a month. Such a test will only surely confirm their love. As to the man who you have both told me of, I confess that I cannot hold his death as being in any way regrettable. I may be wrong, for I know that all life is sacred, but his sort bring misery and death in their wake."

"I tend to agree with you," Miss Shilitoe said. "As you are aware, I belong to a society that renounces violence, but then as you also know only too well the flesh is weak. And no, I ask for no absolution from you, I confer my own strictures for my part in the affair, as I always do. I need no priest to stand between me and my God, not even a good friend like you, and surely I am harder on myself than you would be."

She then took her nephew aside and said, "Charles, the priest has given Elena her penance, and part of it is that she may not see you for a month. That is not a long time to wait, if you love her, so be patient. Now you must do your part, for your share in committing perjury. Let me tell you something. In the past I have had several lovers. Don't look so shocked. I have always made my own atonement for the sins. The first three were also desired by friends of mine, whom I judged in each case to love them more than me, but who unlike me had withheld their favours. I also knew that they would marry them, which I wouldn't, for I have never wished to be in a situation where I was subservient to anyone. I gave each of them up, as penance for my sin, and blessed the unions when they occurred. All of them are now my good friends, both husbands and wives alike. You too, Charles, must do your own penance in this case. When you marry Elena, where do you intend to live?"

"Why, Aunt, I will take her back to England. I have my job and life there. But what has that to do with it?"

"No, Charles. She is pure Spanish. A child of Andalucía," his aunt said, ignoring his question. "She would die in England, she needs the sun, the fiestas, the flamenco. Believe me, I know, for I too could not live without them, English that I am. In her case it is even more so. Your atonement is that you must make a life here, with her. Take this month, whilst you wait for her, to learn the language better and find a job. I will be able to help you do that, for I have plenty of friends and one of them at least will offer you a post. In this way you will both be happy, and forget the violence that almost tore you apart."

He looked at her and nodded agreement, he was aware that she was right in her assessment of Elena. He also knew, deep down, that he too loved this country and its people, and that it was not only his attachment to his aunt that had brought him back time and time again.

"Yes, you are right, I will do as you order," he said, then continued. "And you, Aunt, what is your penance for your own complicity in the affair?"

Today she was back in the dress and with the air of her English persona. His prim and fearsome maiden aunt. She looked at him with a wry smile.

"I shall give up my latest lover."

She was truly a formidable old lady.

HER KNICKERS WENT
TO BUCHAREST

FOR THEIR FIFTH WEDDING anniversary Damien and
Bernice Whiteside decided on a week's holiday in southern
Spain. It had to be on a tight budget as Damien worked as a
groundsman for a cricket and bowls club, and Bernice was
a teaching assistant. Neither had large salaries and once rent,
rates, food and so on were deducted, not much was left over
each week for frivolities. They studied options on the
internet and decided on a small, a very small, self catering
house in San Marcos, one of the white villages of the
Axarquía in southern Spain. Casa Rosalinda was the
smallest, and therefore the cheapest, of all the houses on the
agent's list. Their next choice was of a car to rent and
fortunately the smallest car available at *'Mario's más barato'*,
Mario's cheapest hire company, was within their budget.
They would need a car, they decided, as San Marcos was well
inland and off a regular bus route, there being only two
buses a day in and out of the village, and these not at
convenient times unless you worked in Málaga.

The next choice they had to make was that of a
reasonably priced airline. They chose 'Sun Line Jets' whose
owner, the Scot Charles McDuff, boasted that the airline was
the 'Best and cheapest for flights around Europe'. Sun Line
flew to a limited number of European destinations, Málaga
being one of them. Charlie McDuff, 'Chas' as he liked to be

called, owned three planes and by careful scheduling managed to fly to eight different holiday locations, some every day and others just three or four times a week. If all went well and there were not overlong delays for bad weather, mechanical faults and other unplanned events, then the schedule was kept to. In the event of delays of one kind or another, Chas and his team were usually able to rent a plane from another airline to plug the gap. The tight schedules and quick turnaround times resulted in his pilots, cabin crews and organisers working to their limits. And sometimes well beyond them.

Damien and Bernice left Stansted for Málaga on the morning of a Friday in April and landed on time, stepping out of the plane into a fine warm day after leaving a miserable rain-swept England. All was going as they had hoped and planned for their anniversary break. They stood, trolley ready, at baggage reclaim with the other passengers off SLJ426 waiting for their two bags. They never appeared. When the last of the luggage had been taken off the belt, they were still waiting. The belt stopped moving and they looked at each other at a loss. An official who fortunately spoke English came up and advised them to go to the lost baggage desk. Their cases were not to be found there and they were sent to the Sun Line Jet office, which was on the floor above, to report the situation. On the way through the arrivals hall they came across a man holding a notice with 'Mr and Mrs Whiteside' on it. It was the agent from Mario Más Barato car hire and they had to explain to him their predicament. He gave them his card and told them to ring when they were ready to pick up the car.

When they reached the airline desk it was unmanned as the desk clerk was still at the check in desk, dealing with passengers going out on the plane that they had come in on. There was only the one flight that day, as there was any day, and she had to be first at the check-in desk and then at the boarding gate until the plane was ready to depart.

She was therefore not around for problems of the new people coming in. When at last she came back she had to deal with a family who were leaving the following day, were ahead of them in the queue, and had been waiting for quite a while. They wanted to take extra baggage with them and needed to pay the extra charge. It was late afternoon before she was able to establish the, probable, location of their luggage.

"It's either gone to Rome or Bucharest," she told them. "We had flights to both of them from Stansted at nearly the same time as yours, and as there's nothing left there, that's where they'll be. Rome would be better as we fly there every day but the next one back to England from Rumania will not be until Monday. So if they've gone there, they won't get back here until Tuesday."

"If it's Rome," said Damien, who seemed to be quite relaxed about the situation, "when will they get here?"

"Back to Stansted tomorrow," she replied. "Then on to here on Sunday."

"So we won't get our things until Sunday or even Tuesday?" Bernice almost shouted, she unlike her husband was getting very agitated and almost crying. "What about our change of clothes? I can't last until Sunday never mind Tuesday without clean things, especially knickers!"

Damien looked quite shocked as Bernice almost shouted "knickers" into the busy departures hall. Quite a few people passing the desk turned to stare. The girl behind the desk shrugged and said that there was nothing she could do about it. It was past her normal time to leave and she wanted to get off home.

"Phone me in the morning and I'll have some definite news then," was all she could offer.

Damien then phoned Mario Más Barato and told them that they were now ready to pick up the hire car. The morning shift had gone home and the afternoon staff were a long time sorting out the situation but at last the minibus arrived to take them to the firm's garage.

It was early evening when they turned off the motorway at Vélez-Málaga to head inland to San Marcos. At the junction they stopped off at the large shopping complex of El Ingenio to buy food and essential things, such as underwear, to see them over until they managed to retrieve their bags. It was then an hour's drive up the hill to the village and then they had to look for Casa Rosalinda. The woman who looked after the house had been expecting them around lunchtime and it was now nearly eight in the evening. In all the trouble and hassle at the airport they had forgotten to ring her and she had long since given them up as not coming, and was out in a bar. It took a further half hour to track her down but at last they were in the small house and able to sit down.

"We can't even have a stiff whisky," Bernice complained. "The bottle is in my bag. Somewhere in either Romania or Italy."

"Let's go out to a bar and have a meal and a drink," Damien replied in an attempt to cheer her up. "You don't want to be cooking on to top of the day we've had."

It was not an auspicious start to their holiday.

They had planned to spend most of their time in Spain walking in the sierras around the area. That first Saturday morning however was mainly taken up with phone calls to Sun Line Jets, who at last found their bags in Bucharest. They could not get them to San Marcos before Tuesday lunch time. They would however, the agent assured them, bring them up to the village. As Saturday turned into Sunday and then Monday, more and more problems arose. Not only were they short of clothes but they were missing other items. Their walking boots and poles, sun cream, socks, hats were just a few. As they were on a tight budget they were also short of money to buy replacements. It all meant that their walking plans were severely restricted by lack of adequate footwear etc.

Tuesday morning came at last and they went early to the bar where they had arranged to meet the driver from the airline.

Alvaro García Sanchez was also in the bar. Alvaro was a cousin of the bar owner and had been born in the *pueblo*, village, and often came up to visit from Málaga where he lived. He was a reporter for the local newspaper 'Málaga Sol' and also worked freelance for several national papers, and an international news agency. He spoke very good English and had been listening with interest to Damien and Bernice telling the sorry tale of their lost baggage to an expat resident who lived in San Marcos. He translated the story to his *primo,* cousin, Pedro the barman. Both men awaited the arrival of the courier from Sun Line flights with almost as much interest and expectation as the three English customers.

At last a van with the airline's logo on the side drew up outside the bar and the driver got out, went round to the back of the van, opened the doors and took out two cases. The feelings of relief were palpable.

"Señores Whiteside?" he asked coming into the room. As his pronunciation sounded more like "Wited" than "Whiteside" for a while no one responded. Alvaro turned to the two English people and said, "I think he means you, Señor y Señora." The cases were handed over and a paper produced for them to sign.

Bernice gave a loud cry. "This one isn't mine. That's yours, Damien but this one…" She stopped, unable to go on. The driver stood perplexed.

"Is the ones I got. This and this." He pointed to them, moving his arms about to make the point. "This is yours, sir no? and this one lady, this is yours, no?"

"No, it's not bloody mine," Bernice wailed. "It's not mine," she almost shrieked. Damien, who was a much more phlegmatic character, tried to calm her down, but even he was by this time becoming annoyed and even, for him, angry.

Alvaro, who was secretly delighted with the turn of events, sensing a story, put on a grave concerned face and helped sort out the situation. One of the cases was wrong. In fact, he could see from the attached label that it should have gone out with that afternoon's flight to Gatwick.

Another angry customer, another error by an overworked and, he thought to himself, underpaid member of the 'budget' (for that read cheap he added to himself) staff.

He examined the label and saw at once how the error had been made. 'Whitehead' on the one in the bar and no doubt 'Whiteside' on the one either being loaded on to a flight to London or already on its way. He at once made the courier ring the Sun Line flight office at Málaga, and then took over the phone. He quickly explained the position and on hearing that the plane was almost due to take off, demanded that it be held, the right bag taken off the plane, and then brought up to the village. He told the reluctant woman on the other end in rapid Spanish just what headlines the airline could expect if she refused. In the end she, visualising the wrath of the owner of the firm Charles McDuff, agreed to his demand and rang through to the boarding gate. The plane, which had already been delayed by a technical fault, was then delayed yet again from taking off until the case had been found and removed. Alvaro meanwhile explained to the Whitesides what he had arranged, basking in their relief and gratitude. Pedro gave them all a free glass of wine and even Bernice became calm and almost happy at the situation.

Alvaro was already working out his story for the paper. 'Our reporter holds up aircraft departure to solve English holidaymakers' problem'. 'Budget airline spoils anniversary holiday by bag catastrophe'. He would scoop the other papers and gain his editor's praise. He also had contacts with an English paper, one that liked lurid headlines and revelled in finding faults in organisations and making headlines out of them. 'Blame and Shame' was their motto. They would no doubt buy the story and he could probably sell it to an international news agency as well. He was very glad he had come up to San Marcos to visit friends and family. What a real stroke of luck.

The only person in the bar who was not pleased was the van driver, who now faced having to return to the airport and then come all the way back up with the correct bag. He went out with bad grace, almost forgetting to take the wrong case back with him.

Sensing the story was not yet over, Alvaro stayed in the bar with the others to await his return. He wanted to be on hand to witness, and be able to record, Bernice getting her case back at long last.

It was early evening before the van returned and by then news of the events had spread, almost by osmosis as it always seemed to in San Marcos, to both Spanish and expat residents of the pueblo, and the bar was full. Wine, beer and spirits were flowing freely and an atmosphere almost of a fiesta was in the air.

The van driver when he entered was tired, hungry and in a foul mood. He looked in disbelief at the crowd of revellers in the room, spotted Bernice now the worse for wear and went up to her. He almost threw the bag at her feet and shouted above the noise, "Your bag, Señora." The case hit the floor with a crash which was followed almost immediately by a louder bang and the pungent smell of whisky filled the air. He had broken the bottle of spirit in the case. Bernice came forward with raised fists and he fled the scene.

Alvaro's heart overflowed with joyful anticipation at the thought of even more drama to put into his news report. Being a well-read man and a bit of a classicist, he saw the screaming headline in an English tabloid: 'Comedy of Errors by McDuff spoils anniversary holiday'.

Wednesday, which was the last full day of Damien and Bernice's holiday, was spent by them at last being able to go for a long walk, fully fitted out with thick socks, walking boots and walking poles. It was slightly marred by a strong smell of whisky coming from Bernice's clothes. It seemed resistant to all attempts to wash it out. Elsewhere that day their plight and story was aired, with varying degrees of accuracy, by several newspapers in both England and Spain, and on radio and television programmes also in both countries. Many of you reading this will recall James Naughtie on the Today programme commenting that at least the whisky was a good scotch.

Charles Duff, 'call me Chas', who was in his own opinion a master of the art of slick marketing, also decided on that Wednesday to make an event of their arrival back at Gatwick the following day. He would, he determined, make a spectacular advertising coup of the whole sorry affair.

"Damage limitation," he told his long-suffering PA, "and a commercial advertising plus. A win win all round," he said using the overused cliché.

The Whitesides would be met at the airport by him, together with a crowd of news reporters. They would be offered a free two-week holiday and a cheque for a thousand pounds to cover their losses, together with a personal apology. His advertising manager was not so sure that this would either placate them or reflect too well on him. She knew his usual bombastic nature and smooth talk, and was of the opinion that it would not go down well. In his usual way of rejecting all advice that didn't go along with his own opinions, he ignored her protests.

"Why does he bother to employ me at all?" she asked her long-suffering partner. Then added, "but I'm glad he does as he pays me well."

On the Thursday, just after 4 pm, the jet touched down on to the runway at Gatwick. The Whitesides had been given seats at the front of the plane and were escorted off by the chief steward, Ewan. "Don't worry about your bags, they'll be collected for you by one of our staff." Bernice, remembering the last time the staff of Sun Line Jets had handled their cases, looked at him hard to see if he was being serious or facetious. Reassured by Damien that all was well, she followed the two men somewhat mollified, being followed herself by a quite strong smell of whisky.

When they reached the arrivals hall, they were greeted by a beaming Chas McDuff with an anxious PA and a worried advertising manager at his shoulders. Around them was a seething mass of the media, cameras and microphones at the ready.

What happened next was of course seen live on a few channels but was then heavily censored after that on the news programmes, so as not to 'interfere with the course of justice'. Alvaro García Sanchez back in Málaga was bitterly disappointed that he had not flown over to England to be there for the event. It would have been a fitting addition to his story of the couple's troubled stay in San Marcos. It was his story, he firmly believed, and not to have witnessed the final act was almost criminal.

Charles McDuff stepped forward with his usual wide smile. "Mr and Mrs... er..."

"Whiteside," whispered his PA into his left ear.

"Damien and Bernice," hissed his advertising manager into his right.

"Er, yes, Whiteside, Daniel and er, Bernie. Welcome home. We have an apology to make for mislaying your bags. To make up for it I hope you will accept this voucher for a free two-week holiday, and this cheque to cover any loss you may have suffered. I also have," here he held up a bottle of whisky, "I also have a bottle of scotch to replace the one unfortunately broken by our representative in Spain."

He turned around to beam at the media gathered behind him. He was, to quote one commentator, full of 'insincere contrition'. He turned back to the by now agitated Bernice and the more stoic and longsuffering Damien, and handed the bottle of whisky to Bernice, sniffing the aroma that came from her.

"I see I've given you the right tipple," he commented. "I can tell you've been celebrating with a drop of it already. So once again I must..."

He got no further, as with an indignant howl she took the bottle and hit him on the back of the head with it. The bottle then slipped from her fingers and fell with a loud crash to the floor, showering spirit and glass in all directions. An act recorded by a hundred cameras and as many hastily scribbling hacks. Back in Málaga, Alvaro, watching on the telly, almost cried with rage at not being in the crowd around the fallen tycoon. He was however on the phone to his newsroom almost at the same time as the body hit the ground amid the shattered glass and liquid.

At the trial the fact was established that Chas McDuff, or Charles Edward McDuff as the judge and counsels for both the defence and prosecution insisted on calling him, suffered from having a thin bone covering on the crown of his head.

"Thick-skinned and thin-boned," the defence barrister stated time after time. His client was 'driven to distraction by the comedy of errors'. He had read Alvaro's account of the week in Spain and thought it worth a quote. She was, he insisted in his summing up, 'enraged by the sham of insincerity wrapped up in a cloak of false contrition and trivial recompense'. He gave a bravura performance.

The prosecuting council made a lacklustre and, it appeared, almost bored summing up. It could be précised as "She did it and doesn't deny it"; "You all saw it on the television"; "She's guilty so convict her". Indeed the full speech was hardly any longer than the summary.

The jury, who had all suffered at the hands of cheap flights in the past, refused to convict on a charge of murder. Also the judge, who had had some bad experiences of his own of low-cost airlines, ruled in his summing up that no premeditation had been part of the act. The jury in returning, as they had to, a verdict of manslaughter, added a strong plea for clemency.

The judge before passing sentence, gave a long, rambling and almost incoherent speech on 'thinness of bones', 'rash thoughtless actions brought on by passion and loss' and 'people who ought to know better before bringing down on themselves actions of others encouraged by their own sanctimonious conceit'. He then passed a ruling of a five years suspended sentence.

Bernice when she had been arrested had been given bail as she, in the words of the police inspector at the time, posed no threat to society. The magistrate at the preliminary hearing also granted bail and therefore she served no time in jail at all.

Damien and Bernice dined out on their story for years and as she always said, "If my knickers hadn't gone to Bucharest, then in all probability Chas would still be alive."

"And two bottles of good scotch wouldn't have been wasted," Damien always added.

SISTERS

ROGER STILL CAME TO stay with me several times even after the death of Kate, his wife and my sister. Bill, my husband, and I were both very fond of his two girls, who we treated almost as our own. Even after the sudden death of Bill, whilst he was in England on business, the three of them visited me as usual. This year however, with both girls away at college, I was surprised when Roger rang to say he'd like to come as usual during the spring half-term. I'd agreed of course and so here we were sitting on the terrace, with Roger mixing gin and tonics at the small bar Bill had built just inside the living room door.

All I could see of him was his back, busily moving from side to side as he opened the bottles and poured out the drinks. I glanced idly at the mirror on the opposite wall and saw him tip something from a small bottle into one of the glasses. This puzzled me, but then I thought, perhaps he's on medication or something and doesn't want to tell me. He came back on to the terrace, placed one glass in front of me and the other by his side on the small table that was between us. It can't be medication, I thought in some confusion, not put into alcohol.

"Do you like my new picture I bought in Fuengirola last week?" I asked, pointing back into the lounge. He turned to look over his shoulder at the oil painting by a local artist of Málaga harbour.

"It's very good, was it very expensive?" he said, turning back.

Just like him to think of the cost, I thought. "No, not very, well, cheers." I picked up my drink and sipped it.

"Cheers, bottoms up," and he downed his drink at one go and got up to replenish his glass. When he came back, I finished mine too and rose.

"No, don't get up, I'll do it myself," I told him as he started to rise and went and mixed myself another.

I'm not describing this very clearly, am I, perhaps I'd better start at the beginning. Kate and I grew up in Ilford in Essex, and we met Roger and Bill at a disco in Leyton about twenty-five years ago. Roger and Bill were long-standing friends and the four of us paired off. Eventually we got married and over the next few years were always close to each other. Bill's father had a small factory in Grays which eventually Bill took over. He built it up, then opened two more and we became relatively rich.

Roger was a biology teacher at a comprehensive in Stratford and they were not anything like so well off. We might have become less close if it wasn't for the two girls. Bill and I discovered quite early on in our marriage that we couldn't have children, whilst Kate and Roger soon had two lovely young girls. Both Bill and I love children, and as uncle and aunt as well as godparents to them both, became very attached to them and we visited each other's houses frequently.

When the girls were six and seven respectively, Bill had a mild heart attack and was told to slow down. What we finally decided to do was to buy a villa out here in Spain where he could relax and run his factories using short visits to England, the telephone and fax, and recently the internet. He had very good managers in all his factories, which now number five in all.

Roger, Kate and the girls visited us every school holiday with us often paying the fares, as Roger's salary could not stretch that far. We were pleased to do this as over the years the girls had become almost like daughters to us. As we had no children of our own and Bill was an only child, and I had no other family but Kate, we even drew up our wills in favour of the girls, or rather in favour of Kate who would, by agreement between her and myself, use it for their education and then when they were twenty-one pass it over to them. Kate and I had always been close and I knew I could trust her fully in this. When the girls reached twenty-one then, we were all agreed, we would draw up new wills in their favour. In the event of Kate's death before this time, we put in a clause naming Roger in her place. You may think it strange that we only put Kate's name on the will, and Roger's only if she died, but to tell you the truth I've never really trusted him. I've always felt he begrudged Bill his business success and envied him too much. He's always going on about the cost of things, like my picture for instance, and how little they have. It used to embarrass my sister, I know. Anyway, Bill didn't want his name on the will either, despite their long friendship, and so Kate alone was named.

Our villa is out past Coín in the Sierra de Canucha, and so was handy for the airport, the beach, the towns of Marbella, Fuengirola, Torremolinos and Málaga. It is also easy to get to Ronda and the lakes near Ardales, both places the girls adored visiting.

This was the way things were until two years ago when Kate contracted cancer, and was dead in less than twelve months. As I've said already, Roger and the girls still came out a few times together after that, and Bill and I were glad to have them come. In fact we insisted they did, for they needed to get away for a break, and we wanted to see the girls. Bill and I did nothing about the will, it's not something we really thought about in any case.

Then just two months ago Bill went to England to do his twice yearly tour of his factories. I'll never forget the day the two Guardia came to my door, one male and one female, to tell me he'd been killed. They were very kind and sympathetic, but I just couldn't believe it. He'd apparently fallen under a tube train in the rush hour at Holborn station. It was an accident of course, no thought that he'd done it deliberately, the platform was crowded and those nearest said he'd apparently stumbled under pressure from behind him.

When I got over the first shock I wrote to the girls, who were now both at University, and told them I was looking forward to seeing them in the summer holidays. I also told them that I meant to change my will to make them direct beneficiaries now, and not when they were twenty-one. They knew all about the conditions in the old will, we made sure of that once they were in their early teens. I didn't write to tell Roger of my intentions and didn't know if either of them had mentioned it to him.

And then, just a week ago, Roger had rung to say he'd like to come out this holiday on his own. He arrived this morning and I met him at the airport as usual. He seemed tense and preoccupied, and explained that it had been a hard term at school, and that Bill's death so soon after Kate's had left him very low.

Now we sat on the terrace, in the warm night air, both sunk deep into comfortable armchairs. My eyes began to close as I sipped my third gin and tonic, and I could see that his were closing too. He was however, I saw, looking at me intently through his half-closed lids. I yawned widely, I had been up since very early to get ready for his visit and meet his flight, then we'd had wine with a late lunch which always makes me sleepy. He stifled a half yawn himself and smiled at me. "Feeling tired, are you?" he asked. "Heavy limbed perhaps?" I nodded silently in reply, sinking further down in the chair, and putting my drink on the floor. His breathing became heavier and he too sank lower in his chair, pouring himself a fourth drink from the bottles he had brought out to the terrace with him. He raised his glass to me. "Cheers, Ruth. Going to change your will, were you? Cut me out and give it all to the girls, eh?"

"Only if I die," I mumbled, stunned by his remark and tone.

"Oh, you're going to die alright. Just as Bill did."

Shock hit me, but lethargy kept me sitting, almost asleep in my chair. "What do you mean, just like Bill?" I muttered.

He seemed to sink even deeper down and answered me slowly and somewhat disjointedly. "Bill... well, he had it all, didn't he... lots of money... prettiest sister."

I almost jerked awake. "No, I'm not, Kate was just as pretty as me, anyway I wanted Bill, I wouldn't have married you even if he'd chosen Kate." I sank back down and repeated more slowly and sleepily, "What do you mean, just like Bill?" His voice came to me once more, slow, jerky, disjointed, but with a note of triumph in it.

"I was with him… on the platform… pushed him, didn't I." For a moment his eyes closed and he looked half asleep, drugged. In the silence the night sounds were loud and clear. The call of "Mulo. Arre, arrrreee," from across the valley, as Paco returned home from his vineyard. The call of a grouse from close at hand, the rattle of a motorbike as it passed on a nearby road. Then he spoke again, sleepily but confident. I listened in horror as he went on. "It was no accident… met him after school, didn't I… wanted a bit for myself… but he wouldn't lend me anything, said I should live on my salary… rich bugger… all this… and anything for the girls… but not for me."

"So," I spoke softly and slowly, coming to terms with it. "You pushed him in front of a tube train. Why? That didn't get you anywhere, did it?"

"S'right, pushed him… sure it did… or will," his voice was becoming fainter and slower as sleep overtook him. "Cos, you haven't… you haven't changed your will yet, have you? And it all comes to me… now that Kate's gone. Put something in your drink, didn't I… not a biology teacher… not a biology teacher for nothing, am I."

He struggled to sit up and open his eyes, fighting his sleep. He smiled then as he looked across at my recumbent figure opposite him. When he spoke again, his voice was firmer, louder, more coherent. "It's something I made up in the lab, you'll just go to sleep and not wake up, nobody will suspect anything. It'll look like a heart attack. Brought on by the events of the last year or so, Kate's and Bill's death, having to cope with his business, that sort of thing." He stopped speaking and his eyes closed again, a snore came from his lips.

I pulled myself together and stood up. "Roger!" I half shouted to wake him. His eyes came half open and he stared at me standing over him, in a dazed puzzled way. "Roger, before you nod off, you ought to know something. I saw you put something in the glass. I didn't know what it was, but noted you had given it to me. I switched glasses when you were looking at the picture. Whatever you planned for me, well, now you have it yourself. No trace, no suspicion, you said, look like a heart attack. Overwork at school, grief over Kate and Bill I expect, something like that."

He was staring at me open-mouthed in horror, then his eyes closed and he slipped into a deep dreamless sleep. It won't bring Bill back of course, but at least he won't be able to cheat his own daughters when I'm dead. That won't be long now, as I've got cancer, which is why I get so tired of an evening. It's obviously a family weakness. So when I die, they'll get it all between them, just as we planned.

BULL IN A CHINA SHOP

ESMERELDA WAS BORN IN a small village in the North Yorkshire Moors, not all that far from Northallerton. Where her mother got the name from no one was ever sure, certainly there were no relatives of that name or indeed anyone else in the village or surrounding area. As a girl growing up she was of course known to everyone as Essie.

Essie was, at least according to her mother, a clumsy child, always dropping things and barging into people, furniture and other objects in the home.

"You're like a bull in a china shop," her mother told her, sometimes several times a day.

Over the road from Essie's house was the farm of Frank Fitzough, a big red-faced Yorkshireman who kept, amongst other stock on his farm, a herd of cows for milk. Essie loved going over to the farm and would spend hours playing there, feeding the hens and helping Joan, Frank's wife, in the dairy. She was especially fascinated by the cows and she used to watch their lumbering progress across the yard and say "just like bulls in a china shop". One day when she was about six years old Frank Fitzough, hearing her call the cows bulls, said, "Nay, lass, them's not bulls. Them's cows."

"What's a bull then, Frank?" Essie asked. "Is it like black Sam in the shed? The one I'm not allowed near, cos he's dangerous?"

"Aye lass. Sam's a bull alright. Now look on, see under

the cows, them's teats where we get t'milk from?" Frank was not hesitant in showing her the difference between bulls and cows, and he lifted her up so that she could see over the half door of the bull's shed. Inside was a large black bull with a ring through its nose. This was the first time Essie had seen him close up, having been careful to keep away from the shed after being told he was a dangerous animal.

"Now lass, look ye at yon beast. See, he's got no teats. See his tackle, well, that's a bull. A cow's got teats for milk, but a bull, like old Sam here, he's got tackle like that."

As Essie grew older, she grew to be quite graceful and it was obvious she would one day be beautiful. She was no longer a clumsy child, but delicate and quite deft in her movements. To her mother, however, she was still a "clumsy article" and the phrase "like a bull in a china shop, you are" was still heard at least once a day.

It became an obsession with Essie. She knew what a bull was, a great big black cow with tackle instead of teats. A man cow, her uncle told her. But what was a china shop? She looked for one every time she went out with her mother shopping, or out for the day in a nearby town. She looked in Northallerton, Thirsk, Middlesbrough, Darlington, even once when they went to see her Auntie Dot in York, but could never find one. There were shops with china in them, but there was always glassware or pots and pans and all sorts of other goods as well. She could never find a shop that just sold china, a real china shop. She tried to imagine black Sam in Binn's department store in Middlesbrough and failed. To get to the china department he would have to go through menswear and down the escalator. It was no good.

"What does a china shop look like?" she would ask her mother.

"Don't be daft, lass. One full of cups and plates and so on. Don't ask such silly questions."

But that was not the answer, she had never seen a shop with just cups and plates and suchlike in, only one with them in a small part of it. As she grew older the obsession with bulls and china shops got worse, instead of just fading away as it should have. Every time she dropped something, or fumbled, or bumped into anybody or anything, she would mutter to herself "just like a bull in a china shop".

And try as she might, she could not get the sight of black Sam and his tackle from her mind, or get over her search for a shop that only sold china. Even when she went to Leeds to university, now a beautiful young woman, she still thought of herself as clumsy, gauche and something of a country bumpkin.

It was not till she visited Spain during her first year at university that she found what she was looking for. She went to Málaga with two friends from her course. They had managed to get cheap return flights for a week and rented a small apartment in Torre del Mar. On their third day in the town they were walking along the Avenida de Andalucía, when she saw it, a Cerámica. Her two friends could not understand her excitement, yes it was cheap, there were lots of lovely things in the shop, but why all the fuss?

"It's a china shop," Essie stood enthralled. "Nothing else, just clayware, china."

At last she had found what she was looking for. She imagined black Sam, now long since gone to the slaughterhouse, rampaging through here, ring in his nose, tackle swinging below. Oh yes, what a sight, what havoc he would cause! This then was what her mother thought of her, for she still scolded her in the same way every time she went home, a big black bull crashing through a shop like this. Gaily painted chinaware of all descriptions, cups, bowls, clocks, vases, plates, egg cups and much much more, all crashing to pieces as she lumbered her way through.

She also found what she was looking for on a visit to Málaga, to the bull ring. She had to go alone on this trip as neither of her companions would go with her.

"I wouldn't go to a bullfight, ugh, nasty cruel things," said one, and "What do you want to go there for? I hate blood sports," said the other. But go she did, all alone, and was spellbound. Bull after bull she saw, all black, all with mighty tackle, but all much more agile and lively than old Sam had ever been. And gaily clad men, in their suits of lights, just like the chinaware in the Cerámica, running and spinning and fighting the maddened bulls. She was enthralled, seeing not the cruelty, not the tawdriness, but only the splendour of the ballet-like dance of death, the beauty of the barbarism. And she thrilled when a bull caught a toreador on the thigh and split it open, red blood splashing out on to the sawdust of the ring. She shouted out with the crowd each time the matador cut off the ear of the dead bull. She had never been so excited in her life. It wasn't till much later back in the villa that she realised from the state of her underwear, that she had been sexually aroused by the bullfight.

After that she spent every holiday in Spain, going time

after time to the local cerámicas, and when it was the season to as many bullfights as she could. None of her friends could understand her fascination with the bullring, and they did not realise that this fascination was turning into an obsession.

When she left university she took a job as a PA to the managing director of a large finance company in London. With her B.A. in Economics behind her she was soon promoted to director level herself. She became well groomed, sleek and ruthlessly efficient. Despite being chased by many suitors she remained detached and rebuffed all their attempts. Sex, it seemed, did not interest her. She acquired the nickname 'The ice maiden'. Esmerelda, for she no longer tolerated Essie, even from such close friends as she had, took no notice of any of this however. At work and in London she was the cool, distant, efficient financial expert.

If any of her work colleagues or friends had seen her on holiday in Spain, they would not have recognised her. Over the years she had learnt Spanish, studied the bullfight, bought a small flat in Torremolinos, and, once there, blended in with the local populace.

Gone was the severe pulled back hairstyle, gone the smart city suits, gone the cool efficient air. In their place came the long swinging hair, elegant Spanish dresses, bronzed sun kissed skin and a wild exuberant lifestyle. She made friends with Spanish women of her own age, and went to the bullfights with them. Her apartment was filled with chinaware of all sorts, "My own china shop" she called it to herself.

She was also attracted to brown swarthy Spaniards, with whom she made wild passionate love, always at home amid her chinaware. Over the years however, brown swarthy skin was no longer sufficient for her and she sought out darker and darker skinned men. First, Spaniards of Moorish descent, then Moroccans and finally black sub Saharan men.

They had to have three qualities, a black skin, good sized tackle and a passion for bullfights. When with such a man, at a bullfight, she could reach a climax watching a good kill. Her excitement would rise as the fight progressed, each pass, each twirl of the cloak increasing her excitement, until clutching her companion's arm she would slump in ecstasy after the kill when the ear was cut off. She found it increasingly impossible to find any man who could either satisfy her after this, or stay with her, because of her increasing demands and her obvious obsessive behaviour.

Returning back to London after one such visit to Málaga, she found that a new director had been appointed who had an office next to hers. He was a tall, powerful black man, lithe and handsome. Just the type she would have gone for when on holiday. But here she was Esmerelda, the ice maiden, cool, efficient, with a big 'No sex please' label clearly showing in the way she dressed and by her cool detached manner.

She was in an internal state of confusion. Her every day, workday normal life was being invaded by her fantasy life of Spain. She found herself standing at times in bewilderment, not knowing what was happening.

Then one day reality clicked in and the newcomer asked her out for a drink, and to everyone's surprise, even her own, she accepted. "The ice maiden's melting" the rumour spread rapidly through the office.

"But with him, a black man," said some of the more prejudiced girls.

"Oh he's lovely, dishy, I wish he'd ask me out," sighed others.

"It's not right, man, he should stay with the sisters, like us," was the opinion of a few of the more militant black women.

The following year Esmerelda and her man went on holiday together to her flat in Torremolinos. When they first got there he was amazed at the transformation that took place. Her hair, her clothes, her language, her friends, her manner, all were entirely opposite to her London persona. He was not sure he liked it, even thought at first that she was not quite sane, but a bit unbalanced. But he went along with it all, all that is except for one thing. Try as she might, he would not go to a bullfight with her.

"I don't like them, hon. Really, I think it's weird you like 'em, you know."

So she was forced to go alone, but it was not the same without him. He met her one day immediately after a bullfight, just outside the ring in Málaga. She called a taxi and they got in. She was obviously in a high state of nervous excitement.

"Torre del Mar," she told the driver.

"Where are we going, hon?" he asked. "I thought we were going out for a drink."

"I want to show you something, something I found on my first visit here. You'll love it," she told him.

She was wearing a multi coloured dress in some sort of shiny fabric that glittered in the sun. "My suit of lights" she called it. When they reached Torre she directed the taxi down the Avenida de Andalucía to the Cerámica, the one she had found on that very first holiday.

She dragged him out of the car and pulled him up to the window, becoming more and more excited.

"What is it, hon?" he asked bewildered.

"It's a china shop," she told him, pushing him inside.

Once there she drew a small sharp wicked-looking dagger from her handbag. She flourished it in front of him and he started back, knocking over a set of china bowls. The loud crash startled everyone in the shop. She advanced waving the knife in front of him and he turned to get away, sending more china spinning to the floor. All around people jumped out of the way of her wildly flaying arms, and turned to run out of the shop. More chaos and crashes followed.

"Bull in a china shop," she screamed. "Hay un toro en la cerámica," plunging the knife into his neck. Blood spurted everywhere and he dropped dying at her feet.

"Olé," she cried, and stooped and cut off his ear, brandishing it aloft. "Bull in a china shop," she shouted once more, climaxed, and dropped in a dead faint in the midst of a sea of broken crockery and blood.

DÉJÀ VU

LEN PETERS CAME INTO the square of Tejedos following the float of San Anton, the town band and a crowd of villagers. It was Saturday evening and the fiesta was well underway. Lenny had followed the procession through the village enjoying the music and the spectacle, and now stood watching the group of men carrying the statue lift it high into the air on outstretched arms. The band played a rousing tune, the villagers clapped and shouted "Viva, viva San Anton", and children ran round the edges of the crowd. Len was thoroughly enjoying himself and silently thanked his cousin Samantha for suggesting he come out to Spain for a break, and lending him her village house to stay in.

The statue had now been lowered so that it could be carried through the door of the church, and the band was playing the *himno nacional*, the Spanish national anthem. Len knew it was the himno nacional, for Samantha when describing the fiesta he would witness had explained in detail what happened and when. He knew that the following morning the square would be filled with animals; horses, mules, dogs and even perhaps cats and rabbits. That the priest would come out of the church after the mass and bless them, sprinkling holy water over them as they paraded in front of him. There would be more music and then on Sunday evening there would be a fireworks display.

He made his way to the bar set up in the square for the

fiesta and wedged himself in the corner where the bar met the wall, from where he could survey the whole of the scene. He waited patiently for the barmen to serve the crowd that had descended on the bar at the end of the procession. On the stage erected to one side of the square a pop group were about to begin their evening session. He ordered a glass of *cerveza,* beer, and observed the other customers. Mainly they appeared to be locals, many of whom he now recognised after a week in the pueblo. There was also a small group of Moroccans and two groups of obvious holiday makers, one English and one, he thought by the language, either Dutch or German. These latter two groups had obviously had a lot to drink and were talking loudly and were quite boisterous. He wet his lips with his beer but did not drink any as he considered if he should simply relax and enjoy himself or take advantage of the situation.

Len, or Lenny the dip as he had been known back in Poplar, was as his nickname suggested a pickpocket, and a good one at that.

He'd been born in Poplar forty years ago and as a teenager had been taken in by his uncle on the death of his parents. His uncle Harry had taught him all he knew about the art of picking pockets. 'Fingers Harry' was an expert and had several strict rules which he had drummed into Lenny. First, never drink when working, it made you careless and over confident, clumsy and easier to spot. Second, never take more than four wallets or purses at any one venue. Never go back to the same place within at least two years, there were countless spots to work, Fingers had stressed, sports venues, tube stations, street markets, crowded streets, theatre and cinema crowds, the list was endless. Only keep cash, credit cards and the like were dangerous and could lead the police to you.

Lenny had listened and learned and now stuck rigidly to the same set of rules. He had only strayed once, and learnt his lesson. On his seventeenth birthday he had gone with a crowd of his mates to a pub and after a drinking session, feeling overconfident, had broken Harry's first and cardinal rule and started lifting wallets. He had been caught and ended up in court. Because it was his first offence, and in the light of his age, he was given a caution and a suspended sentence. After that he never strayed from his uncle's rules and was never caught again. When he was twenty he moved from Poplar, where he was well known by the police even if they couldn't catch him, and went to live in a flat in Loughton near to his cousin Samantha. Harry had been his father's brother whilst Samantha was the daughter of his mother's sister, and she knew nothing of his activities. She thought he worked somewhere in the city. He did, often, but not at the sort of job she imagined. Over the years they became good friends. In November Len went down with a bout of food poisoning and was slow in recovering to full health. Samantha, who had a holiday home in Tejedos, suggested that he go out in January to rest and speed his recovery. You could be there for San Anton, she had told him, and then explained in some detail what the fiesta would be like. She said that she usually went out herself but this year had other commitments. She also told him that though it was January, the weather could be warm and sunny, in fact often was.

So he had come out and so far had had a good time and was now well on the way back to full health. He had hired a car and gone down to the coast, the weather had indeed been good, if chilly in the evenings, and he had walked on the beach, sat in *chiringuitos*, bars, on the prom and walked in the sierras above the village. He had also taken two longer drives, the first to Ronda and the second to Nerja Caves. In Ronda he had visited the museum at the bullring and another devoted to outlaws of the region. He had also crossed the ancient bridge over the deep gorge, where people had been flung to their death during the Civil War.

Until now he had not once thought of his trade or practised it since leaving Stansted airport. On his arrival at Stansted he had mingled with the crowds in arrivals, in quick succession lifted three wallets and then immediately gone to departures taking with him enough money to cover his air fare and car hire and also with some over for spending money.

The group on stage were now playing a pasodoble and people were dancing. The square was full of people and movement. Ideal for him, Lenny thought, and decided to act. First he had to get rid of his beer, no drinking and working being the number one rule. Making sure, as he thought, that no one was watching, he poured the liquid into the gap between the bar front and the wall. Then to keep up a normal appearance he ordered a coke, and slowly sipped it whilst waiting his chance.

José Luis Santiago Cabello, to give him his full name, Negrito to his friends, saw Lenny pour the cerveza away and covertly watched him. José Luis was from the pueblo and often returned from time to time, especially for fiestas. This time he was here on duty as well. He worked for a plainclothes department of the Policía Nacional, similar to the English Special Branch. He belonged to a small team in that section whose speciality was that of being watchers, expert in the art of surveillance. They cultivated a persona that was nondescript and average, with an ability to blend into the background. To watch and follow people without being noticed.

He had been sent to Tejedos because he originally came from the village, to watch a Moroccan who was suspected of links to Al Qaeda. His task was to either confirm or not the connection. So far the man had raised no suspicions but simply mixed with the few well-liked and integrated Moroccans of the village. He was now at the bar together with a few of them, watching the fiesta.

Negrito, who was bored, continued to watch as Lenny passed the two groups of *extranjeros,* foreigners, at the bar lifting wallets from four of them on his way to the toilet. A few minutes later he returned to the bar, finished his coke, paid for it and left the *plaza,* square.

José Luis also slipped from his place and followed Lenny through the almost empty small streets. He watched as Lenny went through an arched opening that led to a small square and then into a house. Five minutes later he knocked on the door.

Lenny had just lit the log burner and taken out his stolen goods when the knock came. Putting the wallets into a drawer he cautiously opened the door. José Luis smiled at him and showing his warrant card, asked in perfect English if he could come in. Lenny's thoughts were in turmoil, how could he have been so stupid as to get caught in a strange country, he asked himself, barely aware of what José Luis was telling him.

He was not interested in the robberies, José Luis explained to Lenny. He was not in the ordinary police and his job was not connected to petty crime. So he was not interested, he repeated, that is if Lenny would do a small job for him. Then, if the Englishman would agree to commit no more crimes, he would take no further action.

Lenny, who was due to return to England on Monday, readily agreed. What did the Spaniard want him to do, he wondered.

José Luis explained. He had noticed a mobile phone in the Moroccan's jacket pocket. Lenny would take it, give it to him, and then a few minutes later return it to the same pocket.

No problem, Len thought, as long as the phone did not ring during the operation.

This settled, the pair returned to the square.

Negrito pointed out the Moroccan to Lenny who duly took the phone. He gave it to the Spanish agent, who removed the SIM card and put it into a small object which could extract and store the data on the phone. With this José Luis could see who the man had been in contact with and this could help decide if he was an Al Qaeda member or not. He replaced the card and handed the phone back to Lenny, who in turn returned it to the Moroccan's pocket. All's well that ends well, Lenny thought.

Nothing else untoward happened during Len's stay in

the pueblo and on the Monday morning he drove back to Málaga airport, returned the hire car, and flew back to Stansted. He was relaxed, back to full health, had enjoyed the holiday and was well in profit from his trip.

He was so pleased with himself that he decided to go by taxi all the way to Loughton and to steal his fare by picking a couple of pockets in the busy arrivals hall.

Keith Watson, one of MI5's watchers who had been notified by the Spanish police of Lenny's identity and flight, watched unseen as Len lifted the two wallets and then went into the toilets, presumably to dump the now empty articles.

As Lenny got into the taxi Keith got in behind him, showing him his warrant card. He explained to the crestfallen man that he was not in the ordinary police, not interested in petty crime, not interested that is if Lenny would agree to do the odd job for the service from time to time.

A feeling of déjà vu came over Lenny the dip.

OVER THE EDGE

THE NARROW ROAD TO Las Hojas climbs over 600 metres from the coastal plain to the village, in a continuous sequence of hairpin bends and long straights. To one side of the road the sierra falls away steeply, whilst on the other it rises almost vertically to join the slope above. On the worst bends the cornice road is protected by crash barriers, some of steel posts and rails, and the others of older low stone blocks set intermittently on the roadside. The remainder, that of the straight sections and gentler bends, is unprotected. As the British agent, who sells many of the houses to the growing expatriate community, tells his clients, "It's not the Guardia Civil you need to worry about if you drive over the alcohol limit, it's avoiding driving over the edge!"

William Ambrose was sitting on one of these low stone crash barriers in a small lay-by, several kilometres below Las Hojas. From where he sat he had a good view of the road winding above and below him. When agitated it was his practice to jump into his car and race down the narrow road for some distance, park, and let his mood change before returning home. Looking up, he saw coming down from the village the unmistakeable car belonging to Roger, "Call me Rog," Bray. Bray was the unwitting cause of his agitation, and on seeing the car fear and panic rose up in him. He ran back to his own vehicle and careered off once more down the hill.

Such was his panic that he approached an unprotected bend too fast, braked too late and too hard, skidded and shot over the edge. His last conscious thoughts were the words of the estate agent, someone who he had long since fallen out with, and who he was no longer speaking to. Poetic justice indeed.

Shortly after, a horrified Roger Bray stood looking down at the remains of the car, together with several Spaniards, as it burnt out in the *barranco,* deep gully, below.

The roots of the tragedy went back many years. William Ambrose, always William, never ever Will or Bill, was an ex-teacher of English and R.E. For many years he had taught at a large Midland Comprehensive. Tall, impeccably dressed, sandy haired with a bristling moustache, he was an imposing figure. He was always over polite and punctilious in his language. Never a "who" when it should be "whom", or "I" when "me" was the correct word, he came across as cultured to some but obsessive to others. The slightly manic gleam in his eyes gave a clue as to the reality.

He had as a schoolteacher three failings. He could not keep a class in order, a weakness exploited mercilessly by his pupils. He had an inability to relate to people and so could not get along with his colleagues, causing unrest in the staffroom. His third failing, which was unknown to most others, except the headmaster, was his fascination with the older girls, especially their lingerie. This last was also known to several of the girls, most of whom kept out of his way, but were resigned to seeing him staring at them on the games field.

One of the girls, Betty Williams, well known for her forwardness, deliberately led him on and then accused him of attempted rape. Her father, a burly building labourer, visited the school, caused a scene and struck William on the nose.

Ambrose was lucky in that the event occurred before the days when an accusation of sexual harassment was sure to cause a national scandal, and also that Betty's father had assaulted him. The incident drove Ambrose, not for the first time, over the edge, producing a nervous breakdown, and he was off work for a lengthy period. During this time the headmaster and Betty's father, who were both aware of her character, struck a deal. No prosecution for molesting the girl or for assault on the teacher. The headmaster was then able to have Ambrose retired, at the age of 49, on grounds of ill health.

Fortune once again shone on William, as he sold his house for an enormous profit at the height of the housing boom, bought his place in Las Hojas inland from the Costa del Sol at a low price, invested the profit and lived comfortably off his pension and investment income. No one had cause to complain, except perhaps the tax payer funding his pension and the purchaser of his house, who was soon a victim of negative equity when house prices slumped.

During all this time he had been supported by his wife Ann. She was several years younger than him, fair haired and 'county' in both accent and dress. Despite his difficult and unstable character she had been quite happy during their marriage, until the move to Spain. She had not wanted to move abroad, and was unhappy living there, and became much more aware of his peculiarities.

He started writing stories, "Not for publication, just for

my own pleasure and reading," he told such friends that they managed to keep in the district. These stories centred on the expat community. Ann would invite them to dinner and from their comments William would evolve their 'life stories'. Most of these were wildly inaccurate but, for him, became reality. Janet Pusey, a blousy well developed matron, really had been, in his own mind, a prostitute in Leeds. Jerry Paxman, who in real life had been a postman, to William was a crooked County Councillor from Exeter, and so on.

A second obsession, which had started in England but was now much worse and more developed, was his insistence that Ann wear sexy underwear. She wore the silk and the transparent lingerie, the easy to undo front fixing bras, and the crotch opening pants unhappily under her flowery conventional dresses.

Some ten years after they had moved to the village, Roger Bray arrived. Rog was a widowed East ender, just older than Ann, with a coarse accent. He had been the owner of a small publishing house in Bethnal Green, until he sold it on to his partner just after the death of his wife, and moved to Las Hojas. He had never let on to anyone what his job was, as if he did he was inundated with manuscripts by would-be authors. He retained this practice after his move to Spain, simply saying he "had had a firm in the East End". On a visit to Roger's house William had seen on the desk a replica pistol, a lifelike gun but in reality a cigarette lighter, given to him by his staff when he sold the firm. William however thought it was real and so built up and wrote a story of Roger being the boss of an East End 'firm' of gangsters.

He left the story, newly typed, on the table where Ann found it, just prior to a visit by Roger. She quickly put it in a drawer but forgot to tell William.

The next morning, after the visit, he hunted in vain for the story whilst Ann was out in the village, and convinced himself that Roger had found it and taken it away. His unstable nature then took over. To him the story was the reality, the gangster Roger would discover that he, Willliam, knew all about him and come after him. In a high state of alarm and agitation he raced off down the mountain and parked in the lay-by. He saw to his horror that Roger was pursuing him, gun at the ready. This drove him over the edge, both mentally and in reality.

Nine months after the funeral Roger went to Ann's house for dinner. Since being the first on the scene of the accident he had been in close and constant contact with her, feeling some sense of responsibility. Tonight he had some bad news for her. He had told her of his past as a publisher and offered to take away William's collected stories to read, and if suitable send them to his old partner for publication.

"They're no good, I'm afraid, poorly written, and in any case highly libellous. I must say I can't see Mrs Pusey as a call girl myself, but enjoyed reading about my East End gang and moll."

Ann blushed, as she had meant to remove that one before giving them to him.

"But they're no good for publication, I'm sorry."

Ann was not at all concerned. She had discovered that with the investment income and the insurance on William's life, she was in no need of any payment for their publication.

She had also become increasingly fond of Roger, finding his easy going nature relaxing after William's punctiliousness. She no longer wished to leave Spain and was now more than happy living in the village. Her voice had become softer, less strident and 'county' in its nature.

Tonight for the first time since William's death she was wearing under her sheath dress, itself a change from her usual flowery ones, a set of exotic translucent silk underwear. Roger did not know this, "At least not yet," she thought.

After dinner, on the roof terrace, she brought out two glasses of brandy and bent over to hand Roger his, allowing him to see her breasts, lifted and separated by the bra, through the gap in her low cut dress.

"Shall we have these inside? It's getting midgey out here, and it's very public."

She gazed around the quiet, empty roofs and terraces surrounding them, turned and swayed gently away from him into the house.

PRESSING CHARGES

ON THE TUESDAY OF Holy Week, towards the end of March, the headlines in the press were all about the same event. The broadsheets were headed by phrases such as 'Philip Ray believed found in southern Spain' and 'Englishman held on traffic charges in Spain thought to be Philip Ray'; whilst the tabloids, never ones to be bothered by irrelevancies such as truth or facts, screamed out 'Phil Ray found on the Costa' and 'Gotcha Phil! (sun, sex and crime over for "Búril Phil")'.

The previous Friday afternoon, two Guardia Civil patrolmen on motorbikes had spotted a car travelling at over 160 k.p.h. on the new stretch of the N340 Autovía, near K275 where it approached the Torre del Mar and Vélez-Málaga turn off. The two officers immediately gave chase, and after some difficulty succeeded in forcing it to a halt on the hard shoulder near the exit ramp at K272. If the driver of the car, an Englishman, had not reacted violently to the event, he would have been sent on his way with no more than a caution or a fine. As it was, he first verbally and later physically abused one of the patrolmen, finally trying to run off down the embankment away from the scene. At the time one of the officers had been casually looking at the man's documents, and then giving them a closer scrutiny as the driver's manner began to annoy the pair. He decided that the papers did not look right, though whether this was more to do with him actually spotting any irregularity in them (which there certainly was), or to do with his growing resolve to detain the Englishman, will never be known. His signal to his fellow Guardia to hold the man, and his waving of the papers in front of the man with the words "Esto no es bueno... is no good", brought about the physical assault by the driver, who knocked the other officer to the ground and turned to run down the slope. The Guardia with the papers smiled slightly, pulled out his pistol and calmly shot the man in the leg, bringing an end to the escape attempt.

A Guardia Civil Tráfico patrol car, called up by them, arrived a few minutes later and took the prisoner first to the Hospital Comarcal, visible from where the incident had taken place, where his wound was attended to, then back under the motorway close to where he had been apprehended, and on to the Guardia cuartel in Vélez-Málaga. It was here, sometime later, that the man whose papers declared him to be Peter Raymond from London was questioned by a tall, moustached English speaking officer of the Criminal Investigation Division. Teniente Raúl García y García had spent some time previous to the interview studying the passport of Peter Raymond, and was suspicious of its validity, with more reason than that of the patrolman. He was also aware that the car documents and insurance certificate were not legal. His talk with the prisoner had also been delayed by his search through the list of wanted men supplied through Interpol. This led to him suspecting that the man he was now facing was not, in fact, Peter Raymond at all, but Philip Ray, wanted by the British police on charges of rape and murder.

The information he had from Interpol included a verbal

description of Ray, together with a photo taken some years before, but no fingerprints or recent picture. Despite this, and some effort by the suspect to alter his appearance, the Teniente was reasonably sure of his identification. When challenged by Raúl García as to his true identity Ray, for it was in fact he, gave a truculent denial and would answer no further questions. Raúl dismissed him back to his cell and gave some more thought to the information he had on Ray.

Ray was a racing driver, once of some notoriety in England, and was apparently a man of independent means. He had several times been suspected of involvement in bank and jewellery robberies, often of a violent nature, but without enough evidence to be prosecuted. The summary from the English police claimed he was of an arrogant and violent nature, and was a well known 'playboy' who moved in high society. He had twice been the subject of rape charges, both of which had been withdrawn before coming to court. Until the latest incident, for which he was being sought, he had an unblemished record legally. The event which had resulted in his flight from the UK before he could be apprehended, was of an alleged attack on two young women who had been driving down a quiet country lane. One of them had been killed and the other left for dead. But she had survived and some days later identified Ray as the attacker from photos. Both the women had been brutally attacked by him and tied up whilst he raped first one and then the other. Thinking he had killed them both he had then driven off.

Unfortunately a reporter had got hold of the identification by the survivor, and the papers' story had hit the streets before the police had been able to find Ray, who had seemingly already gone into hiding. He had then apparently fled the country and 'sightings' of him had been reported from all over Europe, Australia and even from the Far East. As he was known to be a violent and dangerous character with a quick, hot temper, the Interpol file carried a warning that he should be approached with caution.

The Guardia Teniente noted that the assault on the women had taken place in the English county of Eastshire, which was also where Ray had lived. All information on him was requested to be forwarded to the Chief Constable of that County. As it was late in the evening before he reached this point in his investigation, it was on the following morning, Saturday, that he put through a call to Police Headquarters in Canford, the county town of Eastshire.

It was not until early on Monday morning that he was at last able to speak to the D.C.C. (Crime) of Eastshire in Canford. The result of this conversation was that the D.C.C. would arrange to send over an officer, "Alright then, Teniente García, two officers," he amended at the Spaniard's insistence, to make a formal identification. Teniente García sat back with a sigh of satisfaction, his request for the presence of two officers was based both on the fact that the Guardia always traditionally worked in pairs, and that he believed two positive identifications would be of a more certain nature than one.

Meanwhile in Canford, the D.C.C. was discussing the matter with Detective Chief Superintendent Hollis, who headed up the Criminal Investigation Department.

"Teniente Raúl García y García of the Guardia Civil is

holding a man who he thinks may be Philip Ray, at the Guardia cuartel in Vélez-Málaga, on the Costa del Sol," the D.C.C., who had no trouble with the Spanish names or accent, told Hollis. "He wants us to send out two officers who have had dealings with Ray to confirm, or not, his suspicions."

Back in his own office Hollis, who did have trouble with the Spanish words, studied the notes he had made of his meeting with the D.C.C.

"What exactly is a 'Teniente' and what's all this 'Garciaegarcia', what sort of name is that?" he muttered to himself. He opened the file that the force held on Ray. His eyes lit up when he saw who had interviewed Ray when he had been brought in for questioning the last time he had been held on suspicion. Hollis was an old fashioned policeman, with many almost subconscious prejudices, against for instance black officers, that he dared not show openly in today's climate. One of these was also against women officers, who he thought fit only for use in family and 'womens' cases. Despite these feelings, he also did know good officers when he met them and was a fair man. The pair who had questioned Ray were D.I. Farthing and his Sergeant, D.S. Collingwood, both of whom he liked and knew to be excellent officers despite both being degree entrants (another of his prejudices) and one being a woman. He was in fact at odds with the D.I. over a bid by him to get his sergeant promoted, but despite his reluctance to promote her, he knew her to be a good officer. And the choice of Farthing to go to Spain to identify Ray added further spice as far as Hollis was concerned, for Farthing had recently acquired a romantic attraction in that country, and could be joshed about that as well.

Hollis had a loud voice and was prone to walk down the corridors in headquarters, shouting out names and information so that all those in earshot, usually a good number, knew who his latest target was and could hear his, to his own mind, witty comments.

"Where's our Spanish expert then?" he roared out as he approached Farthing's office, and then broke into an off key rendition of "We're all off to sunny Spain, sing VIVA ESPAÑA" the last two words at high volume. As usual, his outburst brought smiles to the lips of some who heard him and cringes from the rest.

"Pack your bags, Andrew," he continued at almost the same volume as he entered Farthing's office. "You and our Pen are going on your hols, at the County's expense." And then in a lower tone, with the door finally banged shut behind him, proceeded to outline the situation.

"You're to liaise with a Teniente, whatever that is, why can't they have Inspectors and Superintendents like any civilised police force?"

When faced with Andrew's explanation that Teniente was equivalent to Lieutenant and that the Guardia Civil was a paramilitary police force, with therefore military ranks, he simply snorted.

"He's called Garcee something or other, it's all here in this memo from the D.C.C., at a place called Vélez-Málaga. Do you know it?"

"Yes, I know Vélez," replied Andrew (pronouncing it 'Beleth' in the way he knew to be correct, bringing a frown to Hollis' face, who didn't know if his Inspector was teasing him or being serious). "Been there two or three times actually. Good market on a Thursday, nice little park with ducks, know a few good bars… "

"Yes, yes, alright, I get the picture, I didn't ask for a bloody tour guide, Señor Farthing, just find Penny and arrange a flight tomorrow, the D.C.C.'s secretary will do that for you and get out there and do the job. The Spaniard said not to come out till after next weekend, but we'll show 'em we British don't hang about, no bloody mañana or siesta stuff for us, get on a plane tomorrow. Back here smart like too, no time to spend on the beach!"

With this parting shot, Hollis marched out slamming the door behind him, in his usual fashion, and retreated to his own office.

"Could have done with a little jaunt myself," he thought. "But then I'd have missed the darts match tomorrow."

When Hollis had left his office, the first thing Andrew did was to put out a call to Penny Collingwood, who was somewhere in the county on an investigation. Then he rang the number he'd been given of the Guardia in Vélez, to leave a message for Raúl García informing of his intention to fly out, details of flight to follow. Next he rang the D.C.C.'s secretary, to get her to arrange flights and then took a call from Penny who was responding to his message, and gave her the news. He instructed her to hand over her present task to her D.C. and return at once to Canford. Finally he rang Spain again this time on his own mobile, to give the news of his imminent arrival to his fiancée's mother in her home in Tejedos, not far from Vélez-Málaga.

The news of the possible apprehension of Philip Ray on the Costa del Sol by the Spanish authorities broke that evening, and was on all the TV and radio news programmes. On the following morning, as Andrew and Penny made their way to the boarding gate at Gatwick airport, the newspapers on the stands outside the bookshop at the airport were displaying the headlines already described.

When they alighted from the plane at Málaga into the already hot sunshine, the pair were greeted by a tall, impeccably uniformed, sunburnt and pencil moustached Guardia officer.

"Raúl García y García, at your service, Inspector, Sergeant," he greeted them, in almost accent-less English. On the runway next to the plane stood a Guardia Civil car, beside which an equally smart driver was standing. Their luggage was intercepted as it left the cargo hold and put into the boot, and without further formality they were driven straight out of the airport, over two flyovers, past the San Miguel factory and 'Toys R Us', on to the 'Ronda de Málaga' and down the N340 to the Vélez-Málaga exit. As they left the autovía, Raúl pointed further down the road.

"That's where Ray, if it is him, and I'm sure it is, was stopped and arrested. We've charged him with speeding, having false papers, resisting arrest and assault of an officer. But if you identify him, we would not oppose extradition to Britain to face your charges of rape and murder."

During the drive to Vélez, Raúl explained that he had arranged to take them to the prison at Alhaurin, where the suspect was now being held, on Thursday morning, as he had a long standing appointment for Wednesday and would not be free. He also told them it would be Monday before anything further could be done about starting the extradition proceedings.

"Holy Week is a time when many places are closed here you know," he explained. "The whole week is taken up by processions and the like, you must see some during your stay here. But Monday, unlike in England, it's back to work as usual. I did explain to your D.C.C. that we could not do much this week, and it would have been better to wait until next week before you came."

"My Superintendent insisted we came at once," Andrew smiled, remembering Hollis' assessment of Spanish practices. "But it's no problem, we don't mind staying on, do we Penny?"

"I even had to press the prison authorities to allow me to visit them at all this week, their staff, as well as the Guardia, are reduced in number during Easter week. The Guardia have a lot of extra duties as well with the increased traffic and so on. We even have our own parades, and as these go on nearly all night many of our men are off duty the following day. So you will have to stay until Monday at least, if you confirm it is Ray. It will be Tuesday before you can fly back, at the earliest."

"No pasa nada," said Andrew, bringing a smile to the eyes of the driver.

The two British detectives had been given a room each in the Guardia cuartel, as accommodation in both Vélez and Torre was fully booked for the holiday period. The Guardia is a semi-military police force and all officers are traditionally posted to areas in Spain removed from their own. For this reason most are housed in 'barracks'. These cuartels are therefore mixtures of offices and living accommodation for single and married officers.

Soon the car arrived at the cuartel and passed under the arch bearing the Guardia motto *'Todo por la Patria'*, All for the Fatherland. When they got out, Andrew asked Raúl where was the best place he could hire a car during their stay. He wanted to be able to drive up to Tejedos to see Molly, his fiancée, and Jane her mother, who had invited both him and Penny to dinner that evening.

Later on that Tuesday evening, they drove up the narrow winding mountain road to Tejedos. The road went through the hilly district of the Axarquía, inland from Vélez. After about a forty minute drive they reached the villa, just outside the village, where Molly and her mother lived. When Andrew introduced Molly to his sergeant, both women eyed each other warily, the first to see if the other was a potential rival for his affections, and the second to vet her superior's choice of partner. Both seemed satisfied by what they saw, and the rest of the evening passed smoothly.

Wednesday was a blank day for the two British officers, with Molly at work and Raúl away in Málaga at his pre-arranged meeting. They spent the day exploring the town, visiting the castle and going to Torre del Mar and on to the beach, which was full of holidaymakers. Even though it was only March, with the sun shining and no wind, it was quite warm.

That night Raúl had arranged to meet them, together with his wife and young children, and take them to look at the parades in the town. At about ten that evening, they met up in a fish restaurant opposite the park, in the Paseo de Andalucía, where they shared various dishes of fish and seafood whilst watching the parades being shown on the TV set in the corner, by Vélez TV. Then they left the restaurant and walked up to the nearby fountain set in a roundabout, around which the first parade would soon be going before marching up the Calle Canalejas to the main square set between the Town Hall and the Carmelite Monastery. From the fountain, Raúl led them into the maze of side streets, which lay on the side of the hill below the castle, through which the parades were at present passing.

Over the still, cool night air came the sound of sombre drumbeats rolling down the slope. Then they heard the shrill dramatic sound of a cornet and drum band. Turning a corner they saw, over the heads of the gathered crowd, a large float on which rode the statue of the Virgin, blazing with lights. Over the course of the next few hours, as they walked around the streets, they saw a variety of floats, each with a Christ figure or a Virgin on them, and each carried by over 100 men. They also saw hooded penitents wearing long pointed hats and elegant ladies in high majestic mantillas following each float. Bands playing sombre march music, and cornet and drum bands, accompanied each float. Everyone, float bearers, penitents and band members, swaying from side to side to the music as the processions passed slowly through the narrow streets.

At last Raúl led them into the main square where, on the stage in front of the Monastery, were the special guests and dignitaries. He pointed out a bishop and the Mayor. Whilst they watched, a small party of people went up on to the platform, accompanied by a Guardia officer wearing one of the traditional three sided hats, now worn only for special occasions. Pointing out the man beside the Guardia, Raúl told them that he was Pedro Fernández, a junior minister in the Aznar government, whose family lived in Vélez.

"He's back home for Semana Santa and is a special guest at the festival. The Guardia beside him and the two behind in plain clothes are there as protection. We always have to be vigilant in Spain, in case of an attack by ETA, the Basque separatists."

It was not until 4 am that the party finally left the parades, which were still in progress, and returned to their various beds. Despite this, when Andrew and Penny entered Raúl's office at nine the next morning, he was already at his desk and hard at work. His alert manner was in sharp contrast to their lethargy. He then drove them to Alhaurin prison where they waited in a small room for the suspect to be brought in.

On entering the room, the prisoner stopped in the doorway eyeing the pair with hostile, wary eyes before being pushed forward into the room by a warder and told to sit down opposite them.

"Hello, Phil," began Andrew, who recognised him at once.

"My name's Peter, not Phil. Peter Raymond."

"What do you think, Pen?"

"Oh yes, no doubt about it, sir, that's Ray all right. I'd know him anywhere."

The prisoner sat eyeing them with arrogant, angry eyes.

"I don't know who you are, but you're wrong. Just watch yourselves, I've friends in England who'll soon sort you out."

Andrew smiled. "So, Teniente, we confirm it, that's Philip Ray all right, wanted by the Eastshire Constabulary on the charges of rape and murder. What's the next step?"

"Wait a minute. It's me that's the injured party. That Spanish bastard shot me, look at my leg, I'm the one who's going to press charges."

The Guardia officer ignored the outburst. "On Monday we will see my Colonel and a judge, and start the paperwork. You can make a formal statement to a Notary. Then you should be clear to go home. I've reserved two places, provisionally, for you on the first flight back to Gatwick on Tuesday morning. So now you can relax and enjoy the weekend. Take him away," this last to the prison guard standing next to the prisoner.

Once more the trio drove along the N340 autovía between Málaga and Vélez. During the drive, Andrew took Raúl's pistol out of its holder and examined it. He thumbed back the safety catch, bringing a warning from the Guardia to be careful as it was fully loaded.

"Your police don't carry guns, do they?" Raúl asked. "Do you shoot?"

"Yes, some of us are trained in shooting. Both Penny and I have to visit the county shooting range from time to time, to test our competency. But we are only issued arms in cases where there is thought to be a need. Penny in fact is a far better shot than me, and always gets a higher score on the range."

"If the need arises then, I'll make sure she gets the first gun," Raúl smiled in his mirror at the sergeant sitting in the back seat.

"I may be the better shot, but I don't think I fancy the idea of shooting in anger," Penny smiled back at him.

When they reached the Vélez turnoff, Raúl took them off on the Torre del Mar slip road. They then went round the football ground and back towards Vélez, past the new El Ingenio shopping centre. Then under the motorway they had just left and into the town by way of the wide Avenida Vivar Téllez. As they entered Vélez, he turned off into the residential area at its side. He explained to them that he just needed to call in at home on the way to the cuartel. As a senior member of the Guardia, he rented a flat in the town rather than live in the barracks.

As they turned into a side street, they had to pull to a stop to allow a car coming towards them to pass another one parked on their side of the road, half blocking it, in front of them. Whilst they waited, a small group of people came out of a block of flats some way ahead. They recognised Pedro Fernández and his wife leading them, with just behind them the same Guardia officer as the previous evening, in his traditional hat. At the same time, a motorbike raced up from behind, passing them and the parked car as the road cleared. They could see that the pillion passenger was holding a pistol. Raúl accelerated quickly after the bike, blaring his horn as he did so.

"My pistol, get my pistol," he shouted to Andrew. Andrew undid the holster on Raúl's belt and took out the gun. He opened the safety catch and leaned out of the window. Raúl swerved the car to the left to allow him a clear shot.

Up ahead the uniformed Guardia, alerted by the horn,

had flung himself on top of the politician, bringing them both to the ground. The two plain clothed bodyguards were trying to force their way through the family members clustered in the doorway. The gunman loosed off a couple of shots, but both were wild as he had been distracted by the sound of the car horn and the Guardia's quick response. He now tried to turn round and fire at the car behind.

Andrew fired three times in quick succession, the reports sounding loud inside the car. A fourth even louder bang drowned out the last of his shots, as one of his bullets hit the back tyre of the bike, which slew round and skidded down the road throwing both of the attackers off on to the ground.

Raúl brought the car to a halt, leapt out and ran towards the attackers, with Andrew close behind him. As they neared the pair, the pillion passenger raised his gun from where he lay in the road, pointing it at the unarmed Raúl. Andrew stopped, took deliberate aim, fired, and hit the arm holding the gun before he could fire it. The other attacker was struggling to his feet and also pulling a pistol from his pocket. From behind Raúl one of the bodyguards fired twice, and the bullets, carefully aimed from a classic firing pose, hit the bike driver in the chest, killing him instantly.

No more excitement occurred during the remainder of their stay. Over the weekend they went back to Tejedos to stop with Molly and her mother, and on Monday put into motion the first steps of the extradition proceedings against Ray. On Tuesday morning they boarded the flight back to Gatwick, arriving there just before lunch. As they walked out of the Arrivals area, they glanced at the newspapers on display, which carried headlines such as 'British detectives at scene of ETA assassination attempt' and 'Inspector Farmer of Eastshire CID wounds ETA suspect in Spain' in the broadsheets, and 'ETA killer slain by British cop' and 'British cops foil ETA Costa squad' blazoned across the tabloids.

"You can tell we're back home, by the accurate and restrained nature of the press reports, Inspector Farmer," laughed Penny.

MOONSHINE

NERJA WAS BOOMING, FULL of holidaymakers from all over Europe. High summer: sun, sangria, sand, sea and sex. It was the height of the boom, fed by bankers, property agents and other respectable sober suited men and women, but mainly men. Just before the bust, when over-mortgaged American house owners brought about the collapse. Started the ball rolling downhill, allowing the same bankers to pay themselves high bonuses, to permit the taxpayers to save their institutions. Moonshine expansion followed by the three card trick, all spun by supposed financial experts on a gullible and willing general public. Without penalty.

There were other less respectable purveyors of moonshine, peddling their magic on selected targets. Quick easy money to be made but risky, and if caught with a price to a pay.

The scam was simple, and often repeated in different locations with success. Now the pair of confidence tricksters had arrived in Nerja. 'Suzy Bright' aka June Wilson and her partner Miranda. Suzy, mid fifties but still attractive, glamorous even, and Miranda, really Betty, her plainer, younger and efficient companion and secretary. Suzy was a born actor and Miranda the brains behind the swindle. The problem this time was that their resources were running low. Their capital was 150,000€, a good wardrobe and a necklace worth several thousand pounds inherited from Suzy's mother; this they never touched or depleted. This, added to Miranda's brains and Suzy's talent, was the basis of their operations. Their money for working expenses was running dangerously low, a quick kill was necessary.

They needed, and found, a good hotel in which to stay, that had a quiet bar with a barman whose English did not run beyond that needed to serve drinks. This Miranda found on her reconnaissance trip, the fact that they could not afford to stay there was irrelevant. They never paid hotel bills being experts in doing runners, the management unconcerned as they thought the pair had deposited a valuable necklace in the hotel safe, the jewellery box being found however to be empty after their departure.

Carlos was the ideal barman, quiet, efficient and competent at his job, but any request more than the ordering of a drink being met by "Que?"

Their arrival was dramatic. "That's Suzy Bright, you know the ex film star. What was she in now... er was it Genevieve? Passport to Pimlico?... some British films then Hollywood for a bit... er Psycho? Some Hitchcock ones I think."

The gossip was that she was looking to invest some capital into the flourishing local property boom. All rumours put about by Miranda.

The other pair on the lookout for gullible mugs was Adam Fairweather and his Spanish partner Mario. Their real names are not important. Unlike the two women they worked alone, supposedly with no connection between them. Suzy Bright's arrival and investment plans became known to them within a day of her entering Nerja.

Two other facts need to be established. Miranda spoke

Spanish and let it be known she did, whilst Adam also did but feigned not to. Adam and Mario knew the bar well, as they knew nearly every other likely bar in Nerja, which they had trawled during their two weeks in the town looking for a suitable mark.

The play went like this. Adam came into the bar where Suzy and Miranda were the only customers. He was in a foul temper, that was plain to see. He slapped a fist on the bar and rattled off a long sentence in English. "Que?" from Carlos. More from Adam, followed by more "Que's?" Miranda came over, "Can I help?" and then translated for him.

He joined them and they all chatted. It became apparent that his client, Adam being a developer, had pulled out leaving a development hanging in mid air.

"I have 120,000€, in cash, in my flat. The developer Mario only deals in cash, typical Spaniard. My client who was supplying the other 120,000 has just pulled out and Mario won't wait. Ah well, I'll just have to write it off to experience."

Suzy quickly came to his rescue.

During the next two days it was arranged, over drinks in the bar. They both bought lockable briefcases from a shop nearby and each put 120,000€ in their own. Suzy unbeknown to Adam bought two more which she filled with newspaper. Adam in his turn bought two more which he also filled with paper. The shopkeeper had never sold so many bags before in so short a time. They deposited the two locked bags with Carlos, promising him a fine tip if he would hold them for a few hours.

Mario came, by arrangement, to agree to the deal. He, supposedly, didn't speak English so Miranda translated. He produced plans, estimates and contracts. All were approved and signed. Carlos had put the bags in a cupboard behind the bar. He of course did not know what was in them or what the arrangements were, all that had been done in English before Mario arrived.

"Right," announced Adam. "Now we'll all go and see one of the sites, and then when we return, if we're still agreed, Mario can take the cash and we'll have dinner together when he's gone."

Mario then left to get his car for the journey to the site, and Adam said he would go outside with him, and ring his wife to tell her he'd be late home.

"We'll go up and change," said Suzy. "Ten minutes ok?"

The bar emptied.

Then things moved rapidly and to two different plans. When the women went upstairs, Adam and Mario retrieved the bags from Carlos and gave him the two filled with newspaper, then left in a hurry, drove out of the car park and didn't stop until they reached Seville.

After a brief time, Suzy and Miranda returned and seeing the two men still absent, also took two bags from Carlos and handed him theirs filled with paper. They also left quickly in a pre-ordered taxi with all their belongings and the briefcases, and were on the next flight to London.

That evening Carlos, who spoke English perfectly, sat in his room drinking brandy, counting the 240,000€. He had also bought two briefcases from the shop, more profit for the shopkeeper, and filled them with newspaper.

Those who sell moonlight sometimes get moonlight in return.

BRYNTOR

THE GUARDIA CIVIL REQUESTED the assistance of the British Consul in Málaga, to help sort out the affairs of an old Scottish woman after her death. She had lived for many years near the remote Alpujarran village of Adrajar and had, as far as anyone knew, no living relatives.

A Vice-Consul of many years standing, a good speaker of Spanish, was detailed to go to the village to help them. Because the meeting was to be early in the morning, the official travelled to Adrajar the evening before and stayed overnight in the village Hostal. After a fairly substantial meal he joined a small group of local British residents in the bar. When they learnt why he was in the area, they inundated him with such information they had of her.

"She was well over 90 you know, lived out at Bryntor, that's the name she gave her finca, since before the civil war... "

"Totally alone, never mixed with us, had Spanish friends I've heard. But batty, eccentric, you know, a recluse."

"She was a harmless old biddy though. I met her once, to talk to I mean, not just pass by in the street. She was well educated, quite a character I thought."

They all had their own opinions, which got less and less likely as time passed and drinks were consumed. One thought she might be a relative of the MacTaggart who had lived near Gerald Brennan in Murtas, at Cortijo del Inglés.

Another claimed, improbably, that she was a direct descendant of Mary Queen of Scots. By the time the last of them had left, just after midnight, he knew little more about her than when he had arrived. Flora Clunny was a 95 year old Scotswoman, unmarried, who had lived in the remote finca some 3 km outside the village since about 1932. She was somewhat of a recluse, eccentric, did not mix with the local expats but was on friendly terms with some of the local Spanish.

After they had left, he went across to speak to the few Spaniards still at the bar. These were three middle aged men carrying on an animated conversation, and an old man sitting quietly beside them.

It was the old man who spoke to him first. "You're here about old Flora, are you?"

Surprised, the official asked, "Do you understand English then?"

"No. But I can pick out the words Flora Clunny and Finca Bryntor and I knew a man from the British Consul was coming to help our great Guardia Sergeant!"

After saying this, the old man lapsed back into silence.

The other three now joined in and told him the same things the British had about her, plus a little bit more.

"She was a good friend of ours."

"She hid many of the comrades who had to live on the hill until the death of the tyrant."

"She helped my elder brother Antonio, son of my father Don Antonio here," said one, pointing to the old man in the corner, who nodded but remained silent.

Soon the conversation widened out.

"Have you been to Adrajar before? No? Then you won't know of the mysteries then."

"It's what you British call a 'Bermuda Triangle'. People disappear." Juan, Antonio's younger son, began the story. "The first was María José, the schoolteacher. It was in 1938. She was a hard one. My father here knew her and told me all about her. She was of the falange and denounced many people after the fascists came. Then one day she went for a walk and was never seen again."

"The next was Pablo Romano," cut in a second man. "He was the mayor. He'd had to leave the village at the start of the troubles and only came back after the fascists took control. He had a villager shot for stealing some vegetables from his plot. Everyone was hungry then. He just didn't turn up at the *ayuntamiento,* town hall, one morning after leaving his house, and he too was never seen again."

In all they told of seven disappearances between the first in 1938 until the last in 1970. All Franco supporters, all in their own way tyrants in a village where almost everyone supported the Republican cause.

At last the old man broke his silence. "You're all wrong, the very first was the Italian officer and two Guardia. It was just after they captured the village. My eldest son Antonio, named after me, had run off into the sierras. They didn't capture him until 15 years later. Then they took him to the Valle de los Caídos, and made him help in the building of the mausoleum for that son of a bitch Franco. Antonio was ten years older than Juan here, so he was just a kid then and not involved in the war at all."

"But I remember when they came and told you of his

death," Juan said. "And I remember now you telling me of the Italian and the Guardia. They went off into the hills, looking for mushrooms, you said, and never returned. No bodies, no sound of gunshots, no blood. Nothing."

"Still, you're alright," they reassured the official. "It's quite safe today, the last disappearance was years ago."

"And then," began old Antonio, then stopped again. "No. Nothing." He lapsed back into silence as the others looked questioningly at him.

The next morning the consular official drove the few kilometres to the finca which was in a small valley. Here Flora Clunny had lived and worked until her death just a few days ago. She had fruit trees, a vegetable plot, hens, goats, pigs and had obviously been almost self sufficient. The previous night old Antonio had explained that his son Juan and his two daughters had helped her over the last few years when the work had become too much for her alone. "She helped my Antonio, and so we repaid our debt."

Waiting at the finca were the Guardia Sergeant, two of his men, Juan and two other neighbours who had also helped the old lady over the last few years of her life.

"If you could sort out her papers, try to find out about family and so on, we will go round the farm, make an inventory of her goods, stock and the like," the Sergeant said.

In the main room was an old intricately carved desk, full of papers which the official started to sort through. There were many photos, some obviously of her childhood in Scotland with 'Mum' and 'Dad' written on the back. One was a picture of two children labelled 'Me and Donald', and then there was a postcard of a small town with 'Bryntor,

Ayrshire' across the front. Also there were quite a few pictures of Flora herself in front of the finca and some of her and a man, with 'Me and Antonio' written on the back. By the likeness this was the elder son of old Antonio, brother of Juan. There were also bills and receipts going back many years, letters and much else besides. It was late in the afternoon before he came across a cardboard box which contained the information he was looking for. Clipped together was a small bundle of papers. There was her birth certificate, passport and Spanish residence card. Below them were the death certificates of her parents and of her brother Donald, killed in action in the second world war. Then came a marriage certificate, in Spanish, issued in Almuñécar in 1941. It was between Flora Clunny and Antonio Roberto García Bravo, presumably the son of old Antonio. Next was a photocopy of a notification to old Antonio informing him of the death of his son Antonio Roberto, "traitor and rebel, in the Valle de los Caídos". Underneath this was a Will, also in Spanish, made in 1980 in Motril. It was the Last Will and Testament of Flora Clunny which stated that she had, to her knowledge, no living relatives. She left all her possessions to old Antonio, father of her husband, and if he died before her, to his son Juan, his daughters and their children.

At the bottom of the box was another sheet of paper but before he could read this there was a commotion outside, and the Guardia Sergeant called him. "Señor, come quickly."

He picked up the documents and ran out of the door. The Spaniards were standing around the door of a small stone shed, which had obviously been forcibly opened.

"We couldn't find a key for this, and so we've just broken in," the Sergeant explained.

The official looked inside and saw a line of skeletons, eleven in number with names on cards at their heads and piles of clothes at their feet. He saw that the first three had uniforms below them and that the fourth was headed 'María José Conde Byass'.

"What's it all about, Señor?" asked the Sergeant helplessly.

The official read out the marriage certificate and the Will as they stood in the dying daylight in front of the macabre remains. He raised his eyes and saw that old Antonio, silent as ever, had joined them. He then read out, more slowly as it was in English and he had to translate as he went, the last sheet of paper.

"Confession of Flora Clunny. December 10th 1974. I, Flora Clunny, confess to the judicial killing of eleven fascist terrorists. Ten by poison that I distilled myself from oleander and gave to them in wine. The other by stabbing. No one else was involved or is guilty of these deaths." Then were listed eleven names, nine men and two women.

He raised his eyes again and once more looked at old Antonio.

"Did you know of this?"

"Yes, Señor," replied the new owner of the finca.

"And the eleventh too? Is that what you started to say last night?"

"Oh yes. She once lived in the village, but had moved to Almuñécar by the time of the wedding. She saw Antonio after the ceremony and he, not Flora, my dear daughter-in-law, stabbed her. Fortunately it was late at night and the street was deserted. He had to kill her to silence her, she was probably the worst of the lot and would have denounced him. We brought her back here and put her with the others. Oh yes, I was at the wedding, that's when I discovered the truth about the disappearances, and found out what a good comrade she was." The Sergeant was looking more and more perplexed.

"At your convenience, could you two please explain just what you are talking about, and what all this is?"

He waved his hand towards the eleven silent sets of bones.

PROCRASTINATION?
ANYTHING BUT

YOU WANTED ME TO tell you about the two weeks' holiday I spent in Torre del Mar on the Costa del Sol, that led both to a change in my life and the terrible incidents that happened during and after them. Well, to do that I'll have to go back, set the scene so to speak. You'll have to bear with me as I explain who I am, or perhaps was, and what led up to the events. You will need patience and allow me to wander a bit; procrastinate? No I wouldn't call it that, more go off the point now and then to explain, elaborate so to speak. Well I'll begin then.

My father, Angus Campbell, had this saying that he used often about people who suffered in one way or another as a result of their actions. He used to say that he, or she, had got their just deserts. About, for instance, those sentenced for criminal behaviour, or others simply caught out in misdemeanours.

"They've got their just deserts," he would pronounce in his Scottish brogue, still strong even after years of living in north eastern England. "He shud'na have got away with that," he would announce with satisfaction.

My mother, in her notable accent, estuary English we would call it today, would purse her lips and narrow her eyes and reply, "...anything but." She too had retained her east London tongue, as he had his Scottish, also despite her years in Teesside, though both used local words and slang as well. This was inevitable because of the years they lived there.

When I was a young child both these phrases perplexed me. "Just desserts," I thought. Why should that be a punishment? I loved them, and would happily have eaten a meal of just desserts. No punishment at all, just the opposite in fact. Not to have to eat the bread and butter, the potatoes, but just the puddings. I loved them and whilst my dad was giving stern approval to whatever fitting punishment was being handed out, my thoughts went to rice pudding, ice cream, jelly, apple pie and other such delights.

My mother's reply also both puzzled and also annoyed me. "Anything but," she would say and often repeat it through pursed lips. Anything but what, I wanted to and sometimes did reply. For if I left a sentence unfinished such as "Can I have some?" or "Can I go?" for instance, she would say "Can you have what?" or "Can you go where, Catrina?" In these cases I thought the answers were obvious, unlike hers. But she would say, "Finish your sentences, girl." When I ventured a "Anything but what, mam?" I was told not to be cheeky or to hold my tongue. Life, as any young child will tell you, is unfair, often inexplicable and almost always unjust.

It wasn't really until I was twelve and a first year student at the girls' high school that I discovered the two spellings of 'desserts' and 'deserts', and how a single letter could change the meaning if not the pronunciation of a word. I never did, and still don't, accept that "anything but" can stand alone without a subject. Even though it often does and even though I use it myself. However these two oft repeated sayings stayed with me all my life, as such things often do, lodged in my subconscious.

Let me fill in some more background before I tell you of the things that happened later. What's that, no I won't just "get on with it". If you want to hear of the recent events in Spain and London then I'll tell it my own way. I know I often do prevaricate, go off on tangents, but that's my normal practice. So, as I say, let me "establish a baseline", to use horrible modern management speak used all the time in the world I now work in.

My father, Angus Campbell, was a highland Scot, or 'hielander' as he preferred it, born and brought up near Fort William. He worked for years in the whisky industry, rising to be a senior sales representative of some sort of scotch whisky marketing body. What he didn't know about whisky couldn't be written on one side of a beer mat. Or a whisky mat as he preferred to call it. His love of course was for single malts from the Highlands and Islands. His thinly veiled contempt for blends and lowland distilleries was as I say thinly veiled. But I have to believe him when he avers that as a marketing man it was well hidden. Even though he no longer works for the whisky trade, his many friends in the industry still keep him well supplied with the real stuff. It's where I've got my taste for smoky, peaty single malts from.

My mother on the other hand is from East London, Leytonstone to be precise, and is a nurse. In contrast to his large strong stature and jet black hair, she is slim, of slight build and has what is usually called ash blonde, almost white, hair.

How did they meet? A good question. As it was

explained to me, not of course being about at the time, my mother went on holiday to Fort William with her then boyfriend. She described him as an east London boy from next door, whilst my father's descriptions are far less generous.

"Barrow boy," "No-good cockney layabout," and "Bloody Brylcreemed spiv," being the most polite. My father was attracted to her and dismissive, at best, of him. Whatever the truth, at the end of the fortnight's holiday, my parents were "an item" as they say today, and courting as it was said then. The young man, spiv or otherwise, was heard of no more. My father lived and worked in Scotland and my mother in London. They settled on halfway.

"A score draw, our lass," as my father told it to me.

"We compromised, Catrina," me mam always says with a smile.

My father took a job in advertising for ICI Wilton on Teesside, my mother became a sister in Middlesbrough Infirmary and they bought a house in Saltburn. Which is where I was born. Eldest of three, me and my two brothers, who have no part in this story so need not be mentioned again. Yes, I'm glad you approve of that, not another side road to wander down.

I inherited some characteristics from each of them. My mother's beauty on a more solid and sturdy frame from me dad. An accent as you can tell, mainly Teesside with bits of scotch brogue and east end nasal twang in it. My hair unfortunately is neither the jet black of his nor the bleached white of hers. It's more of a 'faded auburn', some say light brown, but not mousy, definitely not mousy. However you describe it I'm not, nor ever have been, short of admirers. I also inherited a bit of a temper and an impetuous headstrong character from the both of them. My tendencies for not being one for restraint or stopping to think were both attitudes they passed on to me jointly.

After leaving school with good 'A' levels I got a place at the LSE to read Economics and Politics. That of course was inevitable as both my mother and father, me mam and dad in the local vernacular, were always discussing current affairs.

The events I want to relate, yes I've got there at last as you say, but without the background I don't think they are intelligible. So prevarication over, as you say, I'll continue. In 1972 towards the end of my second year at the LSE three of my friends, Sandra, Camilla and Estelle, with whom I shared a flat, decided to go on holiday on the Costa del Sol, and I agreed to go with them. As students of course we had little money. I had, truth to tell, none at all. However a visit home one weekend and a chat with me dad ended with him giving me a few hundred quid to help finance the trip. Later me mam quietly added a hundred of her own and I was home and dry. On my return to London I went to see Sanjiv. In those days the budget airlines hadn't really got going and to get cheap flights the norm was to go to a 'bucket shop'. These places got hold of cheap unfilled seats on the flights that charter firms used for their holidays, and Sanjiv was the king of bucket shop men. I and my family had used him several times and he always came up trumps. He had a small office on the first floor above a shop, just off Oxford Street, near to Tottenham Court Road tube station. He never forgot a face or a name and greeted me smiling.

"Well, Catrina, what can I do for you today? You want to fly again." Like most Indian men he was polite and helpful, and soon tracked down four tickets to Málaga and back on the relevant dates in July.

On the Saturday of the flight we left Gatwick in mid morning, having been up quite early to get to the airport by tube a good two hours before takeoff. Then after a flight of two and a half hours or so, we took the train from Málaga airport to the bus station, and an Alsina Graells bus to Torre del Mar. We had chosen Torre as it was cheaper than somewhere like Torremolinos, Marbella or Nerja. Cheaper both to rent a flat quite near the beach, and also in the bars and restaurants of the town. We had a ten minute trudge with our luggage to the block of flats, and then a trip to a supermarket to buy basic foodstuffs for breakfast in the morning. So it was nearly ten when we finally, quite exhausted, were all done and we were well ready for bed and sleep. I had a bottle of quite good malt, donated by my father, at hand for a nightcap. The other women spurned the whisky, preferring an inferior vodka bought at the airport duty free. Good luck to them, I thought as I slipped into sleep.

The next day, Sunday, was hot and sunny and after a quick breakfast, we went straight down onto the beach and spent the day there. Not even coming away at lunchtime, but having a sandwich lunch at a *chiringuito,* beach bar. We spent all the time sunbathing and swimming. Sandra and I went topless, whilst Camilla kept her bikini top on most of the time. Estelle on the other hand wore a loose cotton top over her bikini. Yes, this is relevant, in fact quite important to the subsequent events, and not just another ramble. So, the sun proved no problem for Sandra and Camilla as they were both black haired and already tanned from a previous camping holiday, nor for Estelle who was protected by her tee shirt. But for me, fair haired and white skinned, who hadn't seen the sun since the previous year, it was a different thing altogether. No matter how the others warned and nagged me not to get sunburn I, impetuous as I am, ignored them. I never even wore a sun hat, unlike Estelle.

I didn't feel any after effects at once of course, you don't do you, but that evening when we were having a meal in an Italian restaurant in Avenida Toré Toré, I began to wish I'd been more prudent. But that's it with me. There's no telling me, as me mam always says, and over the years I've lived to regret that rashness. That's another of her favourite sayings, "You'll live to regret it, our Cat". During the meal I developed a headache and felt slightly giddy, mild sunstroke I expect. Also my skin was on fire, shoulders, arms, legs, my back, my breasts, the lot. Over dinner Estelle and Sandra were planning to go to a disco, and Camilla to meet a boy she had met on the beach. I wasn't going to play gooseberry of course, and the last thing I wanted was to go into a crowded noisy disco. The thought of loud music and continually bumping into people, no, no way, I told them. They didn't take much persuasion to go off and leave me. I'd be ok, I said, I'll go back to the flat, have a hot drink and go to bed.

So there I was alone outside the Italian about a ten minute walk away from the apartment, feeling sorry for myself. I began to walk back, dreading being alone in an empty room. No comfort in telling myself it was my own fault, no comfort at all. Walking down a narrow side street I came upon a small bar, light, laughter and noise spilling on to the street. I went in and decided to have a drink, drown my sorrows and perhaps even anaesthetise my pains and woes. It was a local bar with few foreigners in it, being mainly full of Spaniards. I looked at the bottles displayed on the top shelf. There I spotted a single malt, Cardhu. Not one of my, or me dad's, favourites but good enough. More than good enough. I debated ordering a double or even a treble, but then remembered the Spanish way of serving spirits. Not measured but simply upending the bottle and pouring. I declined a coke with it. Imagine that, coke with a malt, I shuddered to think of me dad's comments. Then I refused ice, water and *casera,* a sort of lemonade. No, I drank malt as Angus did, neat.

The bar was smoky and on a television on the end wall a game of football was being played, ignored by all but a few. These days, since the smoking ban, it's hard to remember smoky bars, as they all were then. I hated smoke and the smell of it on people's breath, hair and clothes, but back then if you wanted a drink you got smoke with it. I have never dated a man who smoked. Well, that's not quite true, in my final year at Saltburn High School, I went out with one. He was about four years my senior, and fancied by all the girls. How could I refuse when he invited me out? At first it was fine, he had borrowed his father's car and dared not smoke in that or he'd never get the loan again and we went for a drive. But after that, later that night, he drove down to the prom and we wandered to the pier and then went onto the beach underneath it. Under the pier was where all the couples went at night if they wanted to do it. At first it was good. We came close and he put his hands up inside my blouse. I was up for it alright, what a thing to tell me classmates. How jealous they'd be. Then he kissed me. It was like kissing an ashtray and I pulled away, and straightened my clothes. He was furious and I thought he was going to hit me, but just then another couple came close and he just walked off. I had to walk home, up the big bank to the town on top of the cliffs, then along Marske Road, past the church to our house. Nearly a mile in high heels and a tight skirt. I never dated a smoker again.

Yes, I know, get on with it, stop wandering away from the story. However I need to explain my thoughts. Smoky bars in those days always reminded me of that experience, and I was there in a smoke-filled bar. It's vital to the tale. And in any case, I'm in no hurry to reach the terrible events that came from that evening.

Now I stood at the bar, sipping my malt, looking around. A single girl in a bar is usually accosted by men but that night, perhaps because they sensed my pain and misery, no one came anywhere near me. Next to me at the bar were two of the few other foreigners in the place. Two Englishmen. The one next to me, facing away, was dressed in a neat suit and wearing, as I saw as every now and then he turned slightly, a tie. He was, I thought, from Birmingham or Warwick, somewhere like that. The other, facing me, a much larger man, was red haired, dressed casually, and a Geordie. Shields, I thought, or Byker, somewhere closer to and on the rougher edge of Newcastle. And they were arguing, violently and loudly. They weren't worried about being overheard.

The bar was noisy and full of Spaniards. No one to hear and anyway tempers were frayed.

It was something to do with a deal that had fallen through, I never knew what exactly, I came in well after the beginning of the row. The one nearest me was some sort of financial adviser and the Geordie thought he'd been cheated. George Butler was the one in the suit. I knew that for he left one of his cards on the bar when he left. George Butler, Financial Advisor, Gestor, Estate Agent. All legal and financial affairs dealt with. That's what it had written on it, I know because I picked it up and put it in my handbag. I'm not sure why but I still have it today all these years later. Since then I've also found out that Gestor is a sort of semi qualified lawyer, one that can do some, but not all, of the tasks that a fully qualified one can. Whether George Butler was actually a qualified Gestor I've no idea at all.

The red haired Geordie was clearly very angry and as he was facing towards me, I could see and hear this in his face and loud voice. He was claiming that he had been swindled out of several million pesetas. At that time a thousand pesetas was worth about five pounds, so a million pesetas was worth about five thousand pounds. I struggled to both work out the sum he said he'd lost and follow the argument. I never managed it, hindered as I was by the noise in the bar, my headache, the shouted conversation and the fact that I am no good at mental arithmetic. It was, I thought, either forty thousand or four hundred thousand pounds. Substantial enough anyway. In the end George Butler left the bar, followed by the larger angry man. I finished my malt, had another and then headed back to the apartment feeling much better than I had done earlier. The effect of the alcohol of course, for the next morning I woke in agony.

The burning hot fire had subsided a bit as had my headache and feelings of light-headedness. They were replaced however by a sensation that the burned skin was now like a tight coating, sore to touch, and a feeling that it would crack at every movement.

All that day I sat in the shade of a large umbrella, completely covered from head to toe, watching my three friends and Miguel, Camilla's boyfriend from the previous evening, sunbathing and swimming. That evening found us all in a bar where we met up with two more boys, Ben Kingston and his Spanish friend with whom he was staying, José María Alguerro. José María had met Estelle at the disco the previous evening and arranged to meet her this evening. Ben and I took an immediate liking to each other and spent most of the evening chatting. He was, you could say, given his rather shy and correct manners, chatting me up. He was unlike anyone else I knew. His father was a bishop and his mother the daughter of an Earl. He had been educated at Harrow and Cambridge and now, four years older than me, was a pupil barrister in Lincoln's Inn. Well spoken and courteous, his idea of courting was perhaps to hold hands at the second or third meeting and exchange kisses sometime after that. I on the other hand came from a different class and background altogether. I had highland relatives on the one hand, farmers, crofters and so on, and east end ones on the other. All my Saltburn friends were, like myself, children of working or middle class parents. We all spoke, not received speech like Ben, but a sort of mixed dialect of Teesside and Yorkshire. My L.S.E. fellow students were of similar backgrounds. On top of this, my nature was somewhat uninhibited and casual. Left to myself I would have been all over him, as I fancied him as I knew he did me. This would have made him run a mile and our paths would never have crossed again. We came from different worlds yet hit it off from the start.

The sunburn saved the day. I couldn't have borne anyone to touch me, let alone put an arm around my shoulders or hugged me. My reticence suited his natural attitude perfectly. I also strove to temper my speech saying for instance, my mother, father and brother, when talking about my family, and not me mam and dad and our kid. By the Friday evening when he was due to fly home the following morning, I having a further week to go, we were close and becoming intimate. If intimate can be used to describe kissing and cuddling, my sunburn now reduced to mild itching as I peeled where I had been badly burned. We exchanged addresses and telephone numbers and despite my not returning to Saltburn until the start of the next term, leading to a period apart of several weeks, we kept in touch and eventually married. Now he is a successful barrister and I am a political and economic newspaper columnist.

That of course was all in the future. As I said in the beginning, that holiday led to a change in my life and how that came about you can now understand. The terrible events were yet to come. The first I heard about it was on the final Friday evening of Ben's holiday, I still having a second week left of course as I have already explained. That evening all six of us went out for a meal in a *bodega,* wine bar, just off the Paseo de Larios. In one corner of the room was the inevitable telly which at one point showed local news. José María was watching it when his attention was caught by the news. I followed his gaze and saw on the screen a face I knew. It was George Butler, and José translated for us what the commentator was saying. George Butler's body had been found on the beach, severely beaten to death. I fingered his business card in my handbag and wondered if I should say anything. Yet what could I say? What did I know of the event? There was nothing to link it to the Geordie in the bar, Butler could have cheated others or his death could have had nothing to do with his business. In the end I said nothing, and months later when talking it over with Ben, by then my fiancée, he agreed that that was the only thing I could have done.

The second terrible thing happened later that year in October, when I was back at the LSE. It was horrific and happened right in front of me when I was shopping one Saturday afternoon in Tottenham Court Road. It was a cold day, overcast with a strong wind making it seem colder and with a hint of rain in the air. I was in a hurry, when was I never, and rushing along to the tube station. The pavements and roads were busy, and what with the wind, paper and rubbish blowing about, the traffic noise, crowds hurrying along in both directions, I was quite flustered. Then I saw him coming towards me in the crowd spewing from the entrance to the underground. I recognised him at once, his face I think had been haunting my thoughts ever since the events in Torre del Mar earlier that year. Red hair, flushed cheeks, large frame, it was the Geordie alright. It was just one of those coincidences that happen in life. I had once met a couple I knew in the visitor centre at Stonehenge. A pair of friends I had not seen for months and who, like me, lived a long way away from there. On another occasion I bumped into an ex-schoolmate in the Machynlleth Centre for Alternative Technology in Wales. There she was sitting on a low wall, eating a sandwich. These things happen.

He recognised me, remember he had been facing towards me in the bar. Our eyes met as we got closer, and I saw he knew that I had recognised him. My eyes must have shown my shock and a flare of fear, just as his revealed his guilt and panic. I could see the thoughts flashing through his eyes. What to do? He couldn't attack me, too many people about, looking over my shoulder he must have seen the two policemen I had just rushed past ambling up to us. My mouth opened to shout and he pushed me violently to one side.

He turned to get away, if he could disappear into the crowd he'd never be found. But progress was hard in either direction because of the large crowds on the pavement. I saw him smile slightly as he made up his mind. Turning to one side, he rushed out into the road to cross the street.

The bus driver had no chance of course. No time even to brake before his radiator hit the Geordie full on and then carried on for several yards as the body went under the front wheels. At least his death was instantaneous.

Over the years and over one shoulder I heard the voice of my father, "…he got his just deserts." Whilst I thought, but surely he didn't deserve to die, prison yes but not that. Over the other shoulder I could hear my mother, "anything but…"

NOBODY'S FOOL

THERE'S NO FOOL LIKE an old fool. Edward Turnbull had built his career, if not his life, around that maxim. It had brought him much wealth and ensured his existence had been comfortable. Now at 56 he had retired, to live a life of leisure on the accumulated gains. Not that he thought 56 was old of course, weren't the 50's the new 30's? he asked himself. And he was still in good shape, still handsome and his hair, his chestnut hair, one of his strong points, not showing any grey. He didn't think anyone could tell that for the past three years he had been discretely colouring it.

Picking up his coffee cup he went out on to the terrace into the already hot June sunshine. The sounds of the Today programme were still audible from the dining room, James Naughtie describing some new health scare. He liked to keep up with events back home, economic, political, cultural, whatever was new in the world. Would Janice be interested, he wondered, would she be content to have Radio 4 on every morning? She was younger than him, by over thirty years. Would she disturb his comfortable routine? He had been living at Casa Molinas in the campo two kilometres from the small *pueblo*, village, of San Bernardo to the east of Málaga for over a year now, since his retirement. He had met Janice just a few months ago. At that time she was living in a flat in Limonar, a part of Málaga, and one day when he was visiting the city they had met in the new marina area of the port. Over coffee and churros they had chatted and found many things in common. After that the relationship had developed until now they had become good friends and Edward was thinking of taking it to a new level. He sighed, it would mean changes, perhaps uncomfortable or even unwelcome ones, but then again she would bring excitement, a new vigour and dynamism into his life.

Undecided and disturbed by his thoughts he drained his cup, strode over to the pool and dived in. Several lengths later he climbed out of the water, a little breathless, and came face to face with Manolo, his gardener who had just arrived to start work. Young, fit and brown from working outdoors, Manolo was a godsend. He kept the gardens in order, grew flowers, vegetables and fruit with seeming ease, and came three times a week at reasonable rates. Edward, who hated gardening and if let loose in one dug up plants instead of weeds and killed everything he touched, could not imagine the grounds without him. Looking at him, his youth, his body, his face and hair, he thought of himself at that age. If Manolo had the nous and the chance to follow a similar path to the one he had, then his future and his fortune were assured. Then however he would lose his invaluable gardener. Thankfully he thought the boy, a rural peasant really, was not likely to, so his garden was safe. These thoughts took him back to his own beginnings.

Edward, then Eddie to all and sundry, had been born and bred on the south bank of the Tees just outside Middlesbrough. A location comprising the suburbs of Grangetown, South Bank and Dormanstown and known locally as 'Slaggy Island'. This was an area of terraced houses, steelworks and, hence the name, slag heaps not far from the docks. Nowadays of course the works, or as the locals had it "t'werks", had mainly gone, as had many of the houses, and the slag heaps had in their turn been used as hardcore under the new road networks.

He had always been a goodly youth and developed into a handsome, well-built and attractive young man. Chestnut hair and light brown eyes made him the sort of man many women found attractive. But he was a true son of Slaggy Island, rough and ready, broad local accent, little education and no social graces at all. All rough edges and destined for the steelworks like his father before him. Then at eighteen he had two strokes of luck that changed the course of his life. They didn't quite occur simultaneously but about eight months apart.

The first was his meeting with Mrs Rowntree, a recently widowed attractive thirty odd year old. She was a black-haired and black-eyed woman who though bereft at the loss of her husband just weeks before their meeting, because of her strong sex drive, missed his presence in her bed even more than his company. She took Edward, always Edward she told him never Ed or Eddie, under her wing and changed his whole personality. She taught him manners, how to speak properly, instructed him in current affairs, showed him the correct cutlery to use at a table, and above all initiated him in the ways of love making. Before Mrs Rowntree, sex to Edward was a quick fumble and climax behind the school science block, with her he learnt foreplay, the art of pleasing his partner and the benefits of mutual satisfaction. On one memorable weekend she took him away for his first ever stay in a hotel. She was an eye opener, an educator, a lover and a rubber away of rough edges.

Fortunately for him his second stroke of luck came just as Mrs Rowntree met Clarence who was to be her second husband, and saved her the unpleasant task of telling Edward it was all over and him the inevitable heartbreak. As it was he couldn't wait to get away and their last meeting brought both passion and relief on both their parts. It ended with insincere "never forget you's" and well meant "good luck's" from the two of them.

Edward's second stroke of luck was a win on the pools. Only £800 but back then that was a sizeable amount. He told no one about it but packed a bag, bought a train ticket and headed for London. His clothes, dress sense, manners and conversation had all not just improved under Mrs Rowntree's instructions, they had metamorphed him from a rough Teeside oik into a cultured young man with a predilection for older women. Young girls bored him.

His career had started. He met, charmed and bedded a succession of older women, all of whom appreciated his attentions and who showered him with gifts and money. They also paid for everything and added to his expertise and accomplishments. All very reasonable. Pleasure and gratitude on the one part and a modest profit on the other. All very reasonable that was, until he grew more avaricious and voracious, wanting more and more rewards for his labours. Mrs Rowntree had not inculcated any morality into his early base character.

That was when he entered his bluebeard era. He had operated in London at first and then, as he became known, he had moved on to other places in England. At the age of thirty he went to New York and here, under a false name, married a wealthy widow. Her death, seemingly natural, brought him his biggest profit to date. It also brought notoriety and unwelcome publicity. When he changed his name again and travelled to California he found the widows and spinsters there altogether tougher and more suspicious. He was also worried by the number of them who owned guns and, deciding that the stakes were too risky, returned to Europe. He spent many years playing the field up and down the wealthy resorts such as Cannes, Monte Carlo, and Biarritz, mainly in France and Italy. During this time he married and killed three more wealthy divorcees and widows, amassing a large fortune. When he was 54, just after his last conquest, he decided to retire and reverting to his real name, found the casa in San Bernardo.

Part of the reason for him retiring was that during his last conquest he had come close to being exposed and caught. The method had been the same as all the previous ones. Death by a drug overdose, Edward the grief stricken widower, who had been unaware of his wife's drug habit. But this time the Italian investigator had been suspicious. There had also been talk of a child, a son or daughter, whereabouts unknown, who may have had a claim on the inheritance. His exit had been quick but clumsy, leaving behind perhaps some clues as to his real nature if not his identity. Also left behind was a substantial part of her fortune. Good luck to the child, he had thought, they are welcome to it, he was just glad in the end to escape into the blue.

He thought back to that first meeting with Janice. He

had been visiting the Picasso museum in Málaga and was lost in thought when he heard a voice near him, talking in rapid Spanish with an odd accent. Then it switched to English, slow and clear. It was Janice and she was talking to two children, telling them that from now on all conversation had to be in English. He found out later that she was a TEFL instructor and worked in a school in Málaga. On this, her day off, she was teaching two young pupils privately to earn a bit of extra money. What caught his attention was her accent. He knew it well, indeed it had once been his own. She was from Teeside. Out of the corner of his eye he studied her. Her voice was coarse, like his had been, her hair pulled back in a pony tail all wrong for her face, her glasses were ill-fitting and she had to keep pushing them back up her nose with a forefinger, and her clothes were all wrong and unflattering. Below all this though he could see her potential. His years as a gigolo had made him an expert at judging people and he had a sudden urge to change her, smooth off her rough edges just as his had been by Mrs Rowntree. It was his Professor Higgins moment.

As the two children and Janice left the building he followed them. He watched as she had handed them back to, presumably, their mother and then had walked down the Paseo de Larios, over the busy Alameda and along the side of the port to the marina. He had followed her and contrived a meeting then invited her to coffee at one of the many bars in the area.

Now she was a changed person, more polished with a new hairstyle, contact lenses and a good selection of clothes. All at his expense. He had swept her off her feet and romance had followed. Today he planned to propose and was worried, but also excited, at the changes that could bring.

He heard the rattle of her ancient car as it pulled up in his gateway, and then the murmur of voices as she chatted to Manolo. Peering through the shrubs and trees he saw them together and felt a stab of fear. They were much of an age, Janice just a few years the older. They looked, he thought, intimate, conspiratorial. Was there something between them? Or were they just chatting? He pushed down his thoughts and smiled as she approached. God, he thought, he had been right that first day, she was lovely. They embraced and she linked arms with him and steered him into the house.

Later, after an afternoon of lovemaking, he asked her to marry him. At first she refused, sending more worried thoughts about her and Manolo, or her and anyone else through his head. When a week later she agreed, relief and excitement flooded through him. Despite his previous four marriages this was, to him, the only real one. The others had been business, this was different and based on love. After the wedding his fears of her changing his life proved groundless. She seemed happy to fit in with his routines and eager to please. When she announced she was pregnant, he was by turns both elated and fearful. Elated at the thought of having a family of his own, and fearful of the changes it would make. Noise and mess, sleepless nights, smelly nappies, sticky fingers over his designer furniture and immaculate clothes. He shuddered to think of it and then was overtaken by pride. A son or daughter to carry on his line, to teach and bring up as he wished he had been. Perhaps, he even dared to hope, there would be others to follow. They would want for nothing but live on the riches he had acquired from his past conquests and crimes. But never know it.

He knew nothing of pregnancy, clinics, doctors or any of the other things necessary. He left all that to Janice, telling her to spare nothing, that money was no problem. He also became aware of his age as 57 was reached and passed. No great age but still old to be a father. He made a new will, leaving everything to Janice, and so leaving nothing to chance. His child would have the best.

A tearful and heartbroken Janice told the investigating officers that she had no idea that her husband took drugs. No idea he was an addict. The consensus was that he had bought an exceptionally pure supply and that it had been too much for his system to cope with. Condolences and sympathy from all who knew them. Manolo when questioned also denied that he knew his employer was a druggie. The consensus also was that Janice was young enough to start again and also, it was whispered away from her ears, with someone more her own age. She certainly was rich enough, the more spiteful ones added, and would need to be on her guard against fortune hunters. Broken hearted, she sold Casa Molinas and dismissed Manolo with a month's extra wages to cushion the blow. She didn't want anyone else to suffer too much from Edward's death and in any case he had played his part, albeit unknowingly.

She then returned to her native Redcar, not too many miles away from Edward's own beginnings and from where her mother had lived before divorcing her father. Her mother who she had not seen since that divorce. Her mother who had married again to a wealthy businessman, the stepfather she had never met. Her mother who had then been widowed and eventually fallen under Edward's spell and who had become his last victim.

It had taken her over a year to track him down, contrive a meeting and then, convinced he had initiated the whole affair, got him to propose.

She wasn't pregnant of course and had had no trouble buying and administering the drug.

There's no fool like an old fool. Edward's maxim and also his downfall.

JUST A PAINTING

ROGER BARRON CAME SLOWLY awake, just as the first light of dawn crept into his uncurtained hotel room. It was already quite warm, indeed it had been all night, and he was naked under a single sheet. But then it should be in late May in the Axarquía, a region to the east of Málaga. He lay half-awake for some time, savouring the quiet of the morning compared to the continual noise, day and night, he experienced at his home in central London. From a location that never slept to one of rural peace.

But of course it was not silent, he realised, already there was birdsong, the humming of insects and the continual sound of cicadas. From the nearby village of Canillas de Albaida came the sporadic barking of dogs, and now and then the sound of a cock crowing. These however were natural acceptable sounds that blended in with the ambience of the situation. After a while the occasional rattle of a moped or drone of a car from the village, as early risers went off to work, drifted into his half-awake state.

When he next became conscious it was nearly seven thirty, just time for a swim before breakfast. He threw off the sheet, pulled on a pair of trunks and put on his towelling robe. Leaving his room he walked down the passage and out on to the sunlit terrace, and down the flight of steps to the pool some way below the hotel. As he crossed the dining area he could hear the rattle of crockery and smell freshly brewed coffee from the kitchen where breakfast was being prepared.

Finca el Cerillo was an old traditional farmhouse, converted into a hotel, set on a steep hillside facing the pueblo of Canillas de Albaida about two kilometres away. The old house had been tastefully and imaginatively restored and extended into a comfortable modern hotel, whilst retaining its traditional feel and look. It was set amid large gardens which cascaded down the hillside, at the bottom of which was a swimming pool surrounded by a tiled area and several pagodas. Roger reached the pool, threw his robe on to a lounger at its edge and turned to dive into the sparkling blue water.

As he was about to plunge into the pool he froze and looked at the water, on the surface of which was the almost naked figure of a woman. She floated face down, arms wide and black hair spread around her head. Roger lowered himself into the water and waded, chest deep, cautiously to her side. He was used to being close to corpses and so was not nervous or even too repelled by coming up close to the body in the water. He had experience of serving in a special unit of the Home Office, which gave protection to politicians, government ministers, ambassadors and the like, and before that had many years of service in the military police. As far as the other guests at the hotel were concerned however, he was a civil servant, a guise he always used when not on active duty. He tried to turn her head, but found the neck locked solid, rigor mortis having set in. On her temple was a large wound, from which blood had seeped into the surrounding water. From what he could see of her face and from the distinctive purple and green bikini bottoms, he knew the woman was Ellie Frazer, a fellow guest.

Roger, Ellie and twelve other guests were at the finca on a painting holiday, under the direction of Regina Bradley the tutor. Each day they attempted different forms of art, including still life, painting using models hired from the village, landscapes and street scenes. The final day, Friday, was to be imaginative composition. That was to have been tomorrow, thought Roger, climbing out of the pool, putting on his robe and beginning to walk up the steps towards the hotel.

Ellie had been an attractive young woman in her twenties, but Roger had not liked her. She flirted with all the men on the course, setting up jealousies between them and between the married couples. She flaunted her body, sunbathing topless and wearing revealing clothes. Roger had sensed a thread of malice running through her dealings with the other guests. Regina, the tutor, had confided to him that she would not have Ellie back on the course next year. Many of the others came back time and time again, enjoying the art, the food and the company. This year Regina had said that Ellie had soured the atmosphere. Well, thought Roger grimly, she wouldn't any longer.

He crossed the reception area and went up the steps to the kitchen. Inside he found one of the Spanish staff. He had hoped that Christine the English cook would be there, then he remembered she didn't do breakfast. He realised that not only did he not know much Spanish but that he also didn't know the woman's name. Hadn't someone once told him that 98% of Spanish women were called María? He tried a tentative sentence.

"María…"

The woman, María del Pilar (Pili to everyone) smiled in response.

Encouraged he went on, "María… una mujer," that was right, he thought, a woman, "muerta." Was that right? "Muerta, dead in the pool… piscina." Yes, that was it. "muerta en la piscina."

Pili rattled off a rapid sentence in Spanish and then, seeing his incomprehension, said slowly, "está muerta en el agua… la piscina…sí, sí."

"Madre mía," she whispered at last. "Mierda, es imposible," but at last she was convinced.

She then went down into reception and called the room of Gordon and Sue, the owners, on the phone.

Soon the small room was full of people. Gordon and Sue dragged early from their bed, Regina the tutor, Christine and David her husband fresh from their home in nearby Cómpeta to start their day's work, and several guests looking for breakfast.

Gordon, as tall as his wife was short, with his unruly hair uncombed, had been down to check for himself on the body, and was now ringing the local Guardia. Sue and Regina were trying to calm the guests and sort out a programme for the day.

By the time Teniente Antonio Pérez arrived to take charge of the investigation it was gone eleven, the doctor had been and the body had been removed. Death had happened, it was estimated, at about eleven the previous night and had been caused by a blow to the head, rendering Ellie unconscious when she had entered the water and had then drowned. Antonio had been sent from Málaga as he spoke good English and was therefore suitable to do the interviews. By the time he arrived breakfast had been served and eaten, and Gordon and Sue, together with the tutor, had calmed the guests down and reconstructed the painting programme. Thursday, which was usually spent either in the *campo*, countryside, painting landscapes or in the pueblo doing street scenes as the participants chose, would now be carried out around the finca, painting either the mountains or the building itself. Friday, the last day, was as usual to be imaginative composition. This would give the Teniente of the Guardia two days of access to the guests before they left the hotel to return home on the Saturday. Friday evening would as normal end with an exhibition of all the week's work, and the awarding of prizes for each of the various types of art and a grand award to the overall winner.

Antonio Pérez began his interviews with Roger, as he was the first on the scene and had discovered the body. Roger revealed his true identity to the policeman in confidence, and his evidence was therefore given close attention by him. After describing the finding of the body, Antonio questioned Roger closely on his opinion of the character of the deceased woman, and her relationship with the other members of the group. Roger explained that he thought Ellie had had a disruptive, almost evil, effect on the group, setting the unattached men against each other and causing problems between the various couples. He went on to add that, in his opinion, she had deliberately sought to attract the men, but that she had not followed through with any of them. She was, he said, a tease a word not known to

Antonio used in this sense. After much time and trouble, and the help of Pili, at last they came to mutual agreement and settled on coqueta or provocativa. The Teniente sat back at last satisfied.

"So," he said. "She was a, how you say, a tease, a flirt. But you don't think she had an actual physical relationship with any of them?"

"I don't think so, no," Roger replied. "But you'll have to ask them to be sure of course. That's if they'll admit to it, if they did."

"Oh they'll admit it," said Antonio firmly and grimly, and Roger looking at him believed it. He was, he thought, a strong and formidable character.

After the interview Roger went out on to one of the terraces, and finding a secluded spot settled down to sketch a view of Maroma, the large mountain behind the finca. He was joined there by Manuel the hotel dog, a friendly spaniel-like dog who was a favourite with all the guests. When asked why he was called Manuel, Sue and Gordon simply said, "Oh, he's from Barcelona," bringing smiles from some and mystification to others who knew nothing of Fawlty Towers.

By evening Antonio had finished all his questioning and discovered that all the men and women amongst the guests who had been Ellie's victims had alibis for the time of her death. Regina Bradley, the tutor, had reinforced Roger's impression of Ellie as a troublemaker and a bad influence on the group, spreading unrest and quarrels amongst them. Regina was the very antithesis of Ellie. A blonde who wore her long hair in a tidy plait down her back, quiet and always well-dressed, she was given to wearing a lot of jewellery, earrings, bangles and rings on most of her fingers. This contrasted with Ellie, loud and vivacious, her long black hair usually left to tumble around her head, and dressed in outlandish and revealing clothes. She too had worn much jewellery, but of a more flamboyant nature with ears, nose and even bellybutton pierced. Her display had put Regina into the shade.

It was noticeable that Antonio seemed to have taken a strong liking to the Englishwoman and took her into his confidence, discussing the case with her and Roger at great length. Roger, who Antonio treated almost as a colleague because of his profession, was amused at the time the Teniente spent with the tutor. One of Antonio's men had found a small bloodstain on the edge of the pool, and before leaving he told Roger that he believed that Ellie had gone for a late evening swim in the still hot night air and, unsteady from too much wine, had slipped and hit her head as she fell into the water. This view was endorsed by the alcohol level in her blood, and the various accounts from both staff and guests alike as to the extent of her drinking that night. He would, he informed Gordon and Sue, be returning on the following day but that unless further facts came to light, he would be sending in a report of accidental death.

Much relieved the entire populace of the hotel, staff and guests alike, felt a vast relief and dinner that night had a festive quality in spite of the recent events. Christine had made a special effort in the kitchen and David was urbanity itself as head waiter, the Spanish women under him especially attentive, friendly and full of smiles. All boded well for the final day's session, prize giving and party, to which Teniente Pérez had been invited as a special guest. Nobody that morning had thought that the week could have been salvaged, let alone finish on such a high note.

Roger woke early again on the following morning and once more lay drowsily in bed listening to the sounds of the countryside as it came to life. Once again he decided to go for a swim, as the day was already warm in the morning sun, as it should be. Wearing shorts and towelling robe, he made his way down to the pool, this time accompanied by a lively Manuel. Today the pool was empty of any other person, living or dead. He swam up and down, pausing to stare at the spot where the bloodstains, now cleaned off, had been found. He was in a reflective mood and after breakfast took himself off to a quiet shady spot on the terrace, to do his final painting of the week, imaginative composition.

He painted all day, with a short break for lunch, almost in a trance as he went over and over in his mind all the events of the day before. He was not really aware of what he was painting, being so preoccupied with his thoughts.

It was after four o'clock when he finished and sat back, waking from his dream state, and looked at his picture. He was amazed at what he saw. Normally an average straightforward artist, he had created an abstract surrealist picture. Regina came over to see his finished work, followed closely by Antonio, who was enjoying her company.

The Teniente looked at the painting.

"It's a cubist picture," he observed. "In the style of Picasso's famous Guernica."

And so it was. At the bottom of the work was a deep blue area with a pale shape recognisable as a woman stretched out, her head surrounded by a tangled mass of black with a red border. Strands of the black hair snaked upward through a kaleidoscope of heads and body parts. The heads were triangular and cubic in form, some in profile but with two eyes on the side, or a full mouth. Some were in full view but with a side profile down the centre. There were recognisable features such as eyes dark with mascara, glasses, moustaches and so on, and many of the staff and guests were easily identifiable. Over the top of the painting was a head with a golden plaited pigtail, strands of the gold threads falling down through the picture to twine and tangle with the black tendrils reaching upwards.

In the future this picture would do many things. It would win best picture of the week that evening at the grand exhibition of all the week's work. A print of it would be hung on the wall in reception at the hotel. A photograph of it, taken on his mobile phone, would sit on Antonio's desk as he tried in vain to find any facts or witnesses to prove the accusation made by the work. It would be sold at auction for a ridiculous sum of money, allowing Roger to retire in comfort.

That was all in the future. At present Roger's and Regina's eyes met above the painting. His steady, full of certainty and knowledge. Hers fearful, guilty and yet with a certain confidence in them as if she was certain of the absence of any direct accusation.

Antonio took a deep breath and gazed from the picture to both of them, aware of the challenge and the tension in the air.

For next to the head was a beringed hand clutching a

stone with a crimson stain on it. Drops of crimson fell from it through the length of the painting to spread out on the edge of the blue water below.

Antonio's men spent many frustrating hours searching for the bloodstained stone without success. Nothing of course could be proved, though the people gathered round the work knew of the truth.

But after all it was just a painting.

BANK ROBBERY

THE FIRST TIME HE went into the bank in Río de los Olivos, he felt almost affronted. It was a branch of the Cajamontes bank, with only room for two staff behind the wooden counter, despite the fact that Río was quite a sizeable town. What he had found almost a slight to him was that there was no security at all. Leaning over the counter he could see an open drawer, almost within his reach, full of banknotes. He had come into the bank with the agent from whom he was buying his villa, and when they were outside, their business complete, he commented on this lack of security.

The agent had looked at him and smiled. "They don't need any, do they?" he had said, looking around. The bank was at one side of a small square through which ran the narrow main road, with trees down each side. At either end of the square the road turned a sharp right angle bend, only wide enough to allow traffic to go in one direction. Mirrors were set on the wall to allow oncoming vehicles to see if the road was clear.

"Not a good place for a speedy getaway, is it," he had continued. "And then, think of where the town is, with only the one road on either side."

Río de los Olivos was about an hour's drive from the main road at the bottom of the hill, in the Montes de Málaga. The road was narrow and winding in both directions, passing through two villages to the west before returning to the coast, whilst the road from the east came straight up the hillside to the town.

"Apart from the problem of getting out of the square, by the time anyone got to the bottom of the hill, the Guardia would have more than enough time to seal the ends of the road," the agent had concluded, stating the obvious.

The man had nodded and smiled back. "Better than grilles, bulletproof glass, alarms and so on," he had agreed. What had disturbed him, and he had found almost an insult, was that for years in England he had made his living from robbing banks and post offices. Well-guarded premises, which nevertheless he had managed to rob, without ever being caught. And here, in rural Spain, was a small unguarded bank, as far as he could see full of cash, and apparently unrobbable. It was a slur to his professionalism, a slight to his ego.

Over the following years, living only a few kilometres from Río, he visited the Cajamontes bank in the town many times, and on each visit worried at the problem of how to raid it. It was as if his honour depended on him finding a solution. After just over three years from his first visit to the bank, he thought he had found the answer. Fortunately for him it was also a good time to spend time on his own doing preliminary research. His last partner had just left in a huff and returned to England. He had met a possible replacement in Marbella, but as yet she had not moved in. He was in the meantime living alone and so had plenty of time to make his plans.

Some way down the road from the town to the east a dirt track branched off and ran for about twelve kilometres to another town, San Marcos, just before joining the main road to Ronda. This track was no good in itself as an escape route, as it would take even longer to drive down than the two surfaced roads, and would also be sealed at the end by the Guardia. However a short way down, it came to within two kilometres from the main road before veering off again. He put on shorts and boots, drove down the dirt track to where the map showed it closest to the Ronda road, and found a spot to park off the track behind some olive trees. Leaving his car out of sight behind the trees, he set off to walk the short distance between the track and the road.

Near the road he found a dry river bed which he entered and walked down. This led him to the road, out of sight of the traffic passing by on it, to the mouth of a culvert which was nearly two metres in diameter. He went through the culvert, under the road, and continued along the bed of the dry river, still out of sight of vehicles passing on their way to and from Ronda. He soon came to a minor road which he saw on his map would take him to the N340, the busy motorway running the length of the Costa del Sol.

He retraced his steps, recovered his car and drove back up to Río. The following day he went down the hill again, along the road to Ronda and turned off onto the minor road he had reached the previous day, and pulled up next to the spot he had walked to, retracing his steps to the culvert to make absolutely sure. Nearby he found a spot where he could park his car out of sight. His preparations were now complete.

Every month the bank in Río paid out the pensions to all the old and widowed people in the town, and on this day there would obviously be more cash in the drawer than normal. He chose the next pension day for his raid. He was so confident of success that he told his new girlfriend that he would come to Marbella two days later, to pick her up and take her to see his villa. His confidence came from knowing that his planning was meticulous and that in the past he had always been successful. He felt happy, keyed up by the prospect of action, and no longer irritated by the presence of the unguarded bank.

Two days before the planned attack, he drove down the track and parked his car once more behind the grove of olives, and again walked down to the culvert. This time he then climbed up to the road and walked to a nearby lay-by where buses stopped. Here he caught a bus to Torremolinos, bought a crash helmet with a darkened sun visor and a workman's full length overall. Late in the afternoon he stole a moped which had been left outside a supermarket and rode it out of town. Once out into the countryside he stopped and removed the number plate, which he threw into the ditch. He then rode back to where he had left his car behind the olives, hid the bike in the same place and returned home in his car.

Mario, a goatherd from San Marcos, who tended his flock on the hill above the spot where he had left the moped, had seen both visits the man had made in his car and had gone down to look at it whilst the man was away walking. Mario was used to the strange ways of the foreigners in the area, and had just assumed the man was out for a day's hike. It was after dark when the man exchanged the car for the moped, and so Mario was back home. The next morning he saw that the car, which had still been behind the trees the previous evening when he returned to San Marcos, had now gone and that it had been replaced by the moped. He walked down for a closer look, but didn't tamper with it or tell anyone about it, but thought that he might come out and take it if it stayed there for any length of time. His daughter was getting married in a few months' time and he could do with some more money to ensure she had a good send-off. He thought he might be able to sell the moped to a dealer in Fuengirola, even without its papers, but he would need to check first.

The following morning the man rose early, drove down the dirt track to the moped, put on the overalls, gloves and crash helmet, and so disguised drove back up to Río de los Olivos. He pulled up outside the bank just after it had opened and entered it, taking out a handgun. The robbery went almost too easily. He had practised the Spanish phrases he would need and herded the waiting queue of pensioners to one side, saying, *"Poneos al lado,"* Move over to the side. He then pushed a sack over the counter to the two bank employees, the manager and his assistant, and told them to put all the money from their drawers into it, *"Pon el dinero en el saco"*. These phrases, even if not grammatically correct, were understood by the people in the bank.

The bank manager remained calm and told everyone to do just as they were ordered, and calmly filled the bag with money. He knew that the thief would not be able to escape but would be caught at the end of the road.

Telling everyone to stay inside for five minutes, the man ran out of the bank and remounted his scooter. It was then that, for him, two unfortunate things occurred. The first was that coming slowly round the corner was a large lorry that even a moped could not pass. He had to sit and wait for several seconds before he could get round the back of the lorry and drive off down the road. The second was that one of the three local policemen walked into the square during these few crucial seconds of delay. One of the old men in the bank, regardless of the bank manager's instructions, put his head out of the door and shouted to the policeman that the moped rider going round the corner had just robbed the bank. As the man rode off, the policeman pulled out his pistol and fired a couple of shots hopefully after him.

Soon the bank manager was talking to the Guardia and telling them of the robbery.

"It was a foreigner, English, I think, by his accent," he said, and shortly after that the roads were blocked by Guardia patrol cars.

The man felt one bullet hit his thigh as he rode away, causing him to wobble but not come off the moped. He rode off down the road, turned off onto the dirt track and reached his hiding spot behind the olive trees. By the time he got there he had lost quite a lot of blood but put on a rough bandage to stem the flow. The bullet was not in the wound, but had simply passed through his thigh and he thought that he would be alright until he reached his car, in which he had a full first-aid kit. It was not the first time he had been shot at during his career, nor indeed the first time he had been wounded, and knew that the policeman had been lucky to hit him at all. He set off walking downhill as fast as he could, leaving the moped, overalls and crash helmet behind.

Walking opened the wound up again and he lost more blood, and this together with the hot sun beating down on him made him giddy and lightheaded. At last he stumbled into the culvert and sank down gratefully into the shade to rest for a while.

He was never seen again. After a few days waiting for him in Marbella, his girlfriend gave up and went off with someone else.

His car was found, broken into by a group of teenagers, driven around by them for a short while and then sold on to a group of car thieves and finally sold in Morocco.

His villa stayed empty for years, slowly decaying. People used to say, "I wonder whatever happened to old what's his name? He hasn't been out for years."

The money was never recovered or a culprit found, and the Cajamontes bank installed some security screens to stop the bank being robbed again.

Old Mario took and sold the moped and the crash helmet to help pay for his daughter's wedding. When he went to get it, he found the overalls torn in the leg and covered in blood. Several days later he listened to the story of the bank raid and heard that the policeman was boasting that he had hit the robber. Nobody believed him, but Mario wondered. He set off down the hill following the path he had seen the man take. Two days later, after searching the area, he came across his body in the culvert, already part eaten by stray dogs or foxes.

Beside the body was a bag containing over six million pesetas. His daughter had a very fine wedding indeed.

DARK ENDING

I'M SITTING OUTSIDE A small bar in a narrow calle behind the cathedral in Málaga, quite close to the Picasso museum, drinking a coffee and waiting for Andrew, a long standing English resident who is going to help me finish a travel book on the Axarquía, a region to the east of Málaga. He knows the area well, having lived there for over 30 years, and has studied the history and terrain of the area. He has agreed to see me and reminisce about the villages, people and stories of the area that he has collected over the years. To enhance my book, dot the i's and cross the t's, gild the lily so to speak with local knowledge, folklore and myth.

I'd better explain. I had been approached by the publishers a few weeks ago with an urgent request to research and write the tourist brochure "A Journey through the Axarquía". It was all in a bit of a rush, due to deadlines, pre-arranged schedules and printing dates. The publishers had contracted with another writer, Graham Hall, who like me was a freelance specialising in travel books. He had apparently almost finished when he, together with all his notes, copy, photos etc, had simply gone missing. The last place he could be traced to was Málaga airport just days before his flight back to the UK. Well one man's loss is another man's gain, or as I prefer to say, "one man lost was another's gain".

You may have read about it in the British press, but as

he vanished just a week before the London Olympics, and a hue and cry was not raised for a few days after that, you may not have noticed the coverage. It was subsumed under a plethora of hysteria over "volunteers", "opening ceremonies", "Queen descending from a helicopter", "James Bond" and the like, and then later by headlines on such things as cycling, marathons, sprints, yachting, world records, gold, silver and bronze medals and so on. The fate or disappearance of Graham Hall was pushed to middle page obscurity, his nemesis hardly commented on. Was he alive or dead? Had he done a Reggie Perrin, a Captain Bob or Lord Lucan? The whereabouts of a minor travel writer with no family could not compete with the likes of Usain Bolt, Bradley Wiggins and Ben Ainslie.

You may not have seen any newspapers at all at that time if you, like me, had sought sanctuary from an Olympic obsessed and crowded London, and retreated to a far corner of the British Isles or indeed the world. I had taken myself on a tour of the highlands and islands of Scotland to write a short book, for the same publishers, on malt whisky. Whilst medals were won and lost, records broken or not, muscles and sinews strained in pursuit of even slimmer thousands of seconds, millimetres of height or distance, I was lost in a taste and a haze of peat, smoke, heather and other subtle flavours and scents.

I read none of it and was not sorry.

But when I returned and handed in my copy I was told the Olympic story by my friends and family who regretted on my behalf my work enforced missing of the games; and by my publishers of the disappearance of Graham Hall and, much more important and inconvenient from their point of view, the accompanying dematerialisation of the proofs of their book, for which they had paid in advance.

I was asked to write a replacement, as quickly as possible, and offered better terms than normal. I quite fancied a holiday in the sun after the rigours of northern Scotland and accepted immediately.

Since then I have been travelling through the Axarquía visiting a score or more *pueblos*, villages, between the Mediterranean coast and the montes and sierras inland to the north. I have driven round several routes devoted to grapes, wine and Moorish remains and influences. I have walked several *senderos,* paths, in the sierras, visited vineyards, almond and olive groves, walked through orange, lemon and avocado plantations, and tasted all their wares. I have been shown where the grapes are dried into raisins and then where they are in turn fomented into *terreno*, the homemade equivalent of Málaga wine. I have visited the factories and co-ops which produce olive oil and diesel from the humble olive. All this and much more, all committed to the page along with maps and pictures.

Now I am sitting in the mid September sun, drinking coffee and *sol y sombra,* brandy and anis, listening to Andrew as he helps me give my travel book a rounded and human feel. At 12.30 we begin to stroll to the bottom of the path that will take us beside the *Alcazaba,* the old lower fort, then along the stone wall of the narrow battlement that links the lower fort to the *Castillo de Gibralfaro,* the castle at the top of the hill. As we climb the steep path, part of Málaga can be viewed below us. The Alameda and Paseo del Parque, a busy road through a tree-lined street and park; the port where two cruise ships and a sinister looking grey warship are moored, and the marina full of the yachts of the rich; the bullring and the eastern beaches of the city. As we get higher the noise of the traffic becomes more muted, pierced now and then by the sharp wail of an ambulance or police car.

We reach the top where the path widens into a small car park where several cars and two tour buses, probably bringing passengers off the cruise ships, and a number 35 service bus are parked. We enter the Parador where we are to have lunch.

It is over lunch that Andrew tells me a disturbing tale. It comes out in dribs and drabs, not in any chronological order and mostly based on rumour, overheard snatches of conversation and speculation, and as none of it can be proved cannot form any part of my book. It may be true, or not, fact or myth, but it is supported by such fact that he, and later myself, have managed to establish.

I have set the tale into context, put it into chronological order and filled in any gaps with probable conjecture. A non-provable but compellingly dark tale, and I set it out below.

Tejedos is one of the *pueblos blancos,* white villages, of southern Spain. Its population is under 800 souls, even including the children and the inhabitants of the many villas in the surrounding countryside. The village has one hostal, four bars, four shops and a chemists, an *ayuntamiento,* town hall, with an *alcalde,* mayor, and seven other councillors. The pueblo is too small to afford its own policía local, so law and order are controlled by the Guardia Civil, Spain's rural police force who have a barracks in a nearby village, and whose patrol car is seen in the village most days; and by the Policía Nacional, whose station is on the coast some 15 kilometres away, and who seldom if ever come to the village. As the pueblo is usually calm and peaceful, and order maintained by the ayuntamiento, the services of either are not often needed.

The hostal, Casa Roja, is situated to the west of the village a few hundred metres before the bus stop and town fountain. It derives its name because before it was built, a house painted red stood on the site, in defiance of the required white of the rest of the buildings. Various reasons are given for this, some say Pedro who owned it painted it red to defy the council, with whom he had had an argument. Others say that red was his favourite colour, but the majority view was that he had bought a job lot of red paint cheap. Whatever the reason, the name stuck and the hostal adopted it when they built their new conventionally white painted building on the site.

It was at Casa Roja that the *extranjero*, foreigner, came to stay in late July. One evening at about ten o'clock at night he walked down the drive to the main road, on his way into Tejedos.

Pepito, a ten year old boy, was wandering along the road on his way back home after an evening spent at a friend's house. Tejedos, like most of Spain, especially rural Spain, is a safe place for both women and children to roam the streets, singly or in groups, even late at night. Ten o'clock on a July evening is not late and even on a cloudy night, as this one was, it was still quite light if not broad daylight, and Pepito was not in the least wary or worried at all. His path and that of the extranjero crossed at the junction of the drive and road, and the stranger had a predilection for small boys and, seeing the road empty and as it was away from any buildings, could not resist temptation. He grabbed the boy, put a hand over his mouth and carried him across the road and into an allotment on the far side. The boy's shouts and struggles were muffled and once inside the allotment and obscured from view by its surrounding bushes, the man proceeded to violate the boy, he knew that when he had finished he would have to kill him and hide the body in the undergrowth.

As fate would have it however Manolo who had been working on his land, which was above and to the side of Casa Roja, was just returning home. He heard the muffled cry of alarm and saw the back of the man, carrying the boy and disappearing into the undergrowth. He ran the last few metres down the path across the road and into the *bancal,* allotment, after them. He came upon the boy on the ground with the man on top of him in the act of violation, and running up to them kicked the man hard on the side of the head with the toe of his metal reinforced work boots. There was a sickening muffled thump and the man fell sideways off the boy without a sound, and lay on the ground with blood welling slowly from a wound on the side of his skull and dribbling out of his mouth.

Ignoring the man completely, Manolo lifted Pepito to his feet and shielding him from seeing the man on the ground, he pulled up the boy's shorts and hugged him tightly until his sobbing slowed and died down. Taking Pepito's hand he led him along the road and into the village.

"Hush now, let's get you home. You must tell no one about this, Pepito, it must be our secret. If anyone asks us now, we'll just say you had a fall, ok?"

Pepito nodded but could not speak. They only passed one or two villagers on their walk and all seemed satisfied with the explanation offered by Manolo. When they reached Pepito's home, Manolo hammered hard on the door and shouted, "Antonio, María, open up."

Once inside Manolo quickly explained what had happened and while María took the boy off to minister to him, the two men discussed what must be done next. They decided that they must deal with the extranjero, dead or alive, protect Manolo from the police and Pepito from public attention, and involve as few people as possible to keep the matter secret.

Leaving Antonio's, they went to his cousin's house nearby and recruited his help. Antonio's *primo,* cousin, Emilio had a mule in a stable under his house and the three men and the mule went back to the bancal where the man lay. On arrival they found him dead, which made their task a bit easier. Lifting the body on to the mule, they set out and went up the path, past Manolo's land and up the hill and on to the open sierra. They walked for over half an hour and arrived at a flattish piece of ground which was not too rocky, and lowered the corpse on to the ground. When they had passed Manolo's land they had taken a pick and a spade from his *almacen,* hut.

Quickly they dug a grave deep enough to conceal the body and keep any stray dog or fox from digging down to it. They covered the body with *cal,* lime, also taken from

Manolo's almacen, and then replaced the earth and stamped it well down.

They had also removed the man's belongings from his pockets to prevent identification if the body was ever found. His passport, credit cards, some photos etc they burned near the grave, and gave his money to Antonio to use for Pepito as some form of recompense for his experience.

The three men then returned to Tejedos where Emilio took the mule back to its stable and the other two went into Casa Roja. There were several villagers and a few extranjeros in the bar, and they called the owner, José, over to one side, and quietly told him of all the evening's happenings.

"He has a room here," said José, "and his hire car is in the car park."

A plan was quickly formed. The three men went up to the room and packed the man's clothes into his suitcase, first removing all personal items which the bar owner said he would destroy. The money they split between the hostal keeper to cover the cost of the man's stay, the remainder Antonio took to add to that for Pepito.

Then Manolo drove the man's car, with Antonio following in his, to the car hire firm's garage at Málaga airport. By the time they got there it was nearly three in the morning and the place was locked up. They parked the hire car outside and posted the keys through a slot in the door for that very purpose. Both men then drove back to Tejedos arriving at dawn.

The secret was well kept but rumours, speculation and wild stories did abound for a short while. Two of the men, who were devout Catholics, made their confession to the parish priest, the other two spurning such practices. But the priest, bound both by the rules of the confessional and his belief that the death of a paedophile, even by murder, was preferable than the defiling and death of a ten year old, was as silent as the grave inhabited by the stranger.

Pepito of course let slip a few of the things he knew about, as any young boy would. But nothing definite, concrete or credible came to light. The Guardia, following up enquiries, established only that the man had stayed at several villages in the region, finishing at Tejedos, and that he had driven back to Málaga a few days before his booked flight to England.

After that all was silent and as quiet as the grave. On the remote hillside of the sierra, the actual grave kept its own silence and the vegetation slowly covered its position once more.

As I said at the beginning, it's a story that is based on rumour, speculation and myth. A fairy tale. Or is it?

Oh, by the way, I never said the name of the extranjero concerned was Graham Hall. Perhaps I had stepped into a dead man's shoes.

Who knows? Not me, I'm just a travel writer.

CONSEQUENCES

THERE WAS NO NEED for Harry to have gone into Nerja shopping that morning at all. But then if he hadn't, he would never have bought the doughnuts. And if he'd not got a pack of six, his wife wouldn't have said, "Harry, we can't eat three with our morning coffee!" and invited Jenny in from next door, to make it just two each. Whilst they were all having their snack, Rollo phoned Jenny to say he was coming home early, from his job teaching English as a foreign language in the Escuela de Idiomas in Torrox, because he had a cold. He had been teaching in the language school for over a year now, and this was the first time he'd ever come home early. If Jenny had been at home, instead of drinking coffee, eating doughnuts and chatting with Harry and his wife, then Rollo would have just driven straight home, about a ten minute journey. When he discovered she was out, he felt so sorry for himself, and not wanting to go back to an empty house, that he decided to go to the bar next to the school and have a couple of brandies to ease his symptoms. So instead of being home in under a quarter of an hour, because he met Paquito, a friend from Nerja, in the bar, he didn't get back for over an hour with six brandies inside him.

Because Jenny was in Harry's and missed his call, she wasn't expecting him home until six in the evening, for he always stayed in Torrox for his lunch which he ate with the other tutors in the same bar he had gone to for his brandies.

If Jenny hadn't been out when he rang, she would have been able to phone Pepe on his mobile and stop him coming to see her. As it was, she had to make her excuses to Harry and his wife when she noticed the time, and rush back to be there to let him in.

Jenny worked two mornings a week in the same language school in Torrox as Rollo, where she was the typist. This suited both of them, as she would go with him in the car and have lunch with him, and then visit the supermarket in the afternoon to get any shopping they wanted and then, in the summer, go on to the beach until he had finished teaching. In the cooler weather she would either sit in the common room of the school and chat to the students and other lecturers, or go and visit friends in the pueblo.

It was during one of these afternoons spent on the beach that she had met Pepe, who worked in a bar restaurant in Torre del Mar, where he did the breakfast and evening meal slots, leaving him free from eleven in the morning until seven in the evening She was an attractive blonde and caught his eye at once when he spied her in a brief bikini, reading and sunbathing. There are few ash blonde Spanish women, and he was smitten at once by the contrast to his usual girlfriends. He was brown, brawny, black haired and full of vital energy, just the opposite to Rollo, who was fair, running to fat and languid. He came as a breath, no a gale, of fresh air, and vanquished the growing boredom of her life.

Soon the only friend she visited on her two afternoons in Torrox was Pepe, who had a flat quite near the Escuela de Idiomas. Two more afternoons, Pepe would drive from Torre del Mar, past his flat in Torrox and on to Nerja, where he would visit her. This arrangement had been in operation for over three months now without any problems. When he came to Jenny's house, he walked along a path to the rear of the row of houses where she and Harry and several other English families lived. Because of the layout of the site and the style of the buildings, he could come to her back door unobserved.

Jenny got back just in time to let Pepe into her house. She was hot and flushed from having to rush back after frantically trying to get away from Harry and his wife, who were both gossips. She had just narrowly missed having to be rude, to manage to get back in time. In the end, Harry's wife had said to him, "Let her go, Harry, she's obviously keen to get away. She's probably got a lover back there. I should be so lucky, stuck with you. It's all these cakes you keep buying, I've put on so much weight I wouldn't attract anyone."

Jenny had flushed red at the remark, even though she knew Harry's wife was only joking. Or at least she thought so.

Because she was so het up, with the rushing and the joke, and to tell the truth a bit full from the two doughnuts which Harry had bought, Pepe and Jenny sat and talked for a bit so that she could recover, before going up to the bedroom. Normally they wouldn't have waited, but rushed straight upstairs the moment he arrived. For this reason they were still in bed when Rollo let himself into the house. If they had been finished and downstairs where they usually had a cup of tea afterwards, Pepe having discovered he liked this strange English beverage, they would have seen him and

Pepe could have slipped out. With no harm done. As it was Rollo came in quickly and they didn't hear him. He thought the house was empty, his wife presumably still out somewhere. Feeling even sorrier for himself, and quite woozy from the drink, he went upstairs and into the bedroom.

When he saw them, naked on the bed in the act of coupling, he went berserk and, picking up a brass candlestick, brought it down first on to Pepe's head and then Jenny's. This violence sobered him and seeing he had killed them both, he went back downstairs and phoned the police.

There was no need for Harry to have gone into Nerja shopping that morning. But then if he hadn't he would never have bought the doughnuts. And if he'd not got a pack of six...... none of this would have happened.

Shopping can be a dangerous pastime.

FLIGHT TO FREEDOM

DAVID GAZED OUT OF the window as the AVE high speed train from Madrid to Málaga slid into Bobadilla station. Just about an hour more, he thought, and then I'll have done it. The elderly Spanish couple opposite him were gathering up their bags ready to get out.

"Adios, buen viaje," they said, as they made their way to the door.

"Adios," he replied. God, but he was tired, he realised, all this travelling. But soon, soon he would see Isabel and they would be free. He stretched his legs, glad to have no one sharing the seats.

"Coach 6, seats 3, 4 and 5." An American voice broke into his thoughts. "Here they are. Excuse us, buddy. How'ya doing?"

Even the intrusion of three loud Americans, two opposite and one beside him, couldn't disturb him now. He had won, got over a million pounds, right here in his briefcase, and Isabel waiting in Málaga. The strident American voices washed over him as he gave automatic answers to their questions.

The train entered the long tunnels south of Bobadilla and he closed his eyes, leaning back to relax. What a journey he'd had. He'd left London after work three days ago and travelled to Portsmouth by train. After a night spent at a small hotel, he'd bought a ticket for the ferry to Santander the next morning. Then yesterday after docking at 12 noon in Santander, he had caught a train to Madrid, arriving in the early hours, slept on the station and caught the 9.30 AVE from there.

All the way he'd kept the briefcase next to him, never letting it out of his sight. This last leg of the journey had been agony. The train had seemed to take forever. Ciudad Real; Puertollano; Córdoba, where the wheels had been altered as they went from international to local gauge, and then slower, Montilla, Puente Genil, Bobadilla, and at last Málaga, under an hour away.

It had been Isabel's idea to travel this way.

"It may be longer, but there'll be no record of your trip, as there would be if you came by plane," she'd argued over the phone, just a week ago.

"You and Paul can come together to Málaga, then he can go where he wants, and we'll go on to Peru after a few days. No one will ever find us. We'll be quite safe."

But of course he'd not come with Paul. He'd never intended to, he wanted all the money for Isabel and himself. He'd moved a day early and left enough clues to ensure that Paul would be easily identified as the culprit. It could be days before Paul managed to persuade the police that David had been his partner, and that he had got clean away with the money. He hadn't even told Paul the full plan, where they were going, just that it was somewhere safe, out of reach of the law, so there was no danger of him being caught in Spain. Isabel of course was from Peru, had friends and family there, and with no extradition treaty with England, even if they were discovered there was no danger of being brought back.

And his wife Rita, who he knew was being unfaithful to him even if he couldn't discover who with, well the first she would have known about any of it would have been when he hadn't come home from work three days ago. But all she would know of course would be only that he'd disappeared. Not till the theft was discovered and Paul had managed to convince the police of David's part in the theft, embezzlement on a grand scale, not till then would she know why he'd gone. Oh, he'd been clever all right, he thought.

Sunshine filled the carriage again as the train left the tunnels and headed on the very last stage of the journey. Looking out of the window he saw olive trees set in low brown hills. Isolated white *cortijos,* farmhouses, standing in their midst. Only a half hour or so to go now. Funny, he thought, it was through Rita that he'd met Isabel. The Peruvian woman was working in England as an au pair and had met his wife at the neighbour's house where she was employed. That was six months ago and over that time Isabel and he had become close. It was Isabel who had suggested a way out.

"Come to Peru with me," she'd said. "Can you get enough for us to live on? Sell something?"

From there the idea of appropriating some of the firm's money grew. This had needed the co-operation of Paul, who was easily persuaded. Paul wanted out as well, with enough money to finance him. Together they had devised a plan whereby some clients' investments had been turned into cash and then picked up by them at the last minute.

The train was entering the suburbs of Málaga now. The

Americans were talking loudly and excitedly next to him. David got up, retrieved his case from the overhead rack and made for the door, clutching it and his precious briefcase. He'd been clever though, he thought, brought things forward by a day, left work that evening just three days ago with the cash, leaving Paul to face the storm the next morning. Rid himself of Rita, who he just knew was cheating on him, and ended up with the money and the beautiful Isabel.

The train drew into the platform at last and there was Isabel running up to meet him. Still clutching the briefcase, he embraced her.

"Where's Paul? Have you got it all? Did anyone suspect?" Questions tumbled from her.

"Yes, I've got it all here," he assured her. "Paul? Oh, he wanted to go off by himself. Come on, let's go to the hotel and I'll tell you all about it. I'm exhausted after all this travelling. When do we leave for Peru?"

When they got to the hotel, David had a large whisky and then went for a long soak in a bath.

"Relax darling," Isabel said, her dark eyes shining. "I'll ring room service and order a meal, you deserve it after all that stress and travelling. Then perhaps we can celebrate together in bed. That's if you're not too exhausted."

David lay wallowing for a half hour, dozing from time to time. He heard Isabel moving in the bedroom and then silence as he nodded off fully. He awoke an hour later in a bath full of cold water.

"Isabel," he called. "Why did you let me sleep? I'm ravenous, has the meal come yet?"

Getting out of the water, he wrapped a towel round his

waist and entered the bedroom. It was empty. The briefcase gone.

Several miles away Isabel paid off her taxi and went into Málaga airport carrying a suitcase and David's briefcase. She checked in and then went to a phone booth and rang a London number.

"I've got all the money, darling. Well, I've left enough for him to pay the hotel bill and a bit more. Don't want to be too hard on him do we, poor dear, after all that hard work. My plane leaves in an hour so I'll be at Gatwick by eight, meet me there and we can go and celebrate together. I'm really looking forward to seeing you again, my love. You can't imagine what these last few months have been like, having to make love to him. Well, perhaps you can. Still, it's all over now and we can be together forever and nobody will suspect us of having the money. How could they? See you soon. Bye for now."

In her flat in Leytonstone Rita put down the phone smiling. She knew David had suspected her of having an affair, but of course he'd not for one moment thought of it as being with another woman. Especially not Isabel, who he himself was chasing. Nor had he suspected that the idea of diverting some of his firm's money was in the first place her idea, not Isabel's. She had outlined the idea to the Peruvian woman, who had played her part to perfection. Seducing David, who had thought he was the initiator of the affair. And then convincing him and Paul that the idea would work. And now she and Isabel would be free to live together in luxury.

Later that evening Rita met Isabel as she came out of

arrivals at Gatwick. Isabel was smiling happily and she raised the briefcase in the air.

"It's all here, and all ours," she said, kissing Rita as they met.

"I'll have that miss, if you don't mind," said a tall stern looking man. "Sergeant McBride, Metropolitan CID. Now if you two will come with us, I'll tell you the story."

Three other men closed around the two women.

"Constable Dodds, carry out the arrest and tell them their rights."

In his hotel room in Málaga, David sat and considered his options. He had only the money left by Isabel and about two hundred pounds he'd had in his wallet. Should he go back and give himself up, or stay here and try to make a living? In front of him was a crumpled note from his wife to Isabel with the flight details of her return to England scribbled on the back. At least he knew what had happened and why and where Isabel had gone. His phone call to Scotland Yard would ensure that they would not benefit from their betrayal.

AN AFFAIR OF THE HEART

ROWENA WAS DISMAYED WHEN she saw George Lumley standing beside the girl from Carlos Tours at the meeting point in Málaga airport. He lived just a few streets from her in Woodford and in her opinion was quite detestable. She was a street collector for Christian Aid, Oxfam and similar charities in her district, and he never gave anything.

"Let them help themselves, work like I do. Not lay about waiting for handouts," was his usual response to her visits. And she knew for a fact that he was loaded. Also, as far as she was aware, he had no close family. His presence on the same holiday as her could quite spoil her own enjoyment.

Virginia Lumley, or Ginny as she preferred to be called, was quite horrified when she was told by her father that he was coming out to Spain, to Torremolinos, on a package tour. She hadn't seen him for over ten years, since his divorce and move to Woodford. She had never got on with him, detested his mean, boorish nature, and knew he would disapprove of her lifestyle. His letter, the first for years and coming out of the blue, had stated coldly, "I am coming out to Torremolinos for a week. I will come to see you when I'm there. Send me a phone number where I can contact you to tell you when. I want to see if you are worth naming in my will as the only beneficiary, or if I've to find somewhere else to leave my money. Your mother of course gets nothing and all your cousins are worthless."

Just that, brief, brutal, and no greetings or tenderness of any kind. He was the most hard hearted man she knew.

"I don't want him here," she had told her partner and hadn't bothered to reply to it.

Ivan Dmitre Berenkov, the floor waiter at the Hotel Los Pinos in Torremolinos, led the group from Carlos Tours up to the sixth floor of the building, which was fully booked by them. In his broken English the Russian émigré showed them into their various rooms. His experienced eye assessed them. This one rich and perhaps worth a large tip; that one young, pretty and gullible, a possible conquest; that one liable to be troublesome; others obviously not well off and so not worth much effort, and so on. George Lumley he assessed as being rich but over demanding, mean and no good for a tip at all. He would have to keep an eye on him to avoid complaints, which he knew would come with little or no provocation. If a safe opportunity came however, he thought George may have some stuff worth stealing as long as no suspicion could fall on him. When he took a tea tray up to George's room soon after their arrival, he spotted some good articles, gold cufflinks, watch, a fat wallet and so on that confirmed this.

Elena, at least that was the name she used in Torremolinos, her own being too difficult to pronounce, was from Bosnia. During the upheavals there she had been smuggled illegally into Spain and made to work as a prostitute. She was part of a syndicate that operated in large tourist hotels locally. She was desperate to get away from her present situation, but without papers or money didn't know how to do it. The only people she knew were the other girls and the pimps in the house where they all lived.

Rowena was further discomforted when she found on their arrival that her room was next to George's. It was inevitable in a way as all the single rooms were situated at one end of the corridor, with the double and family ones occupying the remainder. She just couldn't get away from him, and he was a bully and always bad tempered. On the plane out from Gatwick he had been two rows behind her and had complained all the time to the cabin crew. It had been bad enough, she thought, to see him on the same plane, but now to be on the same package, it was too much. His grumbling had continued at the airport.

"Why do we have to wait for the plane from Manchester?" he had said to the tour rep. "Why can't we go straight to the hotel now, and then they can follow in another bus."

He had gone on and on; what a way to start a holiday, she had thought. She would have to make sure that she never sat anywhere near him at mealtimes or saw anything of him on the beach or in the street.

Ginny lived in a village some way to the east of Málaga, with a group of English expatriates that she knew her father would disapprove of. He would label them as 'hippies' or 'drop outs' if he came to visit her. Any sight of them would most certainly lead to her removal from his will, she knew that at present she was his sole heir. This of itself did not worry her too much, but on the other hand she did not see why, in the event of his death, strangers should benefit when she didn't. She knew when her father would be in Torremolinos, as he had put the dates in the letter to her. She decided to sort out some clothes he would find suitable, more conventional than her normal ones, and go to visit him. She need not stay long, and even if they had never got on in the past, he was after all her father. He might, she vainly hoped, have mellowed or changed over the years.

On Wednesday Rowena had gone straight to her room after the evening meal to read. Before the meal that same evening George had rung the number given to him by the barman, and arranged for a girl to be sent to his room, later after he'd eaten. He gave instructions to the receptionist that if a girl, his 'cousin' he said, asked for his room she was to be given a room key and sent straight up. The attendant agreed with a knowing wink, receiving a furious tirade from George in reply.

Ivan Dmitre was on duty that evening and had decided, as there was a lot of toing and froing as a result of a disco in the hotel, to see if he could safely rob George, who he had definitely chosen as a target. He had arranged to go to the room of the pretty young girl he had formed a relationship with as soon as he came off duty at ten o'clock. Her room was just opposite George's and she would provide a suitable alibi, if he came under suspicion. He could also hide his spoils in her room and collect them later in the week when it was safe to do so.

Elena had been given the number of George's room by her pimp and went straight up without calling at reception and being given the key. He opened the door at her knock, and for once could find nothing to grumble about. She looked, he thought, clean, young and extremely sexy. She for her part was revolted, though she didn't let it show. He looked, to her, old, overweight and extremely unfit.

A short time after Elena's arrival, Ginny went up to the reception desk and asked for Mr Lumley's room number.

"His cousin, are you?" the clerk asked knowingly.

"No, his daughter," she replied, and was given his key and a wink by the man. Mystified, she took it and thought, "I'll just go straight up then."

She entered the room just after her father climaxed. This effort, together with the shock at seeing her enter, caused him to have a fatal heart attack. Her shout of alarm and Elena's scream brought Rowena out of her room next door and into his. The three women stared at his body and as Elena quickly got dressed, they exchanged stories as to who they were, why they were there, and their relationship with George. As their shock wore off, they all started to giggle at the farcical nature of the events. Ginny picked up George's wallet, and gave it to the Bosnian girl.

"Your fee," she said. "Don't worry, I'm his only daughter and I'll inherit the lot."

Then they left the bedroom, shutting but not locking the door behind them, and went next door into Rowena's room. Here they made plans for Elena to go with Ginny to her village.

"Don't worry about papers, most of our lot are here illegally, no one will bother you," she told the young girl. "And when I inherit his assets, which is quite a lot, as well as the house in Woodford which I'll sell, I'll be able to buy you a passport. I have friends who know how to go about doing that."

Turning to Rowena, she said, "When it's all sorted out, I'll send some cash to you. You can pass it on to your charities to make up for what he wouldn't cough up over the years. Oh, don't worry," she added as Rowena started to protest. "He really was loaded, and had plenty of investments. There's more than enough for me as well."

As they sat and chatted in Rowena's room, Ivan Dmitre went into George's room next door which he found to be unlocked. Thinking George to be asleep he quickly pocketed his watch and as many other valuables as he could find. He looked for the wallet which of course he couldn't find. The silence in the room began to alarm him and looking at George, he noticed that he wasn't breathing. Realising he was dead gave the Russian quite a shock and he sat for a few minutes to recover. Then he carried out a more thorough search but still could not find any cash. Fearing a police investigation he went back over everything he had touched, wiping off his fingerprints. All this took a long time and the girl in the room opposite gave up on him and went down to the disco, locking her door behind her. When at last he left George's room, he couldn't get into her room and started off down the stairs to try to find her.

Rowena had rung down to reception to say that she had heard a commotion coming from the room next to her own. An under manager was sent up to see if all was well and discovered the corpse. He met Ivan Dmitre at the top of the stairs on his way and took him with him to the bedroom where they found George's body.

When the police were called they questioned the Russian and found the stolen property on him. He was arrested and charged with theft and 'causing a heart attack whilst carrying out a robbery'.

It was as Rowena always said afterwards, a hard heart is easily broken but an open one is stronger and lasts longer.

EL CIEGO, THE BLIND ONE

THE FIRST THING I noticed as I walked down the steps off the jet standing on the runway was how the hot air hit me. After the cool of the air conditioned plane it was almost like meeting a solid wall, that at least had not changed. Walking across the tarmac I entered the bus that would take me, and the rest of the passengers of the flight, to the arrivals area of the airport. I reflected that that too had not changed over all the years when I had visited my aunt Sasha during my childhood and teens, it had always been the same. What had changed were the smells. In those days, it must be nearly twenty years ago now, the first thing to strike you as you descended the steps was the smell. After the anonymous air of Gatwick or Heathrow, the aroma of Spain appeared to me to be exotic. A mixture of what I took to be perfume from olive trees, stagnant water festering in the heat and cheap cigarettes, but perhaps was something quite other, invaded the nostrils at the same time as the heat struck. Now the air smelled quite different, neutral, just the same as that of Gatwick that I had left just over two and a half hours ago. Perhaps, in reality, nothing had changed except my perceptions. The difference between the impressions of a youngster to that of a more cynical, middle aged… businessman, was what had really altered.

Shortly after, walking out of the arrivals hall into the blinding June sunshine of Málaga, I saw that I did not recognise anything. The last time I was here, just before my aunt's death, I remember walking across the car park, over a footbridge to the railway station. In front of me now the car park, though different, was still there, but there was no obvious way to the trains across it. I remember my cousin George, Sasha's son, writing that the terminal had all been altered, in one of the few letters he had written after her death. As I had only ever written back once, too busy with the difficulties of setting up my operations in the UK and northern Europe, his too had soon stopped. I didn't even know if he still lived in the same old rambling converted stone farmhouse near Coín, or whether, after his mother's death, he had moved nearer to Málaga. He had told me that he was starting work with the Policía Nacional in the city. As a child born in Spain of a marriage between my aunt, an Englishwoman of Russian descent, and a Moroccan resident in Spain, and speaking English, Spanish, Russian and Arabic fluently, he had had no trouble in finding employment. He was aiming for the detective branch or even, if possible, the Spanish secret service. How the two careers of cousins can go in completely opposite directions, I thought now.

I had no need now of trains though, and walked towards the taxi at the head of the line, waiting for passengers. My operations were now very successful and these days I didn't travel by bus or train anymore. I had mixed feelings about coming back to Spain, especially on business. I had made a rule not to work in America or southern Europe. Too many guns, especially carried by policemen. However this time I had made an exception at the request of an old friend. And the fee was very high.

Thinking of friends, I thought naturally of Ciego. During my childhood, when on holiday in Coín, George (Jorge in Spanish, I remembered), Ciego and I were inseparable. Now, business commitments and my personal safety permitting, he was someone I might look up, if I could find him. José María, El Ciego. Perhaps I'd better explain, *El Ciego,* which means the blind one, was his nickname. Well, not his nickname as such, we called people *gordo,* fatty, or *rubio,* blondie. But Ciego was different, something we don't have in English, but which is the norm around here. It was his apodo and as such applied to all his family. Virtually all the families had an apodo, some with specific meanings like Ciego, and others just made up words. These replaced surnames, which are complex in Spain, I can't even remember José's surname, if I ever knew it. He wasn't blind of course, his father and grandfather were called Ciego too, and all his brothers, it was the family apodo. Presumably one of his distant relatives had been blind and the name had stuck.

The taxi took me to a small, mid priced hostal, quite near the port. I'd specified this, not because I couldn't afford a pricy hotel, but because when I was working I wanted somewhere small and quiet to stay, unobtrusive, away from the crowds. I put my three cases on the bed and took a selection of objects from each. They had been scattered through my luggage to avoid detection and now I began assembling them into one unit, which I checked to see was undamaged and in working order before dismantling it once again and hiding the various components in different locations in the room.

The next morning I went back to the airport and hired a car, and then drove east along the N340, turning off at Algarrobo Costa and up into the hills to the largish village of Las Yucas. It was an area I didn't know at all, and I spent several hours exploring and making sure I knew the town well. I found a clump of olive trees on the hillside facing the main square which would be ideal for my purpose. I then walked through the square and studied the front of the town hall, where I had been told the dignitaries would gather at the fiesta that weekend.

After a beer and a couple of tapas I drove back past Málaga and up to Coín, turning off towards Cártama just before entering the town. This is where Sasha's villa had been and I drove past it, reliving old memories. José María had lived a short distance away down a dusty track. José María, I thought, together with the female equivalent María José, was a common name in Spain. Joseph and Mary, Mary and Joseph. I had known at least three other José María's in Coín alone as a child. Coincidentally the subject of my present visit is also a José María. José María Ramos Sanchez, Mayor of the town Las Yucas, and a well known local businessman, and socialist member of the Junta de Andalucía. His business and political activities have apparently angered my present clients and are causing them financial and judicial problems.

I returned to Coín and stopped at a small bar and bought a coffee. Obliquely, because I didn't want to bring attention to myself, I asked about George (Jorge) and Ciego. One thing that has surprised and pleased me since I have been back in Spain is how the language has come back to me. As a youngster, spending all my holidays at Sasha's and mixing with the village kids, my Spanish became fluent. Even after the gap I seem to be able to speak it quite well. None of the people in the bar however knew anything about either of them, but one old man did remember Sasha and her family. I didn't press them much and left quickly, as I half thought I recognised the old man, Paco he was called, but that's no help as there are numerous Pacos around here, and I was worried he might also have recognised me.

The next three days before the fiesta, which was due to start on Friday evening, I spent scouting the area between Las Yucas and the coast road. I was worried that there were only three possible roads, and all of them narrow and winding. I did however manage to find two or three unsurfaced tracks that I could also use. These would take me away from any road blocks that might be set up.

I had a lot of time to think of course, and a lot of my thoughts turned to the three of us and our childhood together. One memory came back of Ciego. When he was excited, or tense, under stress or the centre of attention, such as when he entered competitions in Coín's fiestas, he had a habit of tugging at his left ear and then sweeping his unruly hair off his forehead. He did this unconsciously and the rest of us would mimic him in merriment much to his embarrassment.

To fill in time before Saturday, I also visited Nerja caves and the castle in Málaga. Walking up to the castle I recalled previous visits with Sasha and George, and how George and I would race round the walls pretending to be Christians and Moors. The days were hot and sunny, as you would expect here in June, and I knew I was becoming too relaxed and nostalgic. It was a good thing I had not found George or Ciego, I realised, or I might have approached them and put the whole mission, and my own safety, in danger. I had to realise, I told myself, that I was now living a different life and had a job to do.

Saturday came at last and I put on shorts and walking boots, and retrieved all the parts of my weapon that I had distributed around the room, putting them in a rucksack together with a bottle of water. I drove once more along the N340 and up the road to Las Yucas. I parked the car about four kilometres away near the start of one of the dirt tracks I had found, and walked the rest of the way to the town.

Then I climbed the hillside to the grove of olives opposite the square and made sure there was no one nearby. It was fiesta and so I hadn't expected anyone to be out in the campo working, but you can't be too careful in my line of work. I had plenty of time as it was only just one and the mayor was not due to leave the town hall until three, according to the programme. I knew that in reality it could be, indeed probably would be, much later than that.

The fiesta had started the previous evening and looking down on the town I could see it had been decorated with flags and streamers, and there were plenty of people in the square, where a temporary bar had been set up. A band was playing in one of the roads leading into the square, where some sort of event had just finished. At two o'clock it quietened down and I took the various pieces out of my rucksack. Quickly I assembled my rifle and fixed the telescopic sight. I checked it was in good order and loaded it. Then I scanned the front of the town hall through the sights. It was so powerful I could see every little detail, I could even read a typed notice pinned to the door. It was now just a matter of waiting.

At about two minutes past three, several rockets were let off from in front of the town hall, and people began to come back into the square. At three fifteen more rockets were let off and presently the doors opened. I looked through the sight after studying once more the photo of José María Ramos Sanchez, which in any case I knew quite well by now. With heavy glasses, a beard and a moustache, he was easy to spot. He came to the door and stood on top of the steps, pausing before going down into the crowd.

I focussed the sight on his heart. Just as I was pressing the trigger he raised his left hand and pulled his ear, and was just in the act of brushing his hair back from his forehead when my bullet hit him.

A groan left my lips, it was Ciego. I had killed my childhood friend. I sat numb and stricken. I knew I shouldn't have broken my rule and taken on a contract outside the UK and northern Europe.

Despite the rifle being silenced, the police in the square easily identified where the shot must have come from, and set off at once to run in my direction. It was a good way to come, over 500 metres, and I knew I'd left enough time to get away. It was all a matter of good planning. But instead of moving away I sat still, the gun on the ground beside me, grieving and waiting.

The first policeman on the scene was in plain clothes, running up the hill and motioning the others to spread out and cover him. Without surprise I recognised George, who unlike Ciego hadn't changed at all or taken to glasses and facial hair. It wasn't a surprise, not really. If a prominent local figure, who had received death threats and was pursuing the mafia gangs of the area, needs protection, and he has a friend in the national police in the CID branch, it's only logical that he is put on the case.

As he got nearer, I raised my gun. I had no intention of using it, but I pointed it at him.

"George," I said, tears in my eyes.

He brought his gun up but did not shoot me, as I hoped he would. Instead, he lowered his gun and took the rifle out of my unresisting grip, motioning for the others, the two local police and the two Guardia, to stop where they were.

"Primo?" he said in Spanish. "Cousin, is that you? Do you know what you've done? You've just shot José María, El Ciego, your friend. It's a good job we insisted he wore a bullet proof vest."

So I'd not killed him. I'd just bruised his ribs and sitting here, awaiting trial, I'm glad. I'll get life of course, as they've connected me to previous jobs I've done.

In fact, I've told them all about them. You see, I just can't live with what I'd become.

Yes, it's me that has become El Ciego. The blind one.

EL ALCALDE

ESTEBAN GIL CONTRERAS, *el alcalde,* the mayor, of Triana
Baja, a small village in the foothills of the Axarquía, was
sitting on the patio of his house drinking coffee. The name
Triana Baja, lower Triana, suggested both that there was a
Triana Alta, higher Triana, and that it was low in the sierras,
perhaps near to the sea. In reality there was no Triana Alta,
in fact no other Triana at all within the locality and it was
set high up the slopes of the Sierra Aldras. It was in fact the
highest of all the *pueblos blancos,* white villages, on that
particular sierra, there being only one road up to it, which
after passing the village dropped down slightly to another
village, Ribita, before returning to the coast.

It was just after eleven on a fine hot June morning and
Esteban had returned home for his breakfast, and to work
on his many duties as mayor of the village. If he tried to work
in his office there were continual interruptions from his
secretary, and from Paco, the main administrator, as well as
his telephone and villagers wanting his attention. When he
walked the streets, as he did regularly, he was beset with
people airing their grievances, seeking advice or
reassurance, or simply wanting to gossip. But here in the
shade of a large avocado tree he could work in peace. He
could do more paperwork, or think through problems, in
an hour here than he could in treble that time at the
ayuntamiento, town hall.

He was a large heavy set man in his fifties with a thick growth of greying hair, a walrus moustache and a spreading waistline, and he had been mayor now for nearly fifteen years. In just over a year's time the elections were due again and many of his thoughts and plans were directed at them. As mayor he had control of the budget and all the village activities. He had to oversee and guide the village fiestas, town trips, the farmers' cooperative, culture week, the village band, choir and dance groups, run the village hall, and many more things both important and mundane. These days of crisis and cutbacks meant that the reduced income had to be used wisely. There were constant headaches of balancing essential expenditure against such things as fiestas and social events. He knew the importance of both to the villagers and to his own chance of re-election to a further term in office.

His wife, a jolly overweight but still glamorous woman with long black hair and the face, if not of an angel, at least of a striking nature, came on to the terrace. She was carrying his lunch, a plate of cheese and jamon along with half a *barra,* loaf. Sighing he thanked her and put the official papers to one side as he ate, to concentrate on two problems which were causing trouble and controversy in the village. Both concerned *extranjeros,* foreigners, of which there were a growing number in Triana Baja, just as there were in most of the other villages in the area. No longer was the inflow of extranjeros restricted to the coastal towns but now the inland region was also being invaded. Most of them were no trouble, except with illegal buildings, and were a welcome addition to the village, bringing with them a much needed influx of money. There were however two exceptions to this which were proving a major problem and even a danger to the indigenous populace.

The first was a Russian who had just arrived and built an illegal house in the National Park. The problem was that he was very rich and had, Esteban believed, bribed an official or councillor in the Junta de Andalucía. Or even, he thought, possibly both, who were blocking all efforts of the ayuntamiento to have it demolished. Not only that but he had imported into his home two hefty Russian bodyguards who were not above causing problems in the village. Esteban thought that the man was probably part of the Russian mafia and out of favour with others stronger than himself. So he had come to the village and was hiding out up the mountain. The last thing the alcalde wanted was trouble in the village by armed thugs, or a mafia war breaking out on his territory.

The second was the presence of two other men in the *campo,* countryside, just outside the village about a mile down a *carril,* track. One was a Belgian and the other an Englishman. They were both drug users and dealers who for various reasons had come to the village. Once there they had teamed up and were renting two houses next to each other. He had used various contacts to find out more about each of them. The Belgian was the most dangerous. He was well known in his home town where he had been the leader of a gang of men selling drugs and trafficking women. He had left Belgium when a rival gang had moved into the area and now only returned from time to time. He was a well educated, cultured and rich person, smart and good looking, and had a succession of women living at the *casa,* house, in the campo. The Englishman was dangerous in a different way. He was a rough tough villain from Manchester, on the run from the English police who wanted him on a number of charges ranging from drug possession, physical violence and pimping. When challenged by the mayor when the two men were selling drugs to some local teenagers, he physically threatened him with a large stick. When the alcalde tried to get the local Guardia, who had a *cuartel*, barracks, in a nearby town to help, he was met by indifference and a reluctance to intervene by the Guardia. Esteban believed that a local man in Triana Baja, who had a brother who was a colonel in the Guardia, was protecting them. He could however prove nothing.

He sat on his patio terrace pondering on how he could tackle these problems and remove these potential dangers from his quiet village. There were local criminals, but their crimes were not as extreme as those of the extranjeros and were more easily understood and dealt with. He sat brooding on it all in the hot morning sunshine, and let his mind drift. He knew nothing of Russia or Belgium, but he did know of Manchester. As a football fan he especially knew of Manchester United and Manchester City. Names such as Alex Ferguson and Wayne Rooney went through his mind. And wasn't it Manchester City that had stolen first Málaga's manager, Manuel Pellegrini, and then their goalkeeper Willy Caballero? Oh yes, he knew all about Manchester…

His wandering thoughts were interrupted by his wife.

"Esteban, your secretary's on the phone, she says can you go to the ayuntamiento, there's an official from the Junta to see you."

The mayor rose and stretched and, gathering up his

papers, went back to the town hall to carry on his day. His problems were unresolved, still at the back of his mind, and were causing a frown of worry on his forehead. It was over a quarter of an hour later that he entered his office to greet his visitor, having been stopped several times by villagers during the three minute walk back. On the way he learned one fact to add to the jumble of his thoughts. The Belgian, Tomas Bergermann, had that morning gone to Málaga airport to return for a few days to his home.

Over the next few days Esteban was involved full time in organising a village outing for pensioners to Ronda, and approving the upgrading of one of the small *calles,* streets, in the pueblo. In the past the village had had many day outings to various places, but of recent years with money tight there had not been any for months. He had however secured some funding both from the Diputación of Málaga province and the Junta of Andalucía for major works to the village streets, and the water supply to outlying areas. By re-allocating some village funding originally earmarked for this work, he had managed to find enough to take the pensioners of the village for a day away at Ronda and organise breakfast, lunch and tea for them.

He was sat in his office feeling pleased with his efforts when his phone rang. It was a police captain ringing from Belgium. He was one of the contacts he had made when enquiring into the background of Tomas Bergermann when he had first come to the village. It was, for him if not for Tomas, good news. The previous day, the police captain told him, Tomas had been shot dead in a nightclub by a rival gang, the policeman thought. With even greater satisfaction for the events of the day Esteban put the phone down. Tomas would no longer pose a problem for the people of Triana Baja. Did this open any possibility of getting the Englishman Barry Gregson, out of his hair and out of the village? With a light heart he turned his attention to the street work and the laying of the water pipeline. He could use the same method to lay the water pipes, he thought, as he had last time. He could hire Alfredo and his *máquina,* JCB, to dig the trench and the village plumber, who was employed directly by the ayuntamiento, could lay the pipe. Unemployed men could be used to put in the new paving. This would reduce the costs considerably. He was a happy man when he went home that evening.

For over a week things went very well for the village and its mayor. The outing to Ronda was a success and the work began on both projects bringing employment to the men of Triana Baja, either directly or by the quincena. The quincena was a system where unemployed men were given fifteen days work. They were paid wages a bit higher than their unemployment benefit for doing this community work. The only problem was that Barry Gregson had become more aggressive and unpredictable after the death of the Belgian. Tomas had been, it was obvious, the stronger of the two and had controlled Gregson, now he was becoming more of a problem.

Esteban was getting more parents than ever complaining to him of the Englishman selling drugs to their teenage children. But he had a lot on his plate, the summer feria was approaching, and with a limited budget needed a lot of organising. In any case he had no answers to give them on how to curtail Gregson's activities. He often bemoaned the fact that such a small remote place could attract so many foreign criminals.

"If it were Málaga or Marbella or some such place," he would tell his wife or Paco his main administrator, or indeed anyone who would listen. "If it were one of those places one could understand it. But here, halfway up a mountain in Triana, why? What have we done to deserve it?"

But life went on and things died down a bit, and he had plenty of other ordinary everyday things to see to and organise.

He was not an overly devout man, but a good Catholic nevertheless, he liked to think. So one day he approached the priest and told him of the Russian Mafiosi, and the English drug dealer.

"Should I pray to God to remove them from Triana, father?"

The priest listened to the mayor and thought for a while. "You could pray, Esteban Gil Contreras," he answered. "But I usually find that the answer I get to such prayers is 'God helps those who help themselves'. However I will pray for you too and also think about the problem."

With this the alcalde had to be content.

The priest at that time was not of the usual sort. The village did not have its own priest of course, but was one of a group of churches serviced by a small team. Usually they always had the services of the same man unless the logistics of the situation made that impossible. In the past they had had very old men, rambling in their sermons and sometimes almost unintelligible, or brisk career priests who came and gave perfunctory service before passing on to greater things. They had once had a young man, straight from the seminary, good looking and attractive. But he had run off with a young woman from the next parish, leaving his parishioners and his vows behind him. "I would have run off with María Dolores myself," Esteban muttered to himself. He knew her as she was a cousin of a cousin. "If I'd had the chance and been a few years younger."

The present priest however was a foreigner, a man from Mexico, and a different sort from normal. After a service he was to be found in a bar chatting and joking to the local men. He would stride through the village calling out loudly to everyone, and turn up at houses asking for a coffee and a chat without notice. All the men, even those who never went nearer the church other than to stand outside in the doorway at fiestas, liked him. The women of the pueblo however were less sure.

Being a Mexican, not long from his home country, he was well used to bandits, drug gangs and the like, so one day the following week he visited Málaga. There he spoke to several other priests working on the coast and, without seeming to, obtained the names of some of the Russians in the area who they thought were probably in the mafia. He went to see some of them and in his usual way drank with them in the bars of the city. They were not Catholics of course, but as good Russian Orthodox men were happy to chat to a friendly priest. They were only the hired hands but he knew they would take the message back to their bosses. It was in this way that the whereabouts of a certain Russian hiding out from his former associates, who he had betrayed and swindled, became known.

It was some days later that an excited villager ran into the ayuntamiento in Triana Baja and shouted to the mayor and Paco, "There's gunfire up in the sierras and it's not the hunting season." Indeed they could hear it and they both ran out to the town hall car, and set off to see what the shooting was all about. Triana Baja was too small to employ its own *Policía Local,* local policeman, and they were the ones who had to sort out any problems or call in the Guardia. Esteban thought he could tell where the shots had come from and they turned up a small road that led into the National Park. On their way up they were passed by a car coming fast downhill and had to serve violently to avoid it. The road led to the house of the Russian oligarch. When they got there, they found the man and his two bodyguards, and two other unknown men, shot dead lying in the main room. Paco was sick on the spot at the sight, and Esteban sent him outside to ring the Guardia on his mobile. He himself, who had a much stronger stomach, stayed inside and examined the scene. He saw a bunch of keys protruding from the pocket of the Russian and carefully picked them up, using a handkerchief so that he didn't leave any fingerprints. He had seen a safe in the corner and soon had it open. Inside he found papers and three hundred thousand euros. He pocketed the money and once again with great care returned the keys to the pocket of the dead man.

Three hundred thousand euros, he thought. I can spend some on the fiesta, some on replacing even more old cobbled calles in the village with smart new paving, and even more building an extension to the sports ground. Perhaps put in a tennis court or a basketball pitch. He would have to get the money on to the town hall books, but that should be no problem. Auditors always looked for funds being stolen rather than added to the accounts, and Esteban had had a lot of experience over the years of, not exactly cooking the books, but more of creative accounting. That would leave, he calculated, about three hundred euros. 1% of the total. It would be his commission for his work in getting the money into the town finances and for his risk.

Paco had taken the number of the car as it had passed them, and gave it to the Guardia Sergeant when he arrived at the scene. The Sergeant passed the number on to the Málaga headquarters for them to follow up. Justice it seemed would be done

"We can't have drug wars in the Axarquía," he pronounced.

Everybody had benefitted, the alcalde thought, the town had got rid of a problem, increased its financial balance, the Guardia were happy, and of course he was a few euros in credit himself. All's well that ends well, he thought.

"I was right to pray for help," he told the priest at their next meeting. The Mexican held his peace and bought the mayor a whisky.

A few days later Esteban, still in high spirits, was walking along a carril just outside the village, looking to see if it would be an easy job to bring water out there to the few casas along its length. Since his injection of money into the coffers of the town, he had some spare cash to use and this carril was one of the few left that did not yet have a mains water supply. It was late in the evening and just beginning to get dark, and he wanted to get back to Triana for his dinner. At this point the track ran at the edge of a deep, steep sided, ravine with a rocky stream at its base. The pipe, he was thinking, would have to run at the side of the road away from the edge, but this side ran alongside the land of old Pedro who would want a lot of money to give up any of his plot. It was going to take a lot of bargaining, he thought, as he contemplated the problem.

This carril was the one that led to the house of Barry Gregson, and as he stood there Esteban saw the man walking towards him on his way into Triana. He was weaving from side to side and appeared glassy eyed.

"He's under the influence or drugs, or drink," Esteban thought. "Or perhaps even both."

When the Englishman came up to the mayor he swore at him and waved his stick.

"Get out of my way, Mr Mayor," he shouted. "I'm sick of you trying to get me arrested and sent back to England."

"I've never done that, just tried to ask you not to sell drugs to the teenagers in the village." Esteban, who had had to deal with English immigrants for many years, had learned quite a lot of their language. It was why he got so many of their votes in the local elections.

"Out of the way, I'll do what I want," and Barry swung his big heavy stick that he always carried at the mayor's head. But he was unsteady on his feet and Esteban dodged it and jumped back. The man came at him again. The alcalde looked around him for help but it was late, the light fading and everyone had gone home. The campo was empty. He dodged the next swing of the stick and in desperation pushed Barry away from him.

With a cry Barry lost his balance, went over the edge of the deep gully and ended up on the rocks at the bottom. Esteban peered over the edge and saw by the angle of the man's neck, just visible in the gloom, that it was broken and that the man was obviously dead. He went on his way home leaving the man to be found in the morning. Esteban knew that the first person to come out on the track would be old Pedro on his way to his goats. "Let him raise the alarm," he thought. Esteban had no time for Pedro and little or no sympathy for him.

The verdict the next day by the doctor who examined the body was death by misadventure. He announced that he had stumbled over the edge under the influence of alcohol.

"And of cocaine," was the verdict of the inhabitants of Triana.

Esteban Gil Contreras, Alcalde of Triana Baja, as he sat on his patio the following morning, drinking his coffee and eating the breakfast prepared by his attractive wife, reflected how a few weeks could change things for the better. The village was rid of its two problems and had had a substantial financial boost, which was more than welcome in these days of economic crisis.

"The priest was right," he told himself. "God helps those who help themselves."

He had certainly done that, he thought, settling down contentedly to finalise the arrangements for the summer feria.

A MATTER OF TIMING

MAUREEN O'ROOKE LOOKED FROM her assistant Julie to the two German customers.

"Can we do that then, Julie, get the key from… " The telephone ringing cut across her words. She frowned and said, "Excuse me a minute," and picked it up. "I asked you not to put through… "

"Sorry, Ms 0'Rooke," broke in the operator in Spanish. "I know, but this is your father ringing from England. He said it was very important. A matter of life and death."

"Oh, very well, put him on." She covered the mouthpiece with one hand. "Sorry, just give me a minute," then, uncovering the mouthpiece again, "Hello, Da. What's the matter?"

The switch of languages, without any hesitation, from German to Spanish and then to English was an indication of why she was one of the chief negotiators in the firm of financial advisors and estate agents in her Estepona office.

"Is that you, Mopsy love?" The unmistakeable Irish voice of her father, Pat O'Rooke, on the other end. "Mopsy, love, something terrible. I've just kilt your ma. I don't know what to do."

His voice rose in a tone of panic. She thought, it's

impossible, poor gentle Patrick, who wouldn't hurt a fly, wouldn't raise a hand against anyone, cowed by his hard voiced, tough East End shrew of a wife. No, it wasn't possible. At the same time her mind clicked in, cool, detached and incisive, another reason why she was so highly thought of by the Spanish brothers whose firm she worked for. She never panicked and could quickly work out the best way forward in any situation. She was speaking even as she covered the handset again.

"Julie, could you take these two into your office and carry on, fix everything up for them." This in Spanish to her assistant, who she knew was more than competent, and then, without a break, she said in German to the two clients, "Sorry, a minor family crisis, could you go with Julie here, she'll see to everything. I'll get back to you later, if I can." Then straight on in English to her father, as the three others rose and left the office.

"Now da, calm down and tell me just exactly what happened."

"Well love," he began, his voice steadier now. "I'd come down for a cup of tea, and perhaps a bite to eat, you know, and when I asked your ma what was for breakfast, she started on at me. You know what she's like."

Oh yes, I know what she's like alright, Maureen thought.

"Well, she went on and on about me being a feckless Irish git, no money coming in and all, and wanting waiting on hand and foot. It's not a bit like that love, I'm in work, on the roads, but we're just laid off for a while because of the frost and a bit of snow. Well, I'd had a bit of a bash last night with Sean, you know, Sean Clarke, my ganger, from the next street. And I had a bit of a head. Then she said I was just like that idle lump Mopsy, not a bit like our Rory. Our Rory, I ask you, he's not been in work since he left school. We've not seen him for weeks now and he's always up to no good. But that was her, as you'll well know, always Rory."

He broke off, lost in what he was saying.

"Yes da, I know," she said gently. "But what happened?"

"Right, yes," he came back to the point. "My head, you know, and her. Yeah, yeah," he said in answer to a heavy sigh from her. "Well, I just snapped, picked up the kitchen knife, you know the really sharp one she uses for… Yeah, well I stabbed her, in the chest, hard, it went in and she fell down, dead. Oh love, what do I do now?"

Maureen paused, thinking hard, making decisions, planning before she answered. She glanced at her watch, 9.45, 8.45 in England.

"Right, listen da. Concentrate and do JUST what I say, to the letter, do you understand?"

"Yes love, just tell me, I'm at a loss… "

"Shut up and listen. First, is it cold there? Yes, of course it is," she answered her own question. "Frost, you said, right, now first, turn up the central heating to full, just be quiet." This to a question forming at the other end. "Just listen to me and do what I say. Next, ring Sean and say you're coming out to see me for a few days, as there's no work due to the weather, and that you'll ring him again in a few days time. Then ring for a taxi to come and pick you up in half an hour to go to Gatwick. Next, go upstairs, take off all your clothes and leave them on the bathroom floor, have a shower and put on clean clothes, pack a bag and be ready for the taxi. When you go out, put the key under the stone by the front door. Tell the taxi driver that you're going to visit your daughter in Spain for a few days. Take all your money with you and buy the first ticket out here you can get. Don't worry about the cost, pay whatever, just come, quickly. When you get to Málaga, wait in the airport bar, have a beer or a coffee, but don't go anywhere. Felipe will meet you and bring you back to our flat. You may have to wait, he's on duty, but he'll come, just wait. Got all that?"

"Maureen, sure. But can't you meet me? And what shall I do with the knife?"

"Just leave the knife where it is, don't touch it. And no, I can't meet you... I'll be... busy. I'll see you later, but you know Felipe, you like each other, he'll see to everything. Right, well start now, we've not much time. Bye."

She hung up before he could answer, and sat thinking. Then she picked up her phone and buzzed her boss.

"Salva. Look, I'm sorry, but I've got a bit of a family crisis, I'll have to go home. I'll try to get in tomorrow but don't worry, Julie can see to everything, she's well up to it."

"OK, Maureen," Salva answered, without hesitation. "Just what you want. Anything I can do to help?"

"Thanks, no, sorry about it, I'll make it up... "

"No problem," he cut in. "Just get on with what you need to do, and don't forget, anything, just let me know."

Next she buzzed Julie and asked her to handle all her appointments for that day and perhaps the next. No problem there either. Then a call for a taxi, right away, to take her back to the flat to change, get a warm coat, hat and gloves, and then take her to the airport.

Outside the semi detached house in Brentwood, a taxi hooted. Pat O'Rooke, out of breath and only just ready in time, rushed down the stairs and went to the front door. He deliberately kept his eyes from looking into the kitchen. Already the house was over hot and the air outside felt icy as he opened the door. He waved to the taxi driver. "Just coming," put his bag down and turned to lock the door. Behind the cover of the bag, he hid the key beneath the large stone at the side of the door. He hurried down the path.

Had he forgotten anything? His mind went back over his actions, never questioning what he was doing. Maureen would have it, she was a bright girl, no question. He didn't know where she got it from, not from him certainly, and not from his ignorant and spiteful wife. His mind refused to think any further in that direction. He concentrated on what he had been told to do. He was good at that, hadn't Sean often said, "Don't ask Pat to think for himself, but tell him what to do now, and you can rely on him to do it, to the letter."

"Gatwick is it, mate?" asked the driver as he let in the gears and the cab moved off, leaving behind the tragic mess in the kitchen.

"Yeah, that's right," his mind clicked back in, following instructions. "I'm going out to Spain to see my girl. Laid off with the bad weather, you see. No work outside on the roads in this lot. I'm working on that new bit of road out past Chelmsford. So, my daughter, she rang me up and said why not come out for a few days, get a bit of sun."

That was it, he'd done what she'd said, so now he sat back and let the cabby take over the talk for the rest of the trip. They went from Brentwood south along the M25 and turned off on to the M23. When they reached it, they went down the motorway spur to the airport. The whole journey of just under 50 miles took them slightly over the hour, and by twelve fifteen Pat was trying to get a seat to Málaga. He was in luck and managed to buy one on a flight that was not full and was due to take off at one forty five. He checked in his luggage and went through passport control, and then into the nearest bar to steady his nerves.

MONDAY 4TH JANUARY 12 NOON SPANISH TIME (11 AM ENGLISH TIME)

Maureen O'Rooke, wearing dark nondescript clothes, in contrast to her usual smart and stylish ones, folded her warm overcoat in the overhead locker and sank gratefully down into the seat of the plane. Since leaving her office it had been one long rush, and she was quite exhausted. The adrenalin boost that had kept her going drained away, and she felt empty and apprehensive about the coming hours.

In the taxi, on the way from her office to the flat she shared with Felipe, she had contacted him on her mobile. He was in the Guardia Civil and she had managed to get through to him. He was at the time standing outside his car watching the traffic pass underneath a bridge on the N340 below him, whilst his partner sat in the car.

"Felipe, listen, it's me, Maureen. Could you do me a big, big favour? Sorry to ring you when you're on duty, but I've a bit of a crisis on my hands. Could you meet Pat at the airport this afternoon? I'm not sure exactly when, but it won't be before five at the earliest. It might even be much later. Just look for planes from Gatwick, he could be on any of them, but he'll wait in the bar. You know da, he'll just sit and drink and wait. Take him back to the flat and see him in. I'll be back when I can, but probably not until tomorrow. We've a bit of a crisis on. I'll explain, well all I can, when I see you."

"Sure, sure, no problem, Mo. I'll be off duty by four and I'll go right out to the airport. I'll just wait about, have a drink, talk to the boys in security. No problem. See you when you get back from wherever you're going. Pat and me, we'll have a night out."

That was typical of Felipe, well typical of Spain, she thought, nothing was a problem for him, unless it was trouble with ETA.

As the plane rose into the air and went steeply over the Montes de Málaga, she sat back thinking. Her father, a mild mannered but large and strong Irish immigrant to England, not bright but always ready with a smile, had met and married Elsie. She was a hard bitten, but in those days, going by her photos, an attractive East Ender from Mile End. Pat was a labourer, a hard working but unambitious man, with no drive, and soon the marriage became one where Elsie's discontent had turned her into a bitter scolding shrew. She had given birth to two children, Rory the first born on whom she doted, and Maureen, or Poor Mopsy, as she always called her.

All her childhood it had been "Our Rory, quite brilliant

you know. He'll go far, will Rory, university, I shouldn't wonder". Her attitude to her eldest son never changed, despite his obvious lack of brains, his failure to even sit, never mind pass, any GCSE's. "Oh Rory doesn't need qualifications, he's turned his back on education. Not worth a light, he says. No, he's going to branch out on his own. Bright lad, our Rory." And so on and on through years of having no job and just keeping outside of the law's clutches. Through years of drink and drugs and petty crime. Always the same refrain, "Bright lad, our Rory, doesn't rate an ordinary job, just waiting for the right moment. Go far, will Rory". Against all the evidence to the contrary, her mother's opinion had never varied.

She was brought out of her thoughts by the arrival of the cabin crew with lunch. I'd better eat it, she thought, I'll need all my strength in England, and with no time to get anything to eat probably. She drank a wine with her meal and then followed it with two small bottles of scotch, purchased at a great price, compared to what they would have cost her in Spain. After, she once more lapsed into memories of her childhood.

Also, against all the proof to the contrary, her mother had always belittled her own achievements, scoffed at her attainments and derided her at all times. "Poor Mopsy" was one of her constant and favourite phrases. "Of course, Poor Mopsy can't hope to get anywhere," she'd said, despite her good grades in Junior School. "What does Poor Mopsy want with education, she's going nowhere, not got it in her," she told everyone. But Mopsy was bright, and determined, and had the support and encouragement of her teachers and the, albeit silent, backing of her father. She'd got high grades in her O and A levels, and shone particularly at languages. "University, what does Poor Mopsy want with university, just a waste of time. Better if she goes to work in Woolworths," her mother had flatly stated. She went however, despite this, getting her father to secretly sign her forms as necessary, unbeknown to Elsie. Maureen also had another talent, she was a good mimic, especially of her mother, and on more than one occasion had rung up her teachers and the college, anyone who needed reassurance that Elsie was amenable to her plans. Elsie, who never once went near the school and refused to speak to any teachers, knew none of this. In time Poor Mopsy gained a good degree in languages, learnt to speak French, German and Spanish, added a diploma in Business Studies, and moved to Spain to take up a job in the firm she still worked for. When asked about her progress by friends and neighbours, her mother would always reply, "Poor Mopsy? Oh, she's doing some sort of job in Spain, just an office assistant. Can't expect more. But Rory now, he's doing real well."

Maureen had been in Spain now for over five years, had risen to be one of the senior negotiators in the firm, and taken up with Felipe, a sergeant in the Guardia Civil. Her father had been out to see her two or three times, and he and Felipe got on well together. And now this. She leaned back and closed her eyes, and tried to get some sleep.

MONDAY 4TH JANUARY 3.30 PM ENGLISH TIME
(4.30 PM SPANISH TIME)

Maureen paid off her taxi two streets away from the house in Brentwood. It was a cold day with a clear darkening sky, frost glistened on the surfaces of garden gates and the edge of the pavement. She shivered and pulled her long anonymous coat around her. In dark coat, hat and gloves, with a scarf over the lower part of her face to keep out the cold, she knew she would never be recognised by anyone she knew. She had not, in any case, been back to Brentwood for over eight years, since she had left to go to college in Leeds. She walked the short distance to her old home, retrieved the key from under the stone and opened the door. She closed the front door and stood for a minute in the hall at the bottom of the stairs. The house was hot, stuffy and silent. Quiet as the grave, she thought, and shivered. Outside, footsteps went past on the pavement, a few cars moved on the road, and some distance away the muted sounds of traffic on Brentwood High Street could be heard. As she stood, steeling her nerves, the distant sound of an ambulance rushing to its destination came clearly over the evening air. She moved slowly down the corridor and into the kitchen. There on the floor, just as her father had said, lay her mother in a small pool of blood, the knife still protruding, not from her chest, but from her left side, the point obviously in or near to her heart. Maureen took stock and quickly went out of the room again, took off her coat, hat and gloves, and put on one of her mother's long work coats and a pair of rubber kitchen gloves. She went past her mother on the floor and out of the back door. Making sure no one was in any of the nearby back gardens, she broke the kitchen window from the outside and opened it. She got some soil on her shoes from the flower bed, having to break through the hard frozen surface to do so. Underneath the frozen crusty top layer, it was damp and soft. She hoisted herself through the window, making sure that pieces of earth were left on the window sill and the kitchen floor and went back past her mother. On the way she bent and touched her mother's body, it was still warm to the touch through the thin gloves. Next she turned off the central heating and picked up the phone in the hall. She dialled the number of her aunt, her mother's sister. When the phone was answered, she said in her mother's voice, "Alice, is that you? Else here, listen, you know what that good for nothing Irish git's done now? He's only gone off to bleeding Málaga to visit Poor Mopsy. I've just got back, been up west to do a bit of shopping like, and he's only left me a note. 'Back in a few days' it says. Turn my back on him for an instant and he's off. 'For a bit of sun, to see our Mops'. I tell you Alice, I'll give him sun when he gets back. What's that? Yeah, OK, I'll come over tomorrer evening, if that's OK wiv you. Go to Bingo, eh? Have a bit of a laugh. OK. See you. What? Oh ta, yeah, bye."

Maureen replaced the receiver with a shaky hand, and then dialled again, this time to Sean Clarke, her father's ganger.

"Sean." Once again her mother's voice. "Sean. It's Else O'Rooke here. Here, do you know what? Pat's gone off to Spain... What?... what's that, you know already? He rang you this morning? Well, it's not on, it ain't, I go up west for a day and come back to find him gone. What? YOU think it's a good idea, what about bleeding ME? Oh, you do, do you, well you can eff off," and she slammed the phone down, stood for a minute to stop shaking and then went into the living room. Two more things to do and then she could start to clear up. First, she took a piece of paper from the pad her dad kept to write his betting slips on. Plenty of his fingerprints on this. Another skill she'd developed as a child was forging both her parents' handwriting, a necessary aid to furthering her education against her mother's wishes and her father's reluctance to oppose his wife.

First she wrote a note in Pat's hand, saying he was off to Málaga to stay with Mopsy. Then she wrote a second in her mother's hand which read: 'Pat... I've gone up west for the day. If and when you ever get up, there's nowt for breakfast. Make yourself a cup of tea. I'll be home when you see me. Elsie.' There, that should do. She put both notes behind the clock, where all such notes, letters, bills and so one were always filed.

She moved back into the kitchen and looked at the clock. Gone six o'clock already. Things were taking longer than she expected, better get a move on. She picked up a china pig off the dresser. This was where her mother kept her secret store of money. No one else knew, not Pat or even her mother's favourite, Rory. Elsie was not such a fool as to let Rory, who had no hesitation in taking anything he could get hold of, know what was in the pig. Maureen knew about it because one day, years before, she had seen her mother put in a five pound note and add it to the thick wad already there. Her mother never knew she'd been seen, and Maureen hadn't told anyone of her secret. She knew that the bottom unscrewed but holding the pig in her gloved hands, she brought it down hard on the kitchen table and broke it open. She picked up the wad of notes, must be hundreds of pounds, she thought, gazing at them. Just then a sound behind her made her freeze.

MONDAY 4TH JANUARY 6PM SPANISH TIME
(5 PM ENGLISH TIME)

Pat O'Rooke came through the barrier at Málaga airport with his bag in one hand and his coat in the other. He was sweating in his heavy suit. Coming from a cold frosty afternoon at Gatwick, where it was only just 2^{0}C, to a mild January evening where it was still about 14^{0}C, he felt as if he had walked into a hothouse. He turned left and headed for the bar. Buying a beer, he made himself comfortable and sat down to wait for Felipe.

Felipe was already at the airport, still in his Guardia uniform, outside the doors that led to the coach park, talking to two of his fellow officers who were on airport duty. He saw Pat come out of the doors, go through the gate and then into the bar.

"That's my father-in-law," he said. "Mo's father, I'll have to go and collect him. See you, amigos."

Felipe went to the counter, bought a beer and moved over to Pat's table, where he was sitting gazing unseeingly into space.

"Hi, Pat," Felipe spoke to him in English. "Nice to see you again. Here for a few days, I hear."

Pat rose and shook hands. "Felipe. Well now, it's nice, it is, to see you. But where's Mo? Why couldn't she come?"

"Don't ask me, Pat. I haven't seen her. She said she was busy, had to go off somewhere. But don't worry, she'll be back. Come on, let's get you home and settled in."

They finished their beers and set off. Felipe looked at Pat, he looked pale and was obviously distracted. His face had an anxious, strained look.

"Are you alright, Pat?" he asked.

"What? Yeah, I'm fine. Or I will be when I've seen Mopsy... Mo and found out what she's been up to. For me, I mean, to help me, you understand. Not up to anything for herself. You know what I mean?" Pat rambled incoherently.

"Yes, I know," replied Raúl, who didn't have any idea what Pat was going on about at all. The two men left the arrivals hall and got into Felipe's car, which was parked illegally near the taxi rank, his Guardia cap displayed on the dashboard to warn off any attempt to tow it away.

They joined the traffic heading past Makro and Toys R Us, and took the N340 towards Estepona.

MONDAY 4TH JANUARY 6.15 PM ENGLISH TIME
(7.15 PM SPANISH TIME)

Maureen turned with a gasp and saw her brother Rory, unkempt and obviously the worse for drink, staring at the scene in front of him from the open kitchen door. He looked from his mother's body to his sister, holding a large bundle of notes, standing behind the kitchen table. His eyes flicked to the broken china pig on the table.

"So that's where she kept it," he said. "And you've done 'er in to get it, eh Mopsy? Well, I'll see to it now and you too."

He stooped down and, grasping the knife, pulled it out of Elsie and advanced towards Maureen. He swung the knife viciously towards her. She jumped aside and avoided the swing thanks to her being more agile than him, and by the fact that he was far from sober. With a grunt he came on again and this time the blade cut through the apron and her dress, nicking her arm. She stooped, picked up a bottle of her father's stout that was on the table, and brought it down on to his head, splitting open a gash on top of his balding skull. The bottle did not break but she got a mist of blood down the sleeve of the overall. Rory fell at her feet, unmoving, and shallow rasping breaths came from his mouth.

She stood shaken and dazed for a few minutes and then, just as she was calm again and ready to see to him, he gave a great moan, a gush of blood came out of his mouth and his breathing stopped. She closed her eyes and stood in silent thought. She'd never liked Rory, he'd always bullied her and joined in their mother's taunts about Poor Mopsy, but he was still her brother. In a daze she bent down and felt his neck for a pulse. There was none. She removed her hand and the gloved finger left a red smear across his neck. Suddenly she snapped into action, no time for regrets or might-have-beens now, it was getting on for 6.30. She must move quickly.

First she took the bottle and gingerly and distastefully pressed her mother's fingers on to the neck and then dropped the bottle beside her. She put one of the banknotes back into the largest half of the china pig and pushed the rest into her handbag. She went upstairs to the bathroom and took off the apron. Then she bathed the cut on her arm and put on a plaster.

She bundled up her father's clothes and the apron, and put them into a bin liner. She then set to and cleaned the bath, basin and bathroom floor to remove all traces of blood. She put the rubber gloves in the bin bag and then put on her coat, hat and gloves. She pushed the bin liner into a suitcase she found in her parents' bedroom. She would take it back with her and put it in a rubbish bin somewhere. She went back into the kitchen and closed but didn't lock the kitchen door, leaving the window open. The house was now icy cold and she went quickly out of the front door, which she locked behind her, putting her father's key into her handbag. She walked to the high street, found a pay phone and phoned for a taxi to take her to Gatwick.

TUESDAY 5TH JANUARY 1 AM ENGLISH TIME
(2 AM SPANISH TIME)

Maureen sat in a jet as it taxied down the runway at Gatwick, and closed her eyes in tiredness. It had been a long and traumatic day. Since leaving her flat this morning she had learnt of her mother's death, covered up her father's part in it, killed her brother and spent a lot of the day in taxis and aeroplanes. She was worn out. The events played out in front of her eyes, what had she forgotten or overlooked?

She had come in the taxi to Gatwick arriving at about 8.30, and started seeking a flight. She had not managed to get one earlier than this one, which was due to leave at 1 AM. She had filled in the time by eating a meal, having discovered to her surprise just how hungry she was, and then drinking several whiskies.

One good thing was that her passport was still in the name of Maureen Carver so there would be no trace of her visit here. She had married John Carver whilst studying for her diploma in Business Studies, but it had not lasted and they split up after just six months, finally getting divorced just two years ago. Nobody, not even Felipe, was aware of her marriage, she had kept it to herself and gone back to her own name after the split up. Fortunately she had not as yet altered her passport. She had paid for her tickets both at Málaga and Gatwick in cash, having stopped on the way from her flat to the airport to draw out enough to cover her flights. So there would be no trace of her visit at all, now all she had to do was to get home and invent some sort of story to satisfy Pat and Felipe.

THURSDAY 7TH JANUARY 11 AM ENGLISH TIME (12 NOON SPANISH TIME)

Sergeant Andy Tyler of Essex CID stood in the kitchen looking at the scene in front of him.

"Just go through it all again for me laddie, will you? Slowly and in order this time," he said to the pale faced young constable, who was obviously having some trouble concentrating.

"Yes, sarge, er, can we go into the living room, away from… " He gestured to the two bodies on the kitchen floor.

"First time is it, son? Always gets to you like that, OK then, come on. Now, let's have it. Angie, take some notes." This last to the woman DC, who had come with him in answer to the constable's call to the station house in Brentwood.

"Right, sarge. Well, we got a call from a Mrs Alice

Mooney first thing this morning. Seems she was the sister of… her in there… and she was in a right state according to the station sergeant." The constable gulped, wiped his brow and continued. "She said that her sister was due to go over last night for a bit of a do. Oh, she lives in Southend, her sister that is, and she, that's Elsie O'Rooke in there, didn't turn up. Sorry, Sarge, I'm not very coherent, am I?"

"You're doing just fine lad, I can follow you easily. You can as well, eh Angie?"

"Sure, Sarge," a nod from Angie.

"Right, well, when Elsie didn't turn up, the other one, her sister, er… " He stopped, obviously confused.

"Alice Mooney," helped out the sergeant, patiently raising his eyebrows at Angie getting it all down.

"Alice Mooney, yes, so she rung up all evening and got no answer. Same early this morning, so she rings the station and Sergeant Crabb, that's the desk sergeant, he told me to come round and see if there was a problem. Just to calm her down like, I had to come this way anyway, as I was going to…"

"Never mind where you were bloody going, what then?"

"Well, I rang the front door bell but got no answer, place seemed empty. She's out, I thought, but I went round the back just to make sure. Sergeant Crabb always tells us to check everything before making a report. So I come round the back and saw the broken window, which was open, so I tried the door handle, I thought there'd been a burglary like. The door wasn't locked so I came in and found… them."

"Touch anything, did you?"

"No, Sarge, nothing, I just went straight back outside and rang the station, and then you arrived."

"Right lad, we'll take over now, the police doctor and the scene of the crime lads will be along in a jiff, just go and stand by the gate and let them pass, but keep everyone away. Right?"

It was over three hours later when the two detectives had as many facts as they were likely to get for a while. The police doctor would not give any time of death, but said that they had both probably been dead for at least two days.

"Difficult to tell really, especially with the house as cold as it is, I may be able to tell you more after the autopsy. I'll get on to that as soon as possible. Bye now." And he had rushed off to other more pressing matters.

"Well, what else have we got, Angie?"

"Right, Sarge, we have a broken window and mud from the garden on the sill and the kitchen floor, indicates a break in." The sergeant gave a grunt and she continued. "A broken china pig with a five pound note caught on one of the shards, possibly could have been more in with it, taken perhaps by our perhaps burglar?" No response from her superior so she went on again. "One corpse, Mrs O'Rooke, stabbed by a knife held by her son, Rory. No blood on Rory, odd that if he stabbed her, he should have got some on him, don't you think?"

"I'm not thinking anything at the minute, Angie, just go on, oh and there was a smear on the end of his sleeve."

Angie grimaced, not much for a slice in the side, she thought. "We have a note from her to her husband, and one from him to her outlining their movements."

"We'll have to get someone to confirm handwriting there, so just presumed from her and him at the moment. Go on."

"We have a phone call she made to her sister at about 5 o'clock on Monday afternoon, telling her that her husband Pat, an Irishman by all accounts, had gone off for a few days to stay with their daughter in Spain. And the house to house have turned up a Sean Clarke, another Irishman."

"You amaze me Angie, Sean, an Irishman? Get on with it."

"Sarge, she phoned him too, also at about 5 on Monday, so she was still alive then. Oh, Sean Clarke is Pat 0'Rooke's ganger on a road building job, and lives in the next street. Then we have a bottle of stout…"

"Would be stout, wouldn't it, if it belonged to a bloody Irishman. Don't think I can take much more of this Ang, it's all perhaps and might be and everything very convenient." He rubbed his forehead and stared at her. "Finish it off, then."

"Well, the bottle had a couple of her prints on the neck and bits of skin and hair stuck to it, and it fits the dent in his head. The doctor says he probably didn't die straight off, but can't say how long he may have lingered, it may have been minutes, or even hours."

"There we go again, probably, may, might," he grumbled.

"Then we have a neighbour over the road who saw Pat O'Rooke leave in a taxi, she thinks, yes, I know, thinks, just before 11 on Monday morning. Nobody saw Mrs O'Rooke come back, or Rory come home, but he wasn't here when she rang her sister that afternoon, or at least not according to her sister. And that's about it. Uh, I've found two numbers for Mopsy the daughter in Spain, home and work. We'd best let her know, and the husband too if he's with her."

"Right, soon, but first things first. Get someone on checking the handwriting. Someone else off to look for that taxi driver, and someone else checking the airports to see if 0'Rooke left that morning. Start with Gatwick and move on to Heathrow, Stansted... Luton, I suppose, he wouldn't go further afield. Formal statements from the sister and Clarke and the nosy neighbour who saw the taxi. I'll go back to the station and ring Spain. See you sometime this evening, OK?"

THURSDAY 7TH JANUARY 5 PM SPANISH TIME
(4 PM ENGLISH TIME)

Maureen 0'Rooke opened the door of her flat to the ringing of the phone. She crossed the room and picked up the receiver. "Dígame," she said.

"Eh? Oh hell, do you speak English?" a voice with cockney overtones asked.

"Yes, I am English, who is that, what do you want?"

"Good. Right then, I want to speak to Pat or Mopsy O'Rooke, if they're there please."

"Pat, my father, is out, and I'm Maureen O'Rooke, not Mopsy." Her voice was icy and controlled, but inside she felt a sudden lurch. She put her finger to her lips, motioning her father who had followed her into the room to be silent.

"Oh, right, yes, Maureen then. I tried your office but couldn't get an answer."

"We close at 2 on a Thursday," she said coldly. "Who is this?"

"Sergeant Tyler, Essex CID, miss," he began.

"Ms," she corrected him, thinking, this is it, here we go.

"Right, sorry, Ms," stressing it deliberately. "Ms O'Rooke. I have some bad news for you, can't put it any other way, no way to soften the news. Your mother and brother are both dead, I'm afraid."

"Ma and Rory? Dead?" She tried to put surprise into her voice. "How? When?" Quickly she covered the handset to hiss "Quiet" to her father, who had started forward. "Rory as well?" he was asking. "Yes, shut up, you're not here." He lapsed into silence.

"... seems to have been a bit of a fight between them."

She had missed the first part of the sentence but could fill it in for herself.

"No," she stated emphatically. "No, that's not possible, my mother doted on Rory, there's no chance they would have come to blows."

"Well, it's early days yet. You have my full sympathy, and your father too, he is there with you, isn't he?"

"Oh yes, just out somewhere, he came out on Monday to stay for a bit. He rang me to ask if he could."

"His note says you rang him," the sergeant answered.

"Note? To who? Oh Elsie, I see, yes it would, Sergeant, he wouldn't want her to know it was his idea. That would just make her worse."

"Can you tell me when he got to you on Monday?"

"Yes, he was met by a friend of mine at six on Monday evening, I couldn't pick him up I was... busy elsewhere, I didn't get home until the early hours." Best to stick to the truth as far as possible, she thought.

"Reliable, is he, this friend of yours? You can be sure the time's right?" Tyler knew that most murders were committed between husband and wife, and here was a possible chink in the armour of 0'Rooke.

"Very. He's a sergeant in the Guardia Civil, a policeman like you, I can get him to ring you if you wish. But just what are you suggesting?"

"Nothing, nothing at all, Ms 0'Rooke." He saw the door shut with a bang on the slim opening. "Well, once again, sorry to have to break the news to you. My condolences to you both. I'll leave my number so you can ring me about when we can release them for burial, and if you come over for the funeral, perhaps you could call in at Brentwood Police Station and we could have a chat."

MONDAY 18TH JANUARY 10 AM ENGLISH TIME (11 AM SPANISH TIME)

Sergeant Andy Tyler and Constable Angie West stood outside the chapel of the crematorium just outside Chelmsford, watching the small group of mourners leave. As the congregation came out of the building, they fastened coats and put up umbrellas to protect themselves from the cold biting wind and the snow which was now falling quite heavily, and beginning to lay over the surrounding lawns. Father Shannon, who had been taking the service, turned to shake hands with the family, his black cloak billowing.

"They're all there Angie, sister Alice, husband Pat, daughter Mopsy, sorry Maureen. And only Alice looks really upset. Look, there's Pat having a joke with his mate Sean, and Maureen clinging to that Spanish cop Felipe. I must say

I took to him, nice easy going chap, but very protective of our Mo, wouldn't you say? But there'll be no wake for the two dear departed, I'll bet."

"She was a bit of a tartar by all accounts, Sarge," Angie answered, trying to shelter in the lee of the building as the wind gusted harder and the snow grew heavier. "Made all their lives a misery, so it seems. And that Rory, we've had our eye on him for a bit. A no good waster, that one!"

"Now Ang, innocent until proved guilty and all that," Tyler said in mock reprimand. "Right, when that left hander, Roman Catholic priest to you Ang, has finished, I just want a word with the daughter before she vanishes back to sunnier climes."

Over by the chapel door, Father Shannon was saying his farewells. "God be with you Alice, and you Patrick and Maureen. I didn't know Elsie or Rory at all well, they never came to Mass, but then so many don't these days. But my condolences to you all, will you be going straight back to Spain, Maureen?"

"I'm staying for the inquest on Wednesday, and then yes, Felipe and I are going home."

"And you Mr O'Rooke, Patrick, what are your plans?"

"Well, father, I'll be following them just as soon as I get the house on the market. Mo here, she reckons she can get me a job with this builder, Spanish he is, but speaks enough English to give me me orders like. Then I'll probably be able to learn the lingo like, after a bit."

Maureen smiled listening to her father, he'd never be able to learn Spanish, she knew, but Felipe's cousin, one of many, had a building firm in San Pedro de Alcántara, just 16 km from Estepona. He spoke English as well as Felipe, and had agreed to take Pat on.

"He's a hard worker, and very good at doing exactly what he's told, and very easy to get on with," both Maureen and Felipe had assured him.

"Well now, that's probably for the best," Father Shannon's Irish accent was quite pronounced. "I'll say goodbye to you all then," and with that he went back into the chapel.

"Excuse me, Ms O'Rooke," Sergeant Tyler stepped forward. "The inquest, on Wednesday, will you still be here? We'd like you to come."

"Yes, Sergeant, I'll be there, and my father. Felipe will be there too if you need him."

"No, no, we'll not need Felipe, at least that's really up to the Coroner, but I think we can manage with our other evidence. We know what plane your father caught, checked it at Gatwick, and what time he left the house. No, we know he's not involved. Seems like it was a fight between the two of them... "

"You know what I think about that, Sergeant," cut in Maureen.

"Well, yes, you've made that plain enough, but we'll see what the coroner has to say. There are one or two odd things that I'm not happy about, still, more of that on Wednesday. The hearing shouldn't last more than a day, so then you'll be free to go."

"We fly back on Saturday, Sergeant. See you on Wednesday."

With that, the small group of mourners turned away to walk to their cars, parked nearby.

The coroner brought the court to order and his clerk began swearing in the jury. Neither the family or the police were represented by solicitors and he did not expect the inquest to be a long drawn out affair. He opened proceedings as soon as the formalities were over.

"We are here to inquire into the violent deaths of Mrs Elsie O'Rooke and her son Rory O'Rooke at 12 Litchfield Rd, Brentwood, which took place sometime between Monday 4th January and Thursday 7th January." He turned to the jury. "You will hear evidence from the doctor, the police and relatives of the deceased, amongst others. It is not your duty to say who is guilty of these crimes, for crimes they undoubtedly were, but just to say how they were committed and to give opinions as to who may have been involved, or to any action you think may be needed."

Maureen sat near the front of the small courtroom which was overbearingly hot to counter the cold winter day. All through the morning the events were laid out by one witness after another, herself included. By lunchtime all the facts were known. Elsie O'Rooke was killed by the knife still in the hand of her son when the bodies were found. Rory, her son, was killed by a bottle with his mother's fingerprints on it. Patrick O'Rooke had left the house to travel to his daughter's in Spain on the morning of the incident, arriving there in the evening. Mrs O'Rooke was alive after he left the house, and phoned her sister and a workmate of his, Mr Clarke, to complain that he had left, simply leaving her a note. She had been somewhere in the West End shopping when he had left. It was all straightforward but there were just one or two awkward facts. First, as Sergeant Tyler pointed out in his evidence, exactly how did they kill each other?

"It's difficult to see how he could stab her after being struck," he'd said. "And she certainly couldn't hit him after being stabbed. The only explanation is that the two blows were dealt simultaneously, but that's hard to envisage."

Then there was the problem of why. Maureen insisted that they were close, and that her mother would never attack Rory. She had to admit under questioning by the coroner that she may have done it in self defence, and that Rory was not that fond of his mother. If the argument had been over the money in the pot, then where was it? Maureen insisted that only she knew of the existence of the hiding place, and that Rory did not, a fact endorsed by Pat in his evidence. There was also the existence of a mystery woman. A neighbour had come forward to say that he had seen a tall darkly clad woman outside the front of the house at about half past three on the Monday afternoon. Who was she and what part, if any, did she play in the tragedy?

The evidence of the police doctor was also not straightforward. He would not, could not, give a time of death for either person. He could state that Mrs O'Rooke died first, but when, he could not say. Given the coldness of the house, he thought she could have died any time between 9 am on Monday morning and 8 pm that night. He was not to know that the house had been overheated until after 5 pm, and that that had slowed down the onset of rigor mortis, whilst he was assuming that in the cold air it would have been hastened. Because of the nature of Rory's injury, he again could give no precise time of the injury. It could have been any time between 5 and 8 pm on the Monday, which was the closest he could come to his time of death. And really he would prefer to widen that time span, but, if pushed, then between 5 and 8 pm was the most probable time. Pressed by the coroner, he agreed that given the evidence of the phone calls then yes, perhaps, the time of the incident could probably be said to have occurred between 6 and 8 pm on the Monday evening. But the doctor was obviously not happy with that conclusion.

"There are too many contradictory factors," he finished by saying.

At one o'clock the coroner broke for lunch, asking everyone to reassemble at three, when he would sum up and advise the jury. At ten past three, just when he was beginning to outline the events, detective constable Angie West came in and carried out a whispered conversation with Sergeant Tyler, who was listening to the coroner. After a few minutes he stood up and the coroner broke off.

"Yes, Sergeant," he said irritably. "What is it?"

"Sir. I'd like the court to hear this recording of a phone call my constable received just half an hour ago," and he held up a cassette.

"Is it relevant to the case?"

"Very relevant, sir."

"Oh very well then, have we a suitable instrument to play it on? We have, good, let's get on."

There was a bustle and stir in the court as the jury spoke

amongst themselves, the tape recorder was set up and two bored reporters on court duty sat up and started getting their notepads out again.

The coroner brought the court to order again and the tape set in motion. A woman's rather coarse cockney voice came clearly over the air. Angie had started the tape at the point where the caller, who had asked to speak to 'someone connected with the Brentwood murders', had begun her story.

"You're on the case, right? Well, don't interrupt, or ask questions or I'll ring off and won't ring back. I'm in a call box so it's no use trying to trace the call. Ready? I'll say this once and once only. On Monday the 4th Rory O'Rooke came to me, to ask for some heroin." There was a noise on the tape as Angie started to speak. "Shut up, I've told you, if you interrupt I'll ring off. That's your last chance. Now, I told him I wanted money up front, as I knew him of old. He already owed me quite a bit and I said I wanted that back too. 'I'll get some,' he told me, and he took me to his house in Brentwood. Not far from where we'd met, as it happens. 'Wait here', he said, and let himself into the front door, he had a key, and locked it behind him. After a while I heard a crash, like a plate dropping or a dish, china breaking, that sort of thing. Then there was a woman shouting and Rory answering, and then a scream and a shout. Well, then everything went quiet, it was spooky in the garden, cold and getting dark, well it was dark really by then. It was about half past six, I think. Well, I waited for about ten minutes and then went up to the front door, but I couldn't get in so I went round the back. That was locked too so I broke a window and climbed in. I had a hell of a shock, I can tell you. On the floor were two bodies, a woman's with a knife in her and Rory with a head wound. As I looked he gave a sort of moan, and his breathing became all loud and rasping. Then it stopped and blood came out of his mouth. I knelt down and touched his neck, but he wasn't breathing. I were right scared, but as I was leaving I saw this pile of money, so I grabbed it and left by the back door. It had a key in the lock, so there was no trouble there. I just shut the door and ran off. That's it."

There was a click and the tape went silent. Twice during the taped message Pat had started forward, a question forming on his lips, both times to be pulled back and hushed by Maureen at his side. "Sh, da," she whispered.

There was silence in the court and then the coroner asked, "Is it genuine, Sergeant? Or is it a hoax?"

"Oh, it's genuine alright, no doubt about that, all the facts fit. And there's one we haven't published at all, just to make sure that anyone giving information is genuine. We get all sorts of nutters contacting us after a murder. We said nothing about the smear of blood on Rory's neck. Yes sir, it's genuine alright."

After that the coroner finished his summary, and the jury returned a verdict of death by violence, due to a quarrel between the mother and son. No further action to be taken. As they left the court, Sergeant Tyler said to his assistant, "Well, that's that Angie, but I still don't know how they managed to hit each other at exactly the same time."

"Just a matter of timing, sir," she answered.

Maureen and her father were also walking away

together, Felipe had not come back to the court after lunch and they were to meet him at the house later. Maureen had outlined to her father what she had done on that Monday. She'd had to, once he heard of Rory's death, to stop his questions and to keep him from letting anyone else, especially Felipe, know what he had done, by his continual comments and questions.

After hearing the tape, his confusion and bewilderment increased. He just couldn't understand it. Who was the woman, how could what she have described taken place when he knew, at least he was sure he knew, that he had killed his wife. And Maureen, or so she had told him, had struck out at Rory in self defence, and killed him when she was trying to cover up for her father.

"I don't understand, Mo," he said for the umpteenth time. "If she did all that, did I dream it all? I've never understood at all how you did all you said you did in the time. You were back at the flat by 5 on Tuesday morning, I heard you come in. Couldn't sleep, could I. How could you have come here and back, and done all you said you did?"

She turned to him, and in the coarse cockney voice he'd heard on the tape, said, "It was all a matter of timing, Da."

A FAMILY CHRISTMAS

SIMON WAS PLEASED WHEN his cousin Rick and his wife Stella invited him to spend Christmas with them. Simon had had a bad year and his normal serious and somewhat reserved nature had become almost puritanical and withdrawn as an outcome. In January his long time fiancée had broken off their engagement, saying he was not devout enough, too much of a liberal, and that she wanted to be with somebody more akin to her own standards. Moira was a fervent born-again Christian who attended an evangelical chapel in Norwich, and sang in their choir. Simon, who had spent the three long years of their engagement struggling to follow her, joining the same congregation and choir, felt the criticism to be unjust. Moira had demanded much from him, forbidding not just sex but even limiting any physical contact, and urging him to study for ordination. She was a lovely young woman and Simon had suffered all her demands, except the last.

"I'm just a normal man, I'm an accountant, not cut out for a Pastor at all," he had said.

Soon after their split up, she became engaged to a young minister who had just moved into the area. Simon's response was to shrink even further into himself, brooding over three wasted and frustrated years.

Shortly after this his mother had become ill. She had had a heart attack in early February and then in mid March died of a second more serious one. Simon had inherited the house in Wroxham, where they had lived together before her death, and just a few weeks later the house had been broken into. The thieves had taken all his electrical goods, TV, video, computer, CD player, and so forth. All these he could, and did, replace when the insurance money finally came, but his mother's jewellery, whilst not valuable, was irreplaceable. Although the theft of the equipment irritated him, and caused weeks of frustration dealing with the insurance company, the theft of the jewellery was a body blow. His mother had had two rings and a necklace, which had belonged to her mother and grandmother before that. Simon had been looking forward to the day when he could give them to his bride, the now unavailable Moira.

Then there was his obsession, his secret vice, which over the late summer and autumn grew increasingly strong, and more frequent. But this was something he refused to think about, or even at times admit to himself.

An only child, he had had only two close friends during childhood and early manhood, his cousin Rick, and Stella who lived next door. The three of them had been inseparable. Rick's father owned a boatyard in Wroxham and they often went sailing on the broad and down the river to Horning and beyond. When Rick and Stella had married and then moved, first to Yarmouth and then to Spain, Simon had stayed in Wroxham, his job being in Norwich, and contact became more spasmodic. The letter in October inviting him to spend Christmas with them was the first ray of sunshine into his life for months, and he accepted at once with a light heart.

The letter had read, "It will be a family Christmas, we've invited Rick's brother Paul and his wife Rita, and Stella's younger sister Rosalind, who you probably remember. These days she is living in London somewhere, we haven't seen much of her since she left when she was sixteen to go and live with her aunt after her mother died."

The invitations had caused quite an argument between Rick and Stella, and their two children, Jim who was six, and Ellie who was four. Rick and Stella lived in a cortijo in the Sierra de Mijas, not far away from the road between Alhaurin de la Torre and Alhaurin El Grande, in Málaga province. They had converted and modernised the farmhouse and outbuildings, which were built round an open square yard, into their living quarters and six letting units, which each slept from two to six people. They had decided not to let any of the units over the Christmas period but have a break.

Because they had not seen Simon for over a year, and knew of his troubles, they had agreed to invite him to stay with them. It was the invitation of Paul and Rita that had caused the trouble.

"I ought to invite Paul, Rita and the girls," said Rick. "We've not seen them for a long time, and father is always on at me to invite them out."

"I'd rather invite your father," said Stella. "He's a sweetie, but Paul, ugh! He's a sexist, racist, homophobic, bigoted… " She stopped as the children were listening.

Jim agreed with his mother and added, "Mary and Sandra are too bossy and snooty. I like Auntie Rita though. What's homophobic, Mum?"

"Never you mind," Stella answered.

"I don't like Uncle Paul," Ellie said, adding her weight to the argument. "And Sandra always pulls my hair."

"Father wouldn't come, you know that, love," Rick answered his wife above the uproar. "But, you know, it is Christmas, Paul isn't that bad and we ought to have them…"

"Only if we invite Ros as well then," Stella compromised. "I've not seen my little sister for yonks."

"Who's Ros?" the children asked.

"Auntie Rosalind to you," their mother answered. "My sister."

And so it was finally agreed that Paul and his family would be invited.

"They can stay in the four bed cottage," said Stella. "And Ros and Simon can each have a two bed one."

Simon left Wroxham on the nineteenth of December and drove to Norwich, where he left his car in the small car park behind the accountants office where he worked, and walked down the hill to the bridge over the river Wensum and into the railway station. It was a cold grey morning, with a biting wind and sleet in the air. He took the London train and then went on the Stansted Express to the airport. Before he left Norwich he bought a copy of the Eastern Daily Press and the Norfolk and Norwich Times to read on the journey, and to give to Rick and Stella. He knew they could buy English newspapers in Spain and even get the BBC radio and television channels, but not, he was sure, buy East Anglian papers.

Both papers carried national as well as local news, but today's headlines were almost the same. "Norfolk rapist strikes again" in one, and "Norwich woman latest rape victim" in the other.

"Sooner they catch that beast the better," said a middle-aged woman angrily, reading the paper over his shoulder on the platform at Norwich. She looked at him in an accusing way and he moved away uneasily in some confusion, mumbling an answer.

His cousin Rick met the plane at Málaga airport that evening, and drove him the short distance from there, along the busy A336 through Churriana and Alhaurin de la Torre, to the cortijo.

"Paul and his family are here already," he said, "but Ros isn't coming until tomorrow, she's flying scheduled from Heathrow. Do you remember her at all? I've not seen her since before we came out here. She was seventeen then, that was about five years ago."

"No, I can't say I can remember her really," Simon replied. "She was just a kid when she went to her aunt's, sixteen wasn't she, and we must have been... what?"

"Twenty-three, it was just a year after Stella and me got married."

"And Paul, how is he?" Simon asked. "I know we both live in Wroxham, but I never see anything of him." And don't want to really, can't stand him, he added silently.

"Oh! He's not changed," said Rick, looking at his cousin with a faint rueful smile. "Didn't he once accuse you of being gay? Not that there would have been anything wrong if you had been. But to him there would have been."

"Yes," said Simon. "Then with perfect logic, at least to

him, a short time later of being a pervert and chasing after underage girls."

With Rick and Stella, Simon could relax his normal quiet, withdrawn nature and talk openly. Something he could not do with anyone else. That's probably why he had developed his secret vice, he thought now, once they'd moved from Wroxham he had had no one else to talk to.

"Never mind, I'll keep him in order," said Rick optimistically. He wasn't sure however if he could, as his elder brother seemed to have got worse since he had last seen him. And poor Rita, his wife, was even more downtrodden.

Paul's greeting to Simon when they arrived at the farmhouse did not bode well for the festive season.

"Oh, it's you, Simon. Sorry to hear about your mother, but now you'll have to stand on your own feet. No more being mamby-pambied by her. Straighten you out a bit," he said and, ignoring Rick's protest at his remarks, took the papers Simon had brought and, reading the headlines, continued, "That pervert's struck again since we left, I see. I know what I'd do with him if I had him in my sights."

The next day Ros arrived and lightened the atmosphere. She had turned into a highly attractive young woman from the gawky teenager they all remembered. Not only that but with dramatic makeup, dangling earrings, spiky black hair and clothes that accentuated her shapely figure, she startled them all. Paul, who couldn't keep his eyes off her, was heard to mutter something about strumpets and jezebels, but his eyes belied his criticism.

Over the next three days until Christmas Eve, an uneasy peace was maintained. The four children, from the youngest

Ellie, at four, to the eldest, Mary, at fourteen, became more and more excited and quarrelsome. Rita, Paul's wife, seemed to shrink even further into her browbeaten self, as she tried to control Mary and Sandra, and cope with Paul's increasingly outspoken comments.

He overheard Simon one day talking to Stella.

"Stella, um, can we, I mean can I, um, ask you about something. Since Moira broke up with me… I've, er, had this problem, this, um, well, it's not nice talking about it, but it's getting worse. Happening more often." He broke off.

"What are you talking about, Simon? What problem, what's getting worse?" she asked.

"Oh, never mind, I can't explain. I'll just have to control myself, try to stop doing it," Simon said, and changed the subject.

Paul was intrigued and determined to find out what it was all about. He had never liked his cousin Simon and had always frowned on his younger brother's friendship with him. He considered Simon a repressed, spoilt, secretive character, and one with a perverted nature. He pondered on the conversation he had overheard and formed a possible theory, but who could he share it with? Rick and Stella wouldn't do, they'd just tell him to shut up and come to Simon's defence. His wife was no good, he had a very poor opinion of her. 'The mouse,' he called her in derision to his drinking cronies in The Swan in Horning. But young Ros, now there was a likely accomplice, a feminist no doubt, he thought in derision, but all the better for that in this case. He sought her out and told her what he had heard and of his suspicions. To his chagrin and surprise, she laughed at him.

"You must be joking, or off your trolley," she said. She did not like Paul or his bigoted opinions, and on the other hand she thought Simon quite dishy, if a bit shy and starchy. But that she knew could be changed.

Christmas Eve arrived at last and Rick told the assembled family over breakfast, "Today, noche buena, that's the Spanish for Christmas Eve, is when the Spanish have their Christmas meal. And we planned to do the same, this evening rather than tomorrow. We thought in the morning we could open our presents, and then later in the day go into Torremolinos or somewhere nearby for a meal in a restaurant. But tonight we'll have our Christmas dinner here."

Paul said, "Bloody Spaniards, can't even do Christmas properly."

"Oh shut up, you miserable xenophobe," Ros told him, bringing a flush of anger to his face and a small smile to Stella's lips. Ros, with her lively manner and outspoken ways, was proving the only one able to squash Paul. The others all agreed with her, even Rita, who was emboldened to say, "I think it's a good idea. When in Rome," the first time anyone could remember her ever standing up to her husband.

That evening they all went into Alhaurin to a bar which was full of people singing carols. They were led by two men, one playing a zambomba, a drum with a stick pushed through the skin which the player rubbed up and down with a moistened hand, producing a zum, zum, zum, rhythmic drone; the second musician held a brass cup, or bell, in one hand, and struck it with a brass rod held in the other. The room rocked with Spanish carols or Villancicos. "Campana sobre campana, y sobre campana una," started one, with a rousing chorus between verses, "Belén, campanas de Belén". The tunes were very lively and the choruses easy to pick up and soon all the family, except Paul, were singing along, with Rick explaining some of the words. "Campana is bell, and Belén, Bethlehem," he said. At half past eight everyone was leaving the bar to go home for the evening meal and the family did likewise. During the time in the bar Ros had been, to Paul's growing annoyance, chatting up Simon, who clearly in some way awed by her appearance and direct nature, was only slowly responding.

The meal, which was a long and conventional English Christmas dinner, went on until well past midnight, when both adults and children went off to bed.

Christmas day dawned clear and sunny and, by the time everyone was awake and swapping presents, was quite hot.

"It's not a traditional Christmas huddled round a log fire here," Simon commented, looking at Ros in brief shorts and a revealing sun top as she lay on a sun lounger talking to Jim, who was showing her a computer game his parents had given him.

Christmas and Boxing day passed with too much eating and drinking, spats between the children, and everyone feeling that they had been together weeks not days.

Simon and Ros were together more and more, and his normal quiet nature which had grown more noticeable since Moira had left him, began to change as he became more settled, relaxed and even happy.

Paul grew even more moody and had several rows with Rita. He also became stricter with his two daughters which brought tears and rebellion from them. He tried to convince his wife, brother and Stella of his theory about Simon which Ros had laughed at, but they would not listen. Simon himself he treated with a growing disdain, just stopping short of accusing him of the crimes he was now convinced he had committed.

"It all makes sense, look at him, sexually repressed, thrown over by Moira, sensible girl, distraught by the loss of his overprotective mother, and just drooling over that young slut Ros. Look at her, flaunting her all."

Stella could not believe her ears, Moira who he had always called a frigid, tight legged Jesus freak, a sensible girl? And Ros.

"That's my sister you're calling a slut, just watch what you say about her, or you can piss off now," she angrily retorted. "And Simon, how could you say that about him, we've been friends for years. I know him much better than you."

The morning of the twenty seventh once more dawned clear and fine and there was a general lightening of the mood. Paul and his family were returning to the UK the following day so the others began to look forward to that with some relief. Simon and Ros however were staying over New Year. After breakfast the four children went off to play with friends of Jim and Ellie. Ros came across from her apartment for breakfast wearing a clinging dress that showed off her figure and buttoned down the front. She had left some of the top and bottom buttons undone showing a lot of flesh.

"Look at that," said Paul in an undertone to his wife, just

loud enough to be heard by Stella who was nearby. "She's not got anything on under that dress. It's what I've been saying, she's just a…," he caught sight of Stella's face and said no more.

"You can't take your eyes off though, can you?" replied Rita with a rare flash of spirit.

After a late and long breakfast the group slowly broke up. Simon was the first to leave, returning to his apartment to read. Shortly after that Ros also left to go back across the courtyard to her own room. Paul and Rita were finally left alone in the kitchen, where Rita was listening to BBC 4 on the radio. Just before lunch Paul went outside into the central courtyard for some fresh air. Here he met Rick and Stella coming back from a short walk. As they stood chatting they suddenly heard cries coming from Simon's cottage.

"That's Ros," Paul said, and before they could stop him he rushed across and burst into the building through the front door which was not locked. The other two followed him and all three crowded into the bedroom from where the cries, now quite loud, were coming from. On the bed was Ros, her dress fully open, and on top of her Simon with his trousers down around his ankles. Ros was shouting and beating Simon on the back with her hands.

Paul rushed forward to pull Simon off her.

"There you are, I told you he was the Norfolk rapist, but you wouldn't listen."

He looked down at Ros' naked body. "Are you all right, Ros, I…"

"What the hell are you doing?" Ros screamed at him. "Rape, oh no, this was mutual."

She made no attempt to cover herself. "Get out of here, you sod."

As he still stood staring down at her as if hypnotised, she stood up and postured in front of him.

"Fancy some yourself? Well you've made that obvious enough, well tough. If anyone's capable of rape, it's you."

And she burst out laughing at him. As he stood before her scorn and laughter, he seemed to shrink.

Rita came in at the end of the scene, drawn by the raised voices. She looked at her husband.

"I've just heard on the news, they've caught the Norfolk rapist, last night. So Paul, what now? You're a fool. Go and bring back the children, it's nearly time for lunch."

This was a rare flash of defiance on her part. As Paul, dazed, turned to obey her, for the first time in years, seeming thoroughly cowed, they all saw that he did not need to go for the children as all four of them were standing behind Rita watching the scene.

"You are an idiot," said Mary, the eldest, to her father primly.

"Idiot," repeated Ellie, the youngest, looking wide eyed at Ros. "Why haven't you any pants on, auntie Ros?" she asked. "Mummy says it's not hy, hygee, proper not to wear pants."

Everyone burst out laughing except Paul, who slunk off. There could be changes in that family, thought Rick, as he and the others left Simon and Ros alone and went back to the main house.

Ros slowly buttoned up her dress as Simon pulled up his trousers.

"Well, shall we continue this after lunch?" asked Ros, smiling at him. "Then I think I may as well move in here for the rest of our stay, if you want of course."

She had had to make all the running in the affair so far, as Simon was conditioned by his years with Moira not to touch, kiss or even consider doing anything else. Now at last he began to regain his own self confidence.

"That would be great. But what about Stella?"

"She's my sister, not my mother, and I am a big girl of twenty two."

She sat on the bed to put her shoes back on.

"Fine, but what about after. In England? I want to continue this," he said.

Ros stood up and put her finger to his lips.

"Sh. One thing at a time. And London's not a million miles from Norwich. And Epping where I live is halfway there. You've got your car and I've my motorbike. We can take it from there."

"You've a motorbike?" Simon asked in amazement.

"Yeah, why not, just the thing for getting around town. And for coming to Norwich," she added. "Just one thing though. What's this guilty secret, this hidden vice, this obsession of yours everyone's talking about? What do I have to fear, if you're not the Norfolk rapist, as Paul kept trying to tell me you were?"

Simon went red. "D..did he say that?" he stuttered. "No, it's just…"

"What? Come on, out with it."

"It's just, look, Moira wouldn't let me touch her, I got so frustrated, then she left and… well, I started going to sex shops to watch porn videos. The urge got harder to resist and more frequent, so… "

He broke off, not knowing how to go on.

Ros smiled. "Is that all?" She began slowly to unbutton her dress once more, slowly and tantalisingly, smoothing her hands over her body as she did so.

"Well, if it's stimulation you need, I can give you that."

The dress fell to the floor and she moved provocatively before him.

"Shall we give lunch a miss?" she asked.

BILLY BONES

MANY OF YOU, ESPECIALLY those of more mature years, will probably remember the name Billy Bones. Billy was active in the East End gangs in the early 50's whilst in his teens, before the rise of the Krays. At the time of his activity in the gangs, the so-called king of the underworld was Jack 'Spot' Comer. Billy Bones, or William Jones as he was christened, was born in Manor Park in east London in 1936. (The popular name came either from his childhood, his thin half starved body, with its protruding bones, earning him the name; or as others claimed from the rhyming of bones and Jones). With the demise of Jack 'Spot' and the rise of the Krays, Billy faded from notoriety in the gangs.

He came to public attention once again when he was named, and hunted, by the police after the infamous Hatton jewel theft in 1976, when two members of the public and a police officer were gunned down in the street. Many will remember how reported sightings of him were claimed in Chile, Argentina, Spain and the Far East. Despite these many reports, his actual whereabouts was never established, and the theory of a fall out between the robbers that had resulted in him being murdered by them became common in the popular press.

Billy had in fact, at the age of forty, rich from the proceeds of that and other crimes, decided that the time had come to retire. He managed to do this, and also completely disappear from view, for several reasons. Jones being a common name, he had no need to assume a false one or live abroad using a false passport. England contains many William Joneses and no current pictures of him were known, those from his early gangland activity being over twenty years out of date by that time. He was able to slip, unnoticed, into southern Spain, which at that time had no extradition treaty with Great Britain, and was notorious as being the 'Costa del Crime'.

By opting not to live in lavish style in one of the more well known spots such as Torremolinos, Benidorm or Marbella but more modestly in a small village in the Alpujarras, his presence was never discovered.

Over the years the hunt for him diminished, and whilst still on the wanted list, his death at the hands of his fellow associates became the accepted view of the police. As time passed he became more and more accepted by the villagers of Arucas, where he was a popular member of the community. He became a Spanish resident and slowly picked up the language.

Because he had no family in England, he was able to sever all ties completely and seldom went back on visits, and never to the East End where he was well known. The investment of the spoils from his criminal activities brought in a more than adequate income to ensure a comfortable and safe lifestyle. From time to time, he acquired a mistress, some English, some Spanish, but none of long standing.

He developed a passion for sea fishing and discovered a cove between two rocky headlands, near La Rábita, from where he could fish from the beach. He was essentially a loner and the usual absence of other fishermen on this stretch of coast added to his pleasure. Here he would go once or twice a week to fish, during the hours of darkness.

He was on this beach one night when he saw a dark shape in the water, some way out, and heard the feeble crying of a baby. He took off his clothes and went out to investigate and discovered a young girl, almost drowning, clutching a small child. He quickly pulled them ashore. All he had with him was a flask of whisky and a couple of sandwiches, not at all suitable for the occasion. Fortunately the night air was warm and so he simply bundled them up in his coat and drove them back to his home in Arucas.

The girl, Amel, and her daughter soon made a full recovery from their ordeal. Amel was an illegal immigrant from the Sudan and the pair were the sole survivors of a small boat which had capsized off Almería. Although she was only twenty two to his fifty five, they soon became very close and after a couple of years they married. Billy took this step to legalise Amel's position in Spain, give her English nationality, and to provide stability for her daughter, who she had named Xanda, after his mother Sandra and her own, Xindu.

He might have lived out his life in peace and comfort, if it hadn't been for his essentially greedy and ruthless nature. On the surface he appeared generous and open handed. Indeed in the pueblo of Arucas he was noted for it, and his treatment of Amel and Xanda also showed this side of his nature. They had come from poverty in a country torn by civil war, to a life of prosperity in Arucas, from famine and strife to plenty and peace. Billy too had risen from the gutters of the East End to the comforts of a rich expatriate lifestyle. But underneath his nature was still that of his early years.

As he neared sixty five, he began to fret that he would not get a pension from Britain. There was no way he could claim one, of course, without revealing his true identity and location to the authorities. He was not in need of the extra income, even though the returns from his investments had reduced, due to the prevailing low interest rates and stock market slump. But in his own mind he felt he was entitled to a pension. The question was how to obtain one, and the answer to this was provided by an item broadcast by an English language radio station on their notice board. The ex-servicemen's organisation, retired British soldiers abroad, chaired by Major William Jones, were holding their weekly social get together for the next few months at Jimmy's Bar in Nerja, on Monday nights. Activities would include bridge, darts and many other pastimes. The Major's telephone number and address were given and prospective members urged to contact him for details.

The following Monday evening Billy was sitting outside the Major's house, which was in a small urbanisation just outside Almuñécar, waiting for him to leave for the weekly meeting. When the Major's car turned out of his drive, Billy followed it into Nerja and to Jimmy's bar. He parked outside and went into the bar and bought a beer. Sitting on a corner table he saw the small group of ex-servicemen gather and go into an inner room. The meeting lasted for two hours and then Billy left the bar once more, following the Major's car back to the same urbanisation. Altogether the Major had been away from home for nearly three hours. Billy thought this quite enough time for what he planned to do, but as a believer in detailed planning he decided to follow the Major the following week, before taking any more steps.

Major William Jones was ex Special Services and had served undercover in many countries, including Eastern Europe, Northern Ireland and the Middle East. He was instinctively aware of the surveillance on him from the moment Billy's car started to follow his own. He isolated and identified Billy within minutes of him entering the bar. What puzzled him was who Billy could be and what his motives were. He knew, by the amateur way that he was acting, that he was not an enemy from his past, a member of the IRA or the Eastern security services for instance, bent on some sort of vengeance. They would have been much more professional and difficult to spot. Whilst being puzzled by Billy's motive, he was at the same time pleased that his street craft was still good and that he had sensed the presence of a tail so quickly.

The following week he once again picked up Billy's presence without difficulty.

On the third week Billy followed the Major to the bar, but then returned immediately to the Major's house. Once there he carefully broke in through the rear door and started to search the premises. The Major was a meticulous man and Billy had no problem finding what he wanted. In the lounge was a desk and in it were all the Major's personal files, notes, etc. One folder contained his pension details, from a copy of the original claim up to all the current documents. With the same name Billy knew that, if the Major were removed, he would be able to keep receiving the pension in future. He took away one document from the bottom of the file, with the Major's signature on it, so that he could practise it for use in the future. He then returned to the bar, to watch once more the group break up and return to their homes. He did not however follow the Major home, but returned to Arucas and Amel, who believed he had been out fishing.

The Major had been, once again, aware of his shadow, noted the changed pattern of the surveillance and this time followed Billy back to Arucas, but without the hound being aware that he was now the fox. When the Major eventually got home he quickly found evidence of Billy's visit. Despite the care he had taken, faint scratches were evident around the back door lock. Small differences in the position of papers in the desk indicated where Billy had been searching and what folder he had examined. The missing paper was soon identified by the Major. His many years of living in hostile countries undercover had made him an expert in being able to spot when a search had taken place and isolate its purpose.

The next day he returned to Arucas and soon became aware that his adversary's name was the same as his own. He gave much thought to the facts that he knew. Someone with the same name was interested in his old age pension details. To what purpose? If the second William Jones simply stole his papers, he would not be able to claim the pension for long, as he, the first William Jones, could report the theft and all would be discovered. He knew there was more to it than simple theft. He decided to set up his own watch on his namesake.

Two nights later he followed Billy from his home in Arucas to the cove and watched him fishing from the beach. He went to a nearby stretch of coast, where several more anglers were operating and by chatting to them soon established that "the Englishman often fishes in the nearby cove, by himself". Later he returned to watch Billy and saw him loading his fishing tackle into his car and then drive back to Arucas.

The following Monday Billy watched as the Major once more left his home near Almuñécar to go to Jimmy's bar. This time however he did not follow him, but waited for ten minutes and then once more approached the back door to force an entry. Major Jones, who had identified Billy's car and observed that he was not being followed, pulled up soon after leaving the urbanisation and phoned the secretary of the ex-serviceman's group on his mobile, to say he was unable to attend that evening due to a minor illness. He then made his way to the rear of his house and observed Billy forcing his entry. He silently slipped in by the front door and from the hall watched as Billy removed the folder containing all his pension details. From behind the kitchen door, he saw Billy going upstairs and into the bathroom, and heard him filling the bath. He saw Billy go back downstairs and out into the back garden and hide in a position where he could see the drive, after first taking the folder to his car.

During this time the Major left the house and returned to his own car, in which he sat until it was time for his return from the club. He drove his car into the drive, entered his front door and stood for a minute listening to the silence inside. Cautiously he went through the ground floor, finding it empty. Whistling quietly he went upstairs and into his bedroom which was also empty. He then approached the bathroom door and slammed it open, surprising Billy who was standing to one side of it with a cosh in one hand.

Both men were in their sixties, both well versed in violence but Billy's street fighting background was no match for the more deadly and lethal methods instilled in the Major by British Intelligence. Instead of Billy holding the Major's head underwater in the bath, he found himself being slowly drowned instead. The Major realised he had been destined to end up as a pensioner tragically drowned whilst taking a bath. Instead he put Billy's body in his car, drove to the deserted bay, set up the fishing gear and left Billy floating face down in the sea. He then walked the twelve kilometres back to his home and went to bed, having recovered his folder.

As there was no hint of foul play, the water in Billy's lungs was not analysed nor his real identity ever discovered. Amel and Xanda, his heirs, inherited all his fortune. In just a few years they had gone from being penniless and stateless to become well off English residents in Spain.

The file on Billy Bones remains open to this day in the archives of the Metropolitan Police.

THE LAST WORD

"I DON'T SUPPOSE YOU'VE ever witnessed a crime? Well, most people haven't, have they?"

My guest paused, waiting for a reply. I remained silent, concentrating on the crossword puzzle which I had half finished. We were sitting on the terrace of my villa in the hills, just above the Andalucían holiday resort of Marbella. I filled in another answer in the puzzle, to the clue: 'Conflict CID started diverted attention (10)', trying not to be, as was the answer 'distracted' by him. My caller was not however to be put off.

"Yesterday, I was sitting outside a bar in Estepona when I noticed a man approaching a woman from behind, as she was walking along the street. He had his hand held out and as he passed her, he hooked the bag off her shoulder and ran off with it." Pausing, he added sugar to the coffee I'd just brought him, and stirred vigorously.

"Great, thanks," I replied, filling in 'snatch' to the clue 'Grasp victory at the last moment (6)', the 'a' crossing the one in distracted.

"What?" he asked. "What's great about seeing a robbery?"

"No, sorry. No, I didn't mean great that you saw… what I meant was that you've just helped me fill in a clue." I sipped some more of my drink, smiling at him.

"Fill in a clue? What are you talking about? Don't you

want to know what I did?" He relaxed back into the cane chair, frowning at me.

I gazed into the distance, not really seeing the brown hillside with its olive groves and white villas, or the distant sea beyond. It was too much, I thought, he had turned up unexpectedly and, as far as I was concerned unwelcome, just after I had settled down with my coffee, to fill in the crossword in today's paper which I had purchased earlier that morning in Marbella.

"Followed," I muttered, half to myself.

"Did you say 'I followed him'? I couldn't quite hear. Well yes, I did. As he ran off I went after him, keeping out of sight as much as I could. In the end he went into another bar some distance away."

As he went on to describe how the thief had met up with an accomplice and how the two of them had rifled through the bag, then how he went back out into the street, found two local policemen, and brought them to the bar, I put 'followed' into the grid. I didn't explain that I'd said 'followed' as I'd deciphered the clue 'Double over short oriental who brought up the rear (8)'. The puzzle was now almost complete, and as I worked out all but the last clue, I listened with half an ear to him describe how he had led the officers up to the two thieves.

My thoughts were diverted from the final clue when he grabbed my arm to claim full attention. He always made sure that he took centre stage in any conversation and allowed no diversions. He pointed to a bruise under his discoloured left eye. "I got that from one of them as they tried to escape," he complained. "And then when we returned to the first bar, the woman was nowhere to be seen. No one seemed to be aware of the incident, which in any case had taken place over half an hour before. I got no thanks from the policemen who seemed reluctant to take any action to find out where she'd gone, and simply took the two robbers away."

He was always moaning, I thought, reading the last clue, and trying to sympathise with him at the same time. "Never mind," I said. "At least you were responsible for their capture. And presumably she would get her bag back when she reported the theft."

"But that's not all," he broke in with exasperation. What more, I wondered, concentrating on the final clue, 'Street conflict over animal bedding (5)'.

"As I went into the bar," he continued, "The barman and another local policeman accosted me. I'd not paid for my tapas and drinks when I'd got up to follow the thieves, you see. So he'd called the police. I ended up, not only with a black eye, but also in the same police station as the bag snatchers. It took me over an hour to sort things out, before I was able to explain everything to their satisfaction, pay what I owed and leave."

It was hard not to smile at his story. "What rotten luck," I murmured abstractedly, still working on the clue.

"It's always the same," he moaned. "But to cap it all, when I got back to my car I'd got a parking ticket. It was the final…"

He broke off, distracted by my stifled chuckle and my muttering to myself.

"What? What are you going on about?" he snapped.

"Straw," I said in satisfaction, filling in the last blanks.

"Yes, I was telling you, it was the final straw." He always has the last word.